The Secret Diary of
Marco Polo

MALCOLM MAHR

D1532058

Fiction Publishing, Inc.
5626 Travelers Way
Ft. Pierce, Florida 34982

ISBN: 978-0-9819727-2-5

Printed in the United States of America

To Fran, the companion of my heart

Also by Malcolm Mahr

FICTION

Don't Feed Peanuts to a Zombie

The Nude Gioconda

NONFICTION

How to Win in the Yellow Pages

What Makes a Marriage Work

You're Retired Now. Relax.

Acknowledgment

My thanks to former Italian Ambassador Siro Polo Padolecchia for his invaluable advice, generously given, and for honoring me with membership into the Marco Polo Society.

Polo Padolecchia is the 34th and last living descendant of the Polo family. He is a native of Venice, a resident of Monaco, and the president of the European Institute for Futures Studies in Monte Carlo. In 2007, Polo invited my wife, Fran, and me to Hangzhou, China, the city where Marco Polo served Kublai Khan as regional governor. Polo fired my imagination with information about his intrepid ancestor: in particular, one relationship about which historians have remained conspicuously silent—the concubine of Marco Polo.

The last descendant in the Polo line, Marco Polo's mysterious Chinese lady, and the mystical West Lake in Hangzhou have all been infused into the novel. But, while there are much of Marco Polo's travels accurately represented, this is, nonetheless, a complete work of fiction.

Book I

As he lay on his deathbed, Marco Polo was entreated by his friends, his priest and relations to retract those unbelievable lies that he had written. To which the old traveler replied, "O amici, vi accerto di non aver scritto neppure la meta di quando mi fu dato vedere. I have not as yet told you half of those things which I saw and did."

—Fra Jacopo D'acqui, Marco Polo's contemporary
and his first biographer. January 8, 1324.

Prologue

IN 1827, VENETIAN COUNT TEODORO CORRER ordered repairs to be made to the palazzo, tower and courtyard he had purchased in the Corte Sabionera, near the Rialto Bridge. The property had formerly been known as *Ca' Polo*, home of the famous explorer Marco Polo.

In the interior of the tower the workmen found a doorway that had been sealed with masonry perhaps hundreds of years before the renovation began. The doorway was broken open, and a wooden box was discovered containing an old manuscript. This manuscript, copied by hand, was entitled *The Description of the World*, by Marco Polo. It was one of 119 manuscripts that had gradually made their appearances in various languages: French, Venetian, Spanish, Bohemian, German, Aragonese and Catalon, besides doubtful copies, compendiums, fragments and extracts.

Count Teodoro Correr's copy of *The Description of the World* was donated, along with his private art collection, to the city of Venice in 1830, all to be housed in the new civic museum located in the Piazza San Marco and named in his honor, the Museo Correr.

The Polo manuscript remained virtually unstudied for centuries, protected under glass, until the time of a museum renovation in 2009. During the installation of Plexiglas with antireflective, UV-blocking properties, the document was being repositioned by the Correr Museum's custodian, Vincente Delgado. As Delgado lifted the manuscript for transfer, a folio containing a sheaf of brittle papers flaked loose under his fingertips. The Correr custodian noted that the pages were old and yellowed parchment.

The director of the Correr Museum, Doctore Dante Foscari, was immediately summoned. Foscari fumbled in his pocket for a pair of bifocals and bent close to carefully inspect the pages of parchment, at the same time trying to suppress his growing excitement. Foscari wiped perspiration from his brow with the back of his coat sleeve and stated, "I believe this document will prove to be an original diary written by the hand of Marco Polo. The famous traveler wished to set the record straight before his death."

...1

I, MESSER MARCO POLO, son of Nicolo Polo and respected citizen of Venice, on this twelfth day of October, in the year of our Lord, 1318, do hereby set forth hitherto undisclosed personal revelations concerning my travels to China and my twenty years' service to the great Kubla Khan. These events were not reported in my book Description of the World *for reasons that will presently be made abundantly clear.*

Twenty years ago in that clammy Genoa prison I dictated to the writer, Master Rustichello, a citizen of Pisa, the story of my travels along the North Silk Road, spanning vast distances from the Mediterranean Sea across the Middle East and Central Asia, passing over the roof of the world, the Pamirs, and finally winding through the bleak desert into the Middle Kingdom ruled by the Khan of All Khans of the Mongols.

The book of my travels has been much read and talked about and translated into every other language of Christendom. The admiration of my book of travels has made me known, however little I may deserve that honor. In my recitation to Rustichello, I did not indulge in describing my personal travel experiences; instead, I deemed it prudent that the pages would contain only details of what I heard or saw on my journey with my father, Nicolo, and my uncle, Maffeo, which would serve as a guide for other merchant travelers.

I was but a lad of seventeen in the year 1271 when, together with my father and uncle Maffeo, we embarked on our long journey, gliding 'neath the Grand Canal's one bridge, the Ponte Rialto—that old, low pontoon bridge with the swing-away section. We sailed with a flotilla of Venetian ships along the eastern coast of the Adriatic, headed for Acre and thence to travel the Silk Road to Cathay. As our ship left the quay, I remember looking back upon my beloved Venice, seeing the great bronze horses of St. Mark gleaming in the sun-

light, and then I turned my eyes beyond the Lido and the lagoons to the enterprise to which I was faring forth.

In my book, I attempted to relate the wondrous sights I beheld: of pygmies, exotic birds and plants, ornate palaces, dragon-like serpents, great sheep with horns, vast deserts, people who decorated their skins with designs, of prodigious white bears and dogs that pulled sledges on snow, of nuts as large as a man's head, of jade-bearing rivers and of seabeds full of pearls, of a land where cattle are sacred and of widows who are burned along with their husbands, of cloth that does not burn, and black stones dug out of mountains that do not flame, except a little when first lighted. I visited a far northern land where all winter there was night and all summer there was day; and many other things equally incredible.

I described fountains in the earth from which black liquid flowed in such abundance that a hundred shiploads of it may be taken at one time. This oil is not fit to use as food, but it is excellent for burning and for anointing camels which have the mange or the itch.

I was disbelieved. The name Marco Millions was used by Venetians as an epithet implying not to my wealth or accumulated ducats, but referring to my supposed lies and exaggerations. This amused me more than it irked, because it suited my purpose, which was to avoid onerous taxes while I was alive and upon my death. And, had I described my personal experiences concerning the virtue of Eastern women and their sexual customs, the book would have offended the sensibilities of the Church, caused blushes or qualms to feminine readers, and created embarrassment and distress to my dear wife, Donna, and my three daughters.

Now, at age 59, I commence to tell everything that has not been told, secure in the knowledge that this private journal will be safely stored in my home until after my death.

And now you will hear all that I can tell you. Thanks be to God! Amen! Amen!

THE ISLAND OF THE DEAD, *San Francesco del Deserto,* is located ten minutes north of Venice, next to Burano. The island is owned by former Ambassador Gianpietro Scarlatti, Chairman of EAM, the Euro-Mongolian International Association. His organization promotes exchange and cooperation between enterprises in Europe and Mongolia.

A red light flashes on the frosted glass pedestal desk in Scarlatti's office. In the swivel chair sits a physically powerful man in his eighties. Scarlatti is big-boned, burly, with a berry-brown complexion and deeply recessed sloe eyes; he is dressed in a double-breasted linen suit and tie in muted colors.

"*Pronto,*" he says, grabbing the phone.

"*Buonasera,* Ambassador Scarlatti. My name is Delgado, Vincente Delgado, custodian at the Correr Museum at number 52 on St. Mark's Square."

"I know where the Correr is located. I'm a donor. How can I help you?"

"Our museum is undergoing renovation," Delgado says nervously. "Today, we transferred a six-hundred-year-old manuscript of Marco Polo's *Travels* into a new niche with a protective shield of Plexiglas. During the transfer, I observed a folio of parchments loosely attached to the underside of the Polo book; papers of a different color and consistency—"

"Get on with it," Scarlatti growls.

"I, of course, notified Director Foscari. He believes that, subject to official confirmation, these papers appear to be a private diary penned by Marco Polo himself in 1318. The director wants to have the pages gelatin tested for age determination. In Polo's time rags were macerated into pulp screened with water to make paper. The finished paper was sized by dipping it into a hot gelatin solution to impart a smooth, stable finish—"

Scarlatti heaves a deep sigh and interrupts, "Enlighten me as to the reason for your call."

Delgado stammers, "Director Foscari instructed me to wrap the parchment in thin Japanese paper and take it to his office, where he intended to lock it in his safe. Before wrapping the diary, I chanced to turn a few pages, with gloves and tweezers. Messer Marco Polo makes mention of freeing his slave, Peter the Tatar, to become a Venetian citizen."

"Many historians have written of Peter the Tatar."

"Marco Polo also noted that the slave, Peter, was the son of a Mongol chief named Jochi and was the grandson of Genghis Khan. I couldn't read everything because the director was waiting, but any Venetian archivist can connect the descendant dots—"

"And what does connecting the dots tell you?"

Delgado pauses. "Ambassador, as you well know, the dots connect to you."

"I've made no secret of my Mongolian heritage," Scarlatti replies. "In fact, it stands me in good stead in Ulaanbaatar."

Delgado continues, "The manuscript also refers to the vast oil and mineral deposits in—"

"*Bravo!*" breaks in Scarlatti. "You are an enterprising custodian."

"Custodial pay is difficult to live on in Venice today, Ambassador. I thought you would be generous and appreciative of my... information."

"Where is the Polo diary now?"

"In Director Foscari's desk, for tonight, at least."

"Be assured, my friend, you will be adequately rewarded. But speak of this to no one, understand? No pillow talk, not a word! Goodbye."

Gianpietro Scarlatti picks up the phone and punches in some numbers. When the call is answered he says, "*Apart from our shadows we have no friends.*"

"*And apart from our horsetails we have no whips,*" the hoarse voice responds.

"I have a job for you," Scarlatti says.

FIRE AT CORRER MUSEUM; ARSON SUSPECTED

IL GAZZETTINO—Venetian fireman were summoned to the Correr Museum at 3 A.M. this morning after late night tourists reported white smoke billowing across Piazza San Marco. Two fireboats pumped water directly from the canal through hoses long enough to reach the museum, which is currently under renovation. Firemen aimed their nozzles at flames burning furiously in the second floor window of the museum director's office.

Smoke damage was reported in other administrative offices, but the Napoleonic wing; the splendid Neoclassical rooms; the Halls of the Procuratie Nuove, designed by V. Scamozzi; the Marco Polo manuscript; and the Correr's other priceless art and sculpture collections were unharmed.

Authorities report similarities between today's fire at Museum Correr and the 1996 fire that destroyed Venice's Fenice Opera House, also under renovation at the time. Kerosene was the incendiary agent in both fires. Mala del Brenta Mafia connections were suspected, but unproven.

In a sadly related event, the body of long-time custodian of the Correr Museum, fifty-year-old Vincente Delgado, was found in the Grand Canal near his home in Cannaregeo. Police suspect that Delgado, after being notified of the fire, was rushing to the museum when he suffered a sudden stroke or heart attack, then collapsed, fell into the canal, and drowned.

...4

THE BODY FLOATS FACE DOWN ON THE OUTGOING
TIDE. At 6:14 A.M., the Fort Pierce Inlet is silent, except for waves
persistently slapping against the rocks. The corpse floats on the surface, tethered by seaweed that restrains it from drifting out toward
the freedom of the open waters of the Atlantic.

Two fishermen stroll along the concrete jetty, lugging their gear.
The taller man, Walter, is a retired Army master sergeant with a dark,
wrinkled face, like an old walnut; his head is topped by a battered
Army fatigue cap. Walter spies an object floating in the water.
"What's that—a manatee?"

His partner peers closer, then jumps back. "It's got clothes on,
Walter."

"Holy shit! Use your cell, Jerry. Call 911."

"Police," Jerry mumbles into the phone. "A dead body's floating in the Fort Pierce Inlet, at Jetty Park."

At 7:05, Dominick Perini, the sixty-three-year-old captain of the
Fort Pierce Detective Bureau, receives a call: "Captain, sorry to call
you at home. We got a floater in the inlet."

"Great way to start the day," Perini growls. "Fill me in."

"A fisherman called 911. I dispatched two cars to Jetty Park."

Perini grimaces. He knows that the media will have a feeding
frenzy over a dead body floating in the inlet. The news will probably
make CNN, and the mayor and city manager will go ballistic. Bad
publicity scares away tourists, snowbirds and real estate investors.
Perini takes pride in the fact that Fort Pierce's crime rate over the
last two years has improved, but compared to posh Vero Beach to
the north, and fast-growing Port St. Lucie to the south, Fort Pierce is
still playing catch-up.

"Seal off the crime scene," Perini orders. "Notify Dr. Miriam
Jolson. I want her to personally handle this case. I'm on my way. Tell
our people not to let anyone near the body, understand?"

"Right, Captain."

The six-foot police captain dresses quickly. He catches his reflection in the mirror—flaring eyebrows, blue eyes, ruddy face, thick jaw, and bush of gray hair receding at the temples. He pats his growing stomach paunch and vows to go back to the gym on Indrio Road.

Aware that TV crews will be hovering around, Perini shaves in the car, a six-year-old navy blue Chevy Caprice with no police markings. When he crosses over the Indian River bridge to South Hutchinson Island, he has to shield his eyes from the brilliant early morning sun, rising above the orange-tinted, blue-gray clouds. Gentle winds fan the palm trees; gray pelicans drift lazily along the shoreline. Herring gulls swoop low over the mouth of the inlet, searching for breakfast. Dominick can hear the ocean, the rhythmic crashing and sucking of the water against the shore. Ahead he sees the flashing blue lights of patrol cars.

A crowd of fishermen, joggers, dog walkers, and immigrant construction workers gathers on the corner of Seaway Drive and A1A—silent, just watching. Perini gestures to his officers to keep the people back. He asks, "Who found the body?"

The fisherman named Walter steps forward. "We spotted the poor bugger snagged on the rocks and hauled him out of the water."

"You should know better than to corrupt a crime scene," Perini grouses.

"Crime scene, my ass. There's sharks in the inlet, Captain. When that tide rolled back in, you'd have nothing but bones and rags."

"Sorry, fellow," Perini mutters. "You did the right thing. Give your name and address to one of the officers so we can get back to you." He turns his attention to the body of the victim, lying on his back, partly covered with a blanket. Perini observes that the old man is white, maybe pushing eighty. The face on the pavement, now an object of curious stares, is waxy and pallid, with receding white hair, a thin white line of a scar on his forehead, and glacier blue eyes staring vacantly at the sky.

Perini eyes the crowd. Two short, compact, dark-haired Hispanic-looking men in white painter's overalls furtively whisper together, then the men drift out of sight.

Dr. Miriam Jolson presses her way through the crowd and extends her hand to Perini. "Good morning, Captain, or maybe not so good, eh? What do we have?"

Perini smiles at the medical examiner. In her mid forties, Miriam Jolson is an attractive, fair-skinned lady, with copper-colored hair casually unkempt. Unmarried, Jolson has recently returned from serving a tour in Afghanistan as a captain in the Florida National Guard. The chief of detectives steps aside so that Jolson can examine the body.

"Fisherman found him," Perini comments. "Pulled him out before the tide rolled in."

The medical examiner scrutinizes the body carefully, making notes in a black leather book, then dons rubber gloves. She notes the victim's soaking and torn clothing: a short-sleeve, open-neck, patterned sport shirt and khaki-colored Bermuda shorts. His feet are bare. Jolson gently unbuttons the sopping wet shirt. Perini is impressed that the deceased is so well muscled for an old man. Purplish bruise marks cover his ribs.

"I don't want to corrupt the autopsy by poking around too much," Miriam Jolson says. "There are multiple scars on his arms and torso. Also bruised ribs, which might have been caused by falling on the jetty rocks."

The medical examiner pauses, touching Dominick's arm. "I don't know what's going on here." She lowers her voice. "Look at the obtuse position of the head. X-rays will be needed to confirm what I'm thinking—"

"Which is?"

"A broken neck. I think death was caused by having his neck snapped. I know it sounds barbaric, but that's the way it looks to me."

"Couldn't it be that the old guy broke his neck by accidentally falling on the rocks?"

Jolson takes out a small penlight and aims it at the victim's neck. "This man didn't accidentally fall. There's a suspicious perforation in the neck that might have been caused by a needle. If a tranquilizer was administered, chemicals may show up in the autopsy."

She removes from her kit an L-shaped ruler and camera.

"What's that?" Perini asks.

"In forensic odontology, when there is a suspicion of death or incapacitation by drugs being administered, we place an L-shaped ruler next to the entry hole and photograph it to scale. After the prints are developed, I'll take them to the pathologist."

Perini turns to his two officers. "You guys get busy. Canvas the area and see if anyone knows the victim or saw anything suspicious. The jetty lights are on all night, so you never know what you might find.

"Miriam," he says, "how long has the man been dead?"

"Hard to be accurate, not knowing how long the body was in the water. But there are lividity patterns on the body. Lividity is what happens to a person's blood after death. The heart stops, blood pressure collapses, liquid blood pools by gravity into the lowest positioned part of the body. After about three hours you begin to see liverish purple stains."

"OK, so what does that tell us?"

"These purple marks aren't contusions from a fall. The victim was killed somewhere else, left lying on his stomach for a few hours, and then moved to the inlet during the early hours. The body hasn't been in the water long enough for serious deterioration to take place."

"This case is going to generate a lot of heat. How fast can we get autopsy results?"

"If they're not too backed up, I think the coroner could perform the autopsy this afternoon. You'll have results in the morning. Toxicology reports usually take two weeks, but I'm prepared to give you an educated guess. That anomaly in his neck is a pinhole with a slight bruise. I'd say your victim was first overpowered, tranquilized and then murdered.

"Let me get a few more photographs, fingerprints, a DNA sample, and a small slice of neck tissue for biopsy, then you can call Tri-County and have the body taken to the new crime lab on the Indian River campus."

"Miriam, can you meet me for lunch at Bessie's Grill on Avenue D around one o'clock?"

"Of course. Why?"

"I need to review this case before I talk to Chief Thompkins. In forty years of police work, I've seen hundreds of dead bodies. This case is somehow different. I feel it in my bones."

Perini releases a long, weary sigh and takes a final look at the old man's thin hawk nose and his high cheekbones that suggest nobility. Perini closes his eyes and pinches the skin at the bridge of his nose. Something niggles at him. It isn't specific. What he feels is an unexplainable sadness and melancholy in the presence of this victim. Something hovers on the tip of his consciousness, a resonant blank from somewhere.

...5

"THE VENETIAN IS DEAD," reports the cool, professional voice on Preston Morgan's private line. "His body was dredged out of a harbor this morning."

Hearing the news, the burly, broad-shouldered Undersecretary of Defense slumps in his chair, lowers his head and presses his marble-veined, coffee-colored palms tight up against his temple. The top Pentagon intelligence chief mutters, "They got to him. Fuck."

The voice continues, "We waited at the Fort Pierce Airport, as you ordered, but the Venetian never showed. At seven o'clock, I called his home and cell phones—no answer. I tapped into the local police band radio. They were jawing about a dead body of a white male floating in the inlet. The airfield is ten minutes from the harbor, so I used a fake press card and——"

Morgan interrupts, "Codling, are you a hundred percent certain it's the Venetian?"

"Yes, sir. It's your man, no mistake."

"How close is the nearest special cleanup crew?"

"Patrick Air Force Base, a few hours north."

"Red alert them in. I want the Venetian's apartment swept clean: computer, discs, notes, papers—everything. He was tracking an international heroin cartel. I want this mess covered up. Make it look like an accident, God forgive me. Put out the word that Polo was an old man with dementia. Contact the head of the VA hospital in Palm Beach to offer confirmation. We can't indulge in the luxury of revenge just yet. These cocky bastards need to keep thinking we don't know shit, otherwise they will roll up their network and move somewhere else. Then we're back to square nothing. I trust you to control the situation, Codling. And, don't forget, the Venetian worked for the OSS. He knew all the tricks—search his apartment carefully, and then make everything look undisturbed."

"What if the local gendarmes show up?"

13

"Tell them it has to do with a terrorist threat and that you're with Homeland Security, the Patriot Act and all that shit. Anyway, terrorism trumps their jurisdiction. I'll clear it from this end. It will take the local cops a while to finish their ham and grits, read the sports pages, and figure out Polo's identity and address. Move quickly!"

"One more thing," Codling adds. "By the time my team gets here it will be at least 9 A.M.; the victim's neighbors may be milling around. I don't think we should use the Homeland Secur—"

"Dammit, Codling, use your imagination. Dress your people as house painters." Morgan hangs up and reaches into his bottom right drawer, encircling the head of a bottle of Cutty Sark scotch. He takes a deep drag, then wipes his mouth with the back of his hand.

In for a penny, in for a pound, he sighs as he picks up the phone.

"Boss," Morgan says to Secretary of Defense Desmond Cody. "We have a problem."

"Preston, I'm due at the White House to give my daily briefing, and I'm running late."

"I'll make it fast. The agent I told you about who was investigating the Florida drug smuggling operation—he was found murdered this morning."

"Your people are soldiers in our war against terrorism," Cody cuts in. "Replace him."

"Mr. Secretary, aside from everything else, this man's death may generate unwelcome media attention. The agent was Nicolo Polo, the last descendant of Marco Polo—the explorer."

Morgan hears a loud sigh. "You're overreacting, Preston. The public doesn't read anymore. They're hooked on computers and television. To them, Marco Polo is the name of a swimming pool game. Now I gotta run."

"Also, Mr. Secretary," Morgan presses on, "our intelligence people in Kabul and Islamabad are picking up coded messages from Kyrgyzstan and Northern Pakistan about someone trying to reunite the old Mongolian empire. Nicolo Polo warned me that heroin was being transshipped from Afghanistan through the Venice area, then into this country. And the drug money was funneled back through offshore banks in the Caymans to buy arms. We also have reports from Israeli intelligence confirming efforts by persons unknown to unify tribal clans in Mongolia, Pakistan, Afghanistan and the mountain tribes in Kyrgyzstan."

"Do you seriously want me to tell the President of the United States that the Pentagon is concerned about the ghosts of Genghis Khan? Are you into your scotch already, Preston?"

"With all due respect, sir, you might point out to the President that if the tribal populations that once made up the Greater Mongol confederation make common cause with extremists, than we are in really serious shit. Pakistan has nuclear weapons and has already sold highly classified technology. It is hard to imagine a greater nightmare for America than the world's second largest Muslim nation, plus Afghanistan and Mongolia, falling into the hands of extremists using the poppy fields of Afghanistan to bankroll their nuclear ambitions."

"Preston, you also watch too much television." The Secretary of Defense hangs up.

Morgan reaches into his desk drawer and withdraws a folder containing a photograph of himself and a man with square shoulders, white hair, hawk nose, penetrating glacier-blue eyes, the thin white line of a scar draped across his forehead, and a diplomat's ready smile. The man in the photo is dressed in a slate-gray silk suit, white shirt with an off-white tie, and a Knight of Malta emblem in his lapel.

The general sips his scotch, staring at the photograph. "I messed up, Nicco. I messed up bad and got you killed." His voice cracks. "I should have listened to you and not talked on the phone or trusted that fucking bureaucrat, Cody." Morgan raises his bottle in a mock salute. He takes a long second draught. "You were the best of the best, old friend," he says. "God bless."

6

DOMINICK PERINI PARKS IN THE RIBBONED SHADE of a palm tree near the water's edge on Seaway Drive. To the north, across the inlet, he can see the tips of high-rise condominiums peeking behind the trees. The smell of salt water is strong. A scattering of power boats glides through the inlet at slow speed towards the ocean.

After finishing his coffee, he snaps open his phone. There are four messages.

"Dom, this is Billy Ray. Please return my call—*ASAP*."

"Dominick Perini, this is James S. Codling from the Department of Homeland Security. It is imperative that you contact me at once. Call 443-999-9000."

"Perini, this is Chief Thompkins again. Everybody but the governor is on my ass. *Call me, dammit*." *Click.*

"Captain, this is Jessie at the switchboard again. A young Hispanic housepainter was rubbernecking with the crowd at the jetty. He identified the body. The dead man was his customer. The painter is probably an *illegal*, that's why he didn't contact us until he talked to his wife first. She made him call. He gave us the deceased's name and address: Nicolo Polo, 3030 Windward Drive in Ocean Village, about a mile south of Archie's Bar on A1A. Detectives Brumberg and Unger are there."

Perini pushes *Send* twice. "Jessie," he says, "get the crime investigation team moving. I'm on my way. And patch me in to Chief Thompkins."

"Dominick, listen to me," Billy Ray Thompkins roars. "The inlet case is now a federal matter. Homeland Security people are involved; national security takes jurisdiction. They insist on a sit down with you."

Perini is silent.

"Are you still there, goddammit?"

"Yes, Billy Ray. I'm here. Tell the Feds to come to headquarters tomorrow morning at nine o'clock, and we'll talk." He hangs up.

PERINI PULLS INTO THE VISITOR'S LANE at Ocean Village and flashes his badge to the guard. "Are there any other access roads into the area?" he asks.

"Yes, sir. There's an entrance off Blue Heron Road, but it's locked at night."

Perini points to the other lane. "Your residents all have car stickers that open the gate?"

"Right."

"Are all nonresidents registered when they enter?"

"Our jobs depend on it."

"No exceptions?"

"No, sir."

"Let me see your clipboard." Perini scans the listing of arrivals at the gatehouse. "This is Florida, right?"

"Yeah, so?" the man says defensively.

"How many units in Ocean Village?"

"Probably five hundred."

"Some of these units are on the ocean. That must be hard on roof air-conditioning units?"

"Guess so."

"How come I don't see one air conditioning repair company listed on your log?"

The guard coughs nervously. "We know who the AC service companies are."

"You recognize them by face or by truck?"

The guard shrugs. "By truck, I guess. They always have new employees."

"And that applies also to landscapers, plumbers, electricians, painters, and movers?"

"More or less."

"Sounds pretty airtight to me," Perini grins. "Have a nice day."

* * *

DETECTIVES BRUMBERG AND UNGER meet Perini as the elevator stops on the third floor. Connie Unger is five-foot two, brown hair and olive skin, large dark eyes, an upturned nose. She moves with the bounce of a fit, muscular woman.

"What have we got, Lou?" Perini asks Brumberg.

The short, stocky, red-haired detective's face is open and friendly. "The unit's unlocked, Captain, but we didn't go in. This building has twenty-four units. Most of the owners are snowbirds up north for the summer. I posted a notice on the bulletin board requesting information, and I'm getting a list of year-round residents."

"Anyone see or hear anything?"

Connie Unger looks at her pad. "A downstairs neighbor, Elaine Gillman, talked to me. Mrs. Gillman was a friend of the deceased. She claims that she heard strange noises during the night and called Mr. Polo first thing this morning, but no one answered, so she went up to his apartment. Painters were there."

"Does she know Polo's dead?"

Unger shakes her head. "I don't think so, but she's worried about him."

"I'll break the news," Perini says. "You two keep the unit secure until the crime investigation team gets here."

When Perini knocks, an old lady opens the door a crack, the length of her security chain. She is too short to reach the peephole. Perini holds up his badge. "Mrs. Gillman, I'm Chief of Detectives Dominick Perini. I would appreciate a few moments of your time."

The chain is slowly unlatched and Perini is greeted by a short, gray-haired lady with a heart-shaped face, intelligent brown eyes, and a dish towel over her shoulder. She says in a controlled voice, "This has to do with Nicco, doesn't it?"

Let's get this over with, muses Perini. He nods. "Yes, ma'am. May I come in?"

She nods and steps aside. "If they send a captain, it has to be bad. Tell me."

"I'm sorry, Mrs. Gillman, but your neighbor, Mr. Polo, has been ... he's dead."

Elaine Gillman pales. She tries to blink away the tears that stream down her face. "I warned him," she mumbles. "I told him,

18

'Don't go out late at night in Fort Pierce. It's a jungle.' He wouldn't listen."

"Can I get you some water?"

"They say 'life goes on,' but it hurts to lose someone you care about."

"I know. I've been there."

She wipes her eyes with the dish towel and with a shattered smile says, "Knowing Nicco was a God-given gift to me late in life. Face it—it's hard for an old single woman to be alone. Nicco was a good man. Why would anyone want to harm him?"

"Would you like some water?" Perini repeats.

She half-smiles. "Nicco always told me that water was for bathing; Kir was for drinking." Mrs. Gillman fills two tumblers with a pink liquid and hands one carefully to Perini. He notices the tremor in her right hand.

"*Cin, Cin,*" she says in shaky voice.

"You're Italian?"

"I'm Jewish. Nicco introduced me to Kir. He said *Cin, Cin* meant 'May you live a hundred years.' And now, he'll never live another year."

"You and Mr. Polo were close friends, I take it?"

Perini can see her eyes fill up as she takes a large sip of Kir.

"Nicco, even at his age, always had an eye for pretty young women. But he took me to all the operas at the Sunrise Theater. On Wednesdays, if Nicco was in town, we would go to Toojays in Vero Beach. That's the day they serve cabbage soup. Sometimes Nicco would take me consignment shopping, and sometimes we ate Chinese."

Keep her talking, thinks Perini. "Chinese food?"

"Yes, Uncle Kai's in Stuart."

"That's a long way to go for Chinese food."

Elaine Gillman brightens. "Nicco enjoyed talking Chinese to Uncle Kai."

"What was Mr. Polo's profession, ma'am?"

"Nicco was a retired consultant. He came from the Washington area. Recently he took on a special project as a favor for an old friend. During the war Nicco was a hero."

"A hero? He told you that?"

She runs a shaking hand through her thinning gray hair. "He was wounded five times." The elderly woman pauses and blushes. "I saw his scars."

"With all respect, scars don't always make a hero."

"Once, when Nicco had the flu, I was looking for a thermometer in his bedroom dresser. There was a drawer full of medals." She gets up unsteadily and refills the glasses.

"Mrs. Gillman, did your friend have any enemies?"

"Nicco? No. He was respected by everyone in the building."

"What was he doing out late at night that worried you?"

"At first I thought it was a woman. You know how men are. He said he was researching a project that could only be done at night. I believed him. He was a man to be trusted." She studies Perini's face carefully. "You know, Captain—and it isn't the Kir talking—you remind me of Nicco."

"I take that as a compliment, ma'am. Thank you. I have just a few more questions. Do you think robbery was a motive? Did Mr. Polo have valuable collectibles?"

She shrugs. "Nicco took me thrifting and consignment shopping, but he never collected things for himself. His apartment is sparsely furnished, as you'll see; he didn't even use all of his storage space in the garage. He kept my storm shutters in his storage unit."

"Thank you, Mrs. Gillman. Here's my card. Please call me if you can think of anything." As he is leaving, Perini turns. "You told my detective that you heard strange sounds from upstairs during the night. Do you remember the time?"

She looks up at the ceiling. "Let me see. I was visiting friends in Jensen Beach and got home before dark. I don't like driving at night. Then I watched TV and after the ten o'clock news I went to sleep. I was going to the bathroom about three A.M. when I heard the noise."

"What did it sound like?"

"Bumping sounds."

"To your knowledge, would anyone besides Mr. Polo have a key to his apartment?"

She shakes her head. "Our keys are made special. They cost fifty dollars each."

"If there was an emergency, who could get into your apartment?"

"I guess the management company has a passkey."

"You also mentioned that there were painters in Mr. Polo's apartment this morning."

"They *said* they were painters, and they wore white coveralls, but I knew something was wrong. Nicco only uses Mario, the Brazilian boy. I use him to paint my apartment too. Also, the men were wearing polished black leather shoes."

"Thank you, Mrs. Gillman. Be well."

"Please find the animals who killed Nicco." She pauses. "Oh, and there's Norman."

"Norman?"

"Norman's our exterminator. He has keys to everyone's apartment."

"THE CRIME LAB SAYS THE APARTMENT'S CLEAN," reports Detective Unger. "No prints, no blood, nothing suspicious."

Perini looks around the dead man's apartment. It's a comfortable space: wood floors, an oriental rug, old-fashioned furniture. A small television set with a black cable box wired to it. Some books neatly arranged on a shelf; a small music system with a rack of operatic CD's neatly filed next to it.

"The desk is empty," Unger adds. "His clothes and wallet were left intact in the drawers. The man was vain; I saw five white shirts initialed with the letters *NP*."

Perini motions both detectives into Nicolo Polo's office. "I don't know how much time we have before this case is lifted from our jurisdiction by the Feds. So we need to act fast. This murder occurred on our watch, and I don't want it buried for political expediency.

"Unger, you check out the victim's bank account at BankAmerica. I saw deposit slips in his desk. Call the local branch on Virginia Avenue. Tell them subpoenas are in the works if needed. Then check the post office and talk to the mailman for this building. See if he remembers any unusual mailings. Did anyone find a cell phone?"

"Negative, Captain," Brumberg says.

"Lou, I want you to check his telephone calls for the last 90 days, at least. The phone company usually cooperates. Get me a complete listing. Then contact the management company, find out which exterminator company handles this building. Find out who else has passkeys."

He touches the wall. "If painters were here this morning, why is there no wet paint?"

PERINI KNOCKS. "Mrs. Gillman, sorry to trouble you again. Didn't you tell me Mr. Polo had a storage space in this building?"

"We all do."

"Do you have a key to his storage locker?"

"No. It's a combination lock. I don't have the combination. It's locker number nine."

Perini goes into the trunk of his car and removes a hammer. The ground floor of the building houses the lobby, elevators, and garage area. Number nine is a 10 x 20 foot storage area of chain-link fencing.

With two sharp strikes of the hammer, Perini opens the lock. On the left of the storage space he sees three plastic shelves filled with dusty paint cans and fishing equipment. Against the far wall are stacked folding beach chairs and a multi-striped umbrella. Mrs. Gillman's metal storm shutters are stacked neatly against the link fencing, marked with her apartment number. In the right corner is an old golf bag filled with clubs that are old and dusty.

He carries the golf bag outside the locker where the light is brighter. Brushing aside the spider webs, Perini withdraws the musty clubs and upends the bag. Particles of dirt sprinkle out. He opens a small zippered side panel and finds old balls, tees and dried suntan lotion. In the larger inside compartment, which has a moldy smell, Perini sees a blue folded Nike windbreaker and cracked golf shoes coated with dry grass and mud. He removes the windbreaker and shakes it open. Two black leather packets encased in plastic Ziploc bags drop at his feet.

"Oh, oh," he mutters.

Opening the larger packet, Perini discovers four passports and four driver's licenses, each with the dead man's photo, but under four different names: Nardo Palmiero, Nono Piersanti, Nataniele Prinzio and Nunzio Polidoro. Two passports are American, one Canadian, and one Italian. *Four aliases with common initials,* thinks Perini, shaking his head, remembering the *NP* monogrammed shirts. *I guess as you get older, you have to keep it simple to remember.*

Along with the passports is an envelope with a key taped inside and an M9 Beretta, a nine-millimeter semiautomatic pistol, wrapped in plastic. It's old and scratched, but well-oiled. Perini notes the single shell locked in the chamber. The magazine is missing. He shakes the packet and finds three spare empty magazines wrapped in plastic, along with a box of 45 standard jacketed cartridges. *Smart,* Perini reasons. *Storing the magazine with fifteen rounds of bullets is for thugs and amateurs, particularly in this damp garage. Over time, the springs in the magazines could malfunction. Better to store the bullets separately.*

In the second packet, Perini discovers a dozen envelopes stuffed with one-hundred-dollar bills. He riffles one envelope and estimates that each contains fifty bills. *An old golf bag with fifty thousand dollars in it,* muses Perini. *I really should take up this game.*

Perini locks Polo's packets in his trunk and returns to Elaine Gillman's apartment.

"What is it now?" Mrs. Gillman mumbles, slightly tipsy. "You want another drink?"

"No ma'am. Did Mr. Polo ever discuss his family?"

"Nicco said he was the last living descendant of the famous Italian explorer, Marco Polo."

Perini grins. "And did he have a bridge to sell you?"

"Huh?"

"Was Mr. Polo a golfer?"

"Not that I know of."

"You were good friends, right?"

She takes a deep breath. "I already told you about that."

"I know this is an awkward question, Mrs. Gillman. Did you two ever discuss... what would happen after either of you died?"

Elaine Gillman chuckles. "Don't be embarrassed to ask. When you get to be our age, one makes plans... you know. I will be buried alongside my husband in Long Island. If I wasn't, my kids would go crazy."

"And Mr. Polo?"

"Nicco wanted to be buried in Venice, where he was born."

"How was that to be arranged?"

"Nicco gave me a letter to mail if he—oh my God. I forgot all about it."

7

My Dear Dante:

The fact that you are in receipt of this correspondence presumes my passage. My life has been full, if solitary. But, it has also been one of my own choosing. Like Don Quixote, I tilted at windmills long past the days I should have lain down my lance. As this letter signifies, the windmills have bested me. And, like Quixote's Dulcinea, the passion of my life was a lusty young Veneto farm girl. So, the Polo lineage finally comes to an end, as all things must.

I appoint you my executor. There are matters that must be attended to. My wish is to be buried in San Michele Cemetery. I know that it was un-Venetian of me, but neither wealth nor recognition were of signal importance in my life. I leave no estate, save a modest savings account in BankAmerica, number enclosed. Please use the balance to pay funeral expenses and donate the remainder to a charity of your choice. My furniture and furnishings I gift to my dear friend Elaine Gillman.

Also enclosed you will find my safety deposit box key for Cassa Di Risparmio Di Venesia, SPA in Dorsoduro. I had you sign a signature card, therefore you should experience no difficulty gaining admission. The bank box contains a valuable artifact, an ivory and gold tablet that the Chinese ruler Kubla Khan gave to Marco Polo's Uncle Maffeo, which then passed to Marco in Maffeo's will. This precious tablet has been handed down through generations of Polos. As I am the last descendant, please accept the Golden Tablet as the Polo family's gift to your museum.

Please do not trouble to mourn me. As Da Vinci said, "A well-spent day brings happy sleep, so a life well used brings happy death." I trust my life was well-used.

Bless you and keep you.
Nicolo Polo

* * *

"I'LL MAIL THIS FOR YOU, Mrs. Gillman," Perini says after reading Polo's letter. He makes another trip to his car, removes the money pouch and returns. Handing Mrs. Gillman the black packet, he says, "Mr. Polo wanted you to have this money. Get a safe deposit box at the bank and keep this for a rainy day." He winks. "You didn't hear it from me, but don't tell your tax accountant or your kids."

MEDICAL EXAMINER MIRIAM JOLSON DRIVES down Avenue D. *How drab*, she thinks. On the southwest corner of D and 13th Street she sees a dull blue concrete block restaurant with the name *Bessie's Bar and Grill* painted in foot-high black letters outlined in white. Two Harleys are parked on the sidewalk, leaning against the building.

Jolson parks and locks her car, aware of the curious glances of four young black men sitting on bicycles, idling on the corner. All four are dressed in black caps, black ankle-length pants, black shoes and oversized tee shirts. Her heartbeat quickens. *Get over it*, she wills herself.

All ten tables in Bessie's small bar and restaurant are filled with mostly black male patrons. Five men sit drinking at the bar. Being a medical examiner, Jolson inhales details— it's second nature. The hand-scrawled menu on the cream-colored wall over the bar announces today's special: *Salmon cakes, grits and eggs*. The wall opposite the bar is covered with framed newspaper reviews, citations, and autographed pictures of Los Angeles Dodgers stars who formerly spring-trained in Vero Beach. Two ceiling fans rotate lazily.

The murmur of voices stops. Heads turn to look at the attractive, young, copper-haired white woman whose hair is tied in back, wearing faded blue jeans, a khaki tee shirt, and sunglasses high up on her head. Jolson threads her way between the bar and food-covered tables towards where Perini sits talking to a slender black woman in her sixties.

She feels a large hand roughly clamp her buttocks. "Hello, Sweetie," says a big, bearded, white motorcyclist dressed in black leather except for his red checkered headband. "You looking for a little fun?"

The place becomes hushed. Perini rises quickly from his seat. The owner's son-in-law, Willie the bartender, pulls a baseball bat from somewhere. Before anyone can move, Miriam Jolson grabs the offending hand and rips up sharply on the index finger, breaking it—at the same time she slams her knee hard into the man's groin. The motorcyclist howls in surprise and pain.

"Hey," Jolson says. "That *was* fun. We should do it again sometime."

Perini pushes the man against the bar roughly. "I'm a police officer. This lady is a captain in the Army Reserves who just returned from Afghanistan. Is she bothering you, fellow? Do you want to file a complaint?"

The angry motorcyclist clutches his broken finger and looks around sheepishly. "Damn, that smarts," he says. "I guess I had it coming. No problem." He gives Miriam Jolson a lopsided grin and a salute. The room bursts into hoots and applause.

"NEXT TIME I PICK THE RESTAURANT," Jolson says as she sits down.

"Bessie, meet Fort Pierce's esteemed medical examiner."

"Girl, you sure know how to make an entrance."

"Miriam, say hello to the poster lady for the Fort Pierce black community. Miss Bessie has the oldest active business on Avenue D."

"Except for Sarah's Memorial Chapel," Bessie adds. "When I started, there were nothing but shuttered and broken-down stores here on the avenue. The neighborhood's been in transition for decades. Now a new mix of Haitians and Hispanics are moving in, and we all get along just fine. But enough about me. What can we feed you?"

Perini sniffs. "The salmon cakes smell good."

"Too late for salmon cakes. You got to get here early; we run out. The meat and sweet potato pie is good, made with butter and sweet potatoes, along with vanilla and cinnamon. And the chitterlings are a recipe of my grandmother's, who was a boardinghouse cook in Georgia."

"Aren't chitterlings pigs' intestines?" Jolson asks.

"That's right. Same as chitlins."

"Sweet potato pie and coffee for me. I see enough intestines in my work."

"I'll take the same," chimes in Perini.

After Bessie leaves, he says, "I eat here regularly. Food's great, prices are right, and nothing goes on in the black community that Bessie isn't privy to. She's a grandmother, bartender and psychiatrist rolled into one, but she has never betrayed a confidence. It wouldn't be good for her business or her health. Sometimes she alerts me to potential trouble and signals me in the right direction."

"Did you find out who the man was who was murdered?" Jolson asks.

"His name was Polo, a distant relative to the Italian explorer. I think the old gentleman was some sort of government agent. The *federales* want to take over the investigation, invoking Homeland Security jurisdiction. So far I've avoided them."

"Can't they overrule you?"

"Probably, but it gives me a little time to check things out."

Willie arrives at the table laden with two sweet potato pies and coffee. "Let it cool a minute, folks."

"Smells good," whispers Jolson, "but loaded with calories." She touches Perini's hand. "Could your job be in danger if you don't cooperate?"

"I've learned to take things as they come. Maybe I should chuck the job, take up golf, marry you and live off your exorbitant medical examiner's income."

Jolson smiles. "I love you, Dom, but not in that way. If the California court's decision on same-sex marriage holds, I might soon be inviting you to a wedding— to escort me down the aisle. How about *your* family? Don't you have a son in the Army?"

"We're not close. Woulda, coulda, shoulda. I was working my ass off twenty-four-seven with the Baltimore Detective Squad. The town was a madhouse. The year I joined, in '68, we had the race riots after Martin Luther King was shot. Then in '78 Baltimore's murder rate was going through the roof because of drugs. All around me, cops were seeing their marriages fall apart. I drank too hard. I put my job ahead of everything... even my kid."

He pauses for a pull on his coffee. "It was a sad, familiar story with cops' wives. Mine left me and took my son, Tony. I was a basket case. Then I started reading union vacancy lists. Saw this job offer in Fort Pierce in the detective division, and I took off. Mary was a good woman. She married a corrugated box salesman a year after our divorce."

"*Was* a good woman?"

"Mary died a year ago while my boy was serving in Afghanistan. Her sister called me."

"And your son?"

"Tony and I were tight when he was young," Perini said. "After the divorce, I had to get away from the Baltimore drug scene, the bullshit politicians, my drinking, and the hole in my heart from losing my family. Tony was angry with me. I guess he rightly felt I deserted him. For a few years I sent Christmas and birthday gifts; when he didn't respond, I just let it slide. He sent me an invitation to his West Point graduation, but at the time it was just after the Rodney King thing in California. Avenue D was a powder keg, and Haitian refugees were piling ashore all over Hutchinson Island. I was trying to help them integrate into the community without getting picked up by immigration and shipped back to Haiti."

"That twists the law. Wasn't it your job to arrest the Haitians as illegal immigrants?"

"Eat your sweet potato pie before it gets cold," Perini says.

"Dom," Jolson continues, "I've been thinking about the inlet murder and the old man's musculature; he wouldn't have been a pushover. I biopsied the neck tissue before releasing the body for autopsy. There were trace elements of reconstructed Rohypnol."

"Isn't that what they call the 'date rape' drug?"

"Yes, it's a form of benzodiazepine, a tranquilizer and central nervous system depressant about ten times stronger than Valium. It causes muscle relaxation, drowsiness, unconsciousness and amnesia. Rohypnol incapacitates a person instantly and dissipates in the body within hours, leaving no residue. If I had waited for the autopsy results, it would have gone undetected. Rohypnol was developed in the Army's Chemical and Biological Center at Edgewood Arsenal in Maryland for use in detention centers in Afghanistan and Guantanamo Bay."

Perini closes his eyes and tightens his jaw muscles.

"I believe the old man was tranquilized with Rohypnol, then dropped in the inlet. With the Rohypnol dissipated and undetected, the broken neck would appear to be a result of falling on the jetty rocks. Do you have any leads?"

"The truth is, I don't know anything. Getting into Polo's gated community isn't rocket science, but gaining access to the apartment of an experienced operative is another matter. If the murder occurred in the apartment, how was the body moved to the inlet without anyone seeing? Also, Polo's unit was swept clean this morning by government people posing as house painters." Perini sighs and shrugs.

Jolson studies the chief of detective's face. "I know this sounds odd, but your resemblance to the murdered man is uncanny."

Perini's phone beeps.

"Captain," says Connie Unger, "we caught a break. I'm at the Orange Avenue post office. I found the man in charge on his lunch break. His name's Theodore. He's Haitian. At first he was uptight, lecturing me about a citizen's right to privacy while he ogled my breasts. At any rate, he checked, as a favor, and there's a rented post office box here assigned to an N. Polo."

"Did you get a look in the box?"

"No way. USPS bureaucracy is about as safe as a Swiss bank."

"Good work, Connie. Regular mail, that's what Polo used. Once the mail was out of his hands it was safe—it was in the system, stored in his mailbox."

Perini flips his phone closed, gives Miriam Jolson a thumbs-up sign, drops a twenty-dollar bill on the table, and waves goodbye to Bessie Carter.

THE FORT PIERCE POST OFFICE parking lot is half-empty in the early afternoon hours. Perini rushes through the narrow, musty-smelling hallway. Metal mailboxes are stacked ten high on either side of the aisle, the biggest boxes on the bottom.

At the counter Perini flashes his badge and asks for Mr. Theodore. People waiting in line eye him sullenly. One Hispanic woman, with a little girl in tow, spies the badge, slips out of the line and leaves the building.

"My name is Theodore. How may I be of service?" says a tall, dignified-looking Haitian.

"Mr. Theodore, as my detective told you, we're investigating a murder. It's important that I check out the rented postal box of the deceased."

"I'm sorry, Captain. The law is very specific. You can apply to the postal inspectors or secure a court order to gain access."

"Look, Theodore. Let's make it simple. I'm on a tight timeline. I can't wait for court orders. Do me a favor and get me the box contents. I won't forget it. I'll owe you a big favor."

"I've heard about you, Captain Perini. You're a good friend to our Haitian community, but it's not worth my job to shortcut the system. Anyone with a key and a box number can get in—no problem. Otherwise, there's no way."

Key and box number, thinks Perini. He bolts to the parking lot and unlocks his trunk. In the black packet containing Polo's passports, he withdraws the envelope. Inside is the taped key and a 2 x 4 card reading: Box #127.

THERE IS NO SHADE on the post office parking lot. Perini pulls down his window visor and sets the air conditioner on high as he studies the three brown kraft envelopes. All are addressed to Box #127, US Post Office, Orange Avenue Station, 1717 Orange Ave, Fort Pierce, Florida 34950-0021. There are no return addresses.

He notes one envelope has a February date, one March and one April. Perini opens the envelope dated April. Inside is a folded sheet filled with numbers and letters. He sighs. Adrenaline has been kicking in ever since he used the key. Finding a listing of oddball letters and numbers is a disappointment. Perini takes a deep breath and slowly rereads the list.

```
04-01-0315-RGU023
04-01-0445-MCT424
04-02-0215-DHK762
04-02-0345-PBY565
04-03-0315-WDS981
04-03-0445-LGT284
04-04-0215-BJU495
04-04-0445-VGH556
04-05-0315-RGU023
04-05-0445-MCT424
```

OK. So 04 is probably the month; the next number is the date, the next group could be military time, and the last batch must be some kind of code. He opens the other two envelopes and, except for the change in month and variations in time, the other data is much the same.

Perini shifts out of park and waits behind a green Toyota for traffic to allow him to exit on to Orange Avenue. He taps impatiently on the steering wheel, idly reading the rear bumper sticker on the Toyota. "When life hands you gators, make Gatorade."

His glance moves to the license plate, FJT699. "Bingo." Perini smiles as he heads east on Orange to US1, then south to Stuart.

UNCLE KAI'S is located on the southeast side of Federal Highway in Stuart. The Chinese restaurant is painted white with a slanted red pagoda roof. A neat row of four-foot yews with fluffy green needles border the metal grate entrance.

A sour-faced Chinese woman of about sixty drops a menu on the table.

"I'd like to speak to Uncle Kai," Perini says.

"Too busy," she grumbles.

Perini sighs and shows his badge. "Rat droppings were seen in your kitchen."

She glares, tightens her lips, and goes into the kitchen.

A tall man approaches the table. His posture is erect, his age indeterminate.

"Uncle Kai?" Perini asks. He shows the owner one of Polo's passports. "Do you recognize this man?"

"Hard to be certain. We have many customers."

"How many customers speak Chinese?"

Perini watches the man's eyes—no emotion. Kai smiles blandly. "Mr. Polo was well traveled—an educated man." Kai barks a few words in Chinese to the old woman behind the counter. She immediately places a bowl of simmering soup in front of Perini.

"Please try the hot-and-sour soup. It is our signature dish."

"Nicolo Polo was murdered."

Uncle Kai's expression is unreadable. "That is regrettable."

They sit in silence.

Perini says, "I'd like to ask you a few questions. Just routine." He knows that line makes most people nervous. "So what did you guys talk about in Chinese?"

Uncle Kai eyes the captain closely. "I come from Hangzhou, a city near Shanghai. Mr. Polo was familiar with my city. We spoke about the exquisite West Lake called *Xi Hu*, the beautiful gardens and temples—"

"By any chance, do you know what business Nicolo Polo was in?"

"I believe he was retired."

Perini sips his soup. It's too spicy for his taste, but he doesn't want to appear rude. He knows from experience that prolonged silence normally causes the other person to feel pressured and to fill the vacuum by talking. *This man is not only stoic, but is controlling the flow of the interview. He's a pro*, intuits the detective.

"How long have you been in business?"

"In Fort Pierce?"

"Yes. In Fort Pierce."

Kai steeples his hands. "In the Year of the Horse, 2002."

"And before that, maybe you had a restaurant in Washington?"

"Sorry, Captain, no. I did not."

Perini finishes his soup and wipes his mouth with a napkin.

The restaurant owner smiles. "It was in Alexandria, Virginia."

"Uncle Kai," Perini asks, "do you live upstairs?"

"Yes. My wife and I live on the premises."

"Hypothetically, if I was to ask your permission to look around your apartment—without a search warrant—would you be opposed?"

"Hypothetically or otherwise, it will be my honor to welcome you into our home."

"Nicolo Polo was more than your customer. Do you know why he was murdered?"

"Captain, I know you by reputation. You are a good man and no fool. We understand one another; therefore I speak plainly. Your city is an offload point for heroin. The money from the drugs finances political problems on China's northern border with Mongolia. Drug money also buys weapons for the Taliban to kill your soldiers in Afghanistan. In this instance, our national interests coincide.

"I received a telephone call two days ago," Kai continues. "Polo was angry. He had accomplished his mission and uncovered the heroin smugglers. Polo complained that his organization was getting as careless and bureaucratic as the CIA, and his handler was an alcoholic. Then Polo had to stop talking because the building exterminator came in to spray. Polo promised to call me back. He never did."

Kai shrugged his shoulders, and his eyes softened. "Captain. I give you the advice I gave my friend, which unfortunately went unheeded. You never wound an octopus; you kill it. To kill an octopus you must cut off its head. If you cut off one tentacle, two or more tentacles grow back. In that case, it becomes a decatopus and is even more dangerous.

"Nicolo was intrepid—like his ancestor. Personally and professionally, I mourn his loss. You may find this strange for me to say, but I wish you no success in tracking Polo's killers locally. They are but one tentacle, which can easily be withdrawn. Unless the octopus' head is cut off, more tentacles will appear, and that is unacceptable." Kai stared into Perini's face. "My friend, you remind me much of Nicolo Polo—men who fulfill their destiny through their duty."

"And your duty is to make hot and sour soup. Right."

"Yes. With octopus eyes."

The two men stand and silently shake hands.

* * *

34

"MRS. GILLMAN," Perini says on the cell phone. "Does your exterminator have a key to your apartment?"

"Of course. How else could Mr. Doyle—?"

"Thank you ma'am," Perini cuts in. Then he punches in Detective Brumberg's number. "Lou, I know how they got through the gate, and I know how they gained access to Polo's apartment. Take some officers and bring in the exterminator; his name is Doyle. "

THE FORT PIERCE POLICE STATION is located in the north end of town off of US1. It is a long, low, one-story brown brick structure with a forest of tall radio masts bolted to the roof. Stainless steel letters spell out "Fort Pierce Police Department" over the entrance. Three flags fly briskly on the flagpole: the large American flag at the top; the Florida flag, with red diagonal stripes and state seal, in the center; and the smaller Fort Pierce flag at the bottom.

Perini hangs his suit jacket on the back of the office chair and loosens his tie. The sparsely furnished room is decorated with off-white walls, tough tan nylon carpet and steel filing cabinets. Reports and memoranda are tacked to a corkboard on the wall. Two visitor chairs covered in black micro suede face the desk. A window with white vertical blinds overlooks the greenery of the Indian Springs golf course.

On his desk, someone has left the morning paper. A front page column is circled with a black marker pen. A Post-It memo is attached with the terse *FYI* and signed with Police Chief Thompkin's initials.

ACCIDENTAL DROWNING IN FORT PIERCE INLET

FORT PIERCE GAZETTE, May 4—Police were summoned to Jetty Park yesterday morning to retrieve the body of Mr. Nicolo Polo, a resident of Hutchinson Island, who died from accidental causes. According to Colonel Charles Landry, head of the Veterans Administration medical facility in West Palm Beach, Mr. Polo, age 82, and a veteran of World War II, suffered from advanced dementia. It is reported that Mr. Polo would often take long, solitary walks late at night. Mr. Polo was the last in the line of a noble Venetian family. His body is being flown to Italy for burial.

...8

PERINI'S INTERCOM BUZZES. "They're here," Jessie says.

"The Federal Bureau of Incompetence?" he chuckles, letting a beat of silence pass, then adding, "Send them in."

Perini observes the older man: tall, straight-backed, over forty-five, with a narrow face, a genial smile and hard, cold, gray eyes. He is still in reasonable shape. The federal agent wears a charcoal gray winter wool suit, white button-down shirt, and a quiet tie. *Didn't have time to change clothes for the Florida weather*, thinks Perini.

The second agent is a heavyset man with a distinctive white streak in his brush cut. The man's eyes are hard and watchful, and his neck is short and thickly muscled: a weight lifter.

"My name's Codling," the leader states, not bothering to shake hands. "My partner's name is Fischer." He tosses his card on the desk and takes a chair. "I'm glad you can spare us some of your valuable time," he says in a dismissive voice.

Perini grins. "I had to juggle my schedule." He eyes the card identifying James S. Codling, Pentagon, Washington. D.C. "On the phone you said you were Homeland Security."

"Spare me, Sherlock. I hear you're a bloodhound and like to do things your own way, but this one is way over your pay grade. You can now go back to arresting hookers on Avenue D."

He's good, Perini decides. *Trying to rattle me.* "Codling, I read the phony obit you put in the *Tribune*."

"I'll lay it out for you, Sherlock, so you don't fuck up here like you did in Baltimore. This case has larger issues that involve national security—"

"Let's get something clear before we go any further, Codling," interrupts Perini. "I can appreciate your needling me to make me lose my cool. It's a good tactic. I use it myself. But if you call me 'Sherlock' again, I'm going to flatten your nose and toss your sorry ass out into the parking lot." He smiles at Fischer. "And your girlfriend with you."

Fischer's eyes narrow, his eyebrows pinch together, and his jaw clenches tightly. His eyes flicker with barely controlled animosity. The will to violence radiates from him.

Codling gives Fischer a quick look and shakes his head. He turns to Perini and lifts his eyebrows and shoulders in an exaggerated shrug of bewildered innocence. "Sorry, Captain. No offense, but there are forces at play here that I'm not at liberty to discuss. Nothing to be gained by a local investigation of the drug network except to scare off important leads to a foreign drug cartel. The official line is that the old man suffered from dementia. He wandered off, fell into the water and drowned. Nobody knows any different, and that's the way we're going to keep it."

"How about witnesses, and the autopsy results showing traces of Rohypnol?"

"What results? The body has been flown to Walter Reed for the autopsy. When it comes to terrorism threats," Codling says with a wintry smile and unblinking eyes, "the government can and will do whatever is necessary. Your pal, the medical examiner, Captain Jolson, has been reactivated for another tour in Afghanistan. She shipped out this morning."

Perini returns him a hard look, and they sit like that for a long moment, facing each other. Codling taps his watch in annoyance. "As to your fishermen, they are not available for questioning. Walter's son is an officer in the Navy SEALS. He took his dad and friend to a remote fishing village in Alaska. A salmon fishing trip as a gift for Father's Day. Nice son, eh?"

"And my detectives?"

"Let me wrap it up nice for you, Perini. Detective Brumberg is with the program. He sniffs a job opening and wants it. Detective Connie Unger may be a problem, but she's your problem. If she talks, her career is over—bank on it. The Pentagon intercepts a lot of threats to national safety. And *we* deal with them. How we deal with them is entirely confidential. Therefore, I am informing you that you are under a legal obligation to drop your personal investigation and never mention this situation to anybody, anywhere, any time. That obligation is rooted in federal statute and the Patriot Act. There are serious sanctions available to us.

"In addition, your pension contract specifies cancellation for malfeasance, which we can prove—if necessary—because you have impeded our investigation, and the Internal Revenue Service can be an annoying and costly organization to fight in court if it really chooses to be."

Codling sighs his irritation. He looks directly at Perini. "Terminate your interest in Mr. Polo immediately. We don't want flags raised on the matter, not under any circumstances."

Perini remains silent.

"Do you understand what I said?"

"I'd like it in writing."

"Verbal will do." Without another word, Codling and Fischer leave the office.

As the government men drive off, shore winds pick up. The insistent breezes cause the three flags in front of the police station to wave and snap like rifle shots.

Perini leans back in his chair and combs his hair with his fingers. He presses the intercom. "Jessie, please call the Veterans Administration in Palm Beach. Tell them we're investigating the murder of one of their veterans. Ask them to fax us up the file on Nicolo Polo."

His cell phone hums

"Dominick, listen to me," whispers Bessie Carter. "Willie heard two guys talking at the bar. One was from Okachoobie. Willie says he's a known dealer. They had a lot to drink, and Willie heard the guy sayin' that he hasta go make a pickup 'cause the eagles landed on Indrio.'"

"Thank you, Bessie."

"I don't want no trouble over this, you hear?" She hangs up.

"THE VA IS STALLING," Jessie reports. "They say Mr. Polo's files can't be released because there are confidentiality issues. They gave me a number to call in Washington, and Detective Brumberg is holding for you."

"Yeah, Lou," Perini says testily.

"Captain. The exterminator isn't our man. He's been in Las Vegas for a week on a gambling junket. I spoke to him on the phone."

"Couldn't somebody else have used his truck?"

"No, sir. I confirmed it with airport security. The truck's parked in the long term parking lot at the Orlando Airport. It has never been moved."

...9

THE METROPOLITAN CLUB AT 1700 H STREET is Washington's oldest, most prestigious private club. Proximity to the White House and other seats of American power makes it a way point for national leaders, including every U.S. President since Abraham Lincoln. The club's unique location provides its members with a convenient haven from the bustle of Washington's official business while offering the amenities of a four-star hotel.

The Assistant Secretary of Defense, Preston Morgan, drinks his second scotch neat. He drums his fingers on the table top while reading a 201 file, sometimes called the OMPF (Official Military Personnel File).

Major Anthony Perini: West Point graduate; two-time All-American lacrosse selection. Ranger training at Fort Benning, Georgia. Graduated third in class from IMCOM, the US Army Intelligence Center at Fort Huachuca, Arizona; served with 569th Airborne Brigade in Afghanistan.

Awarded Combat Infantryman Badge, the Silver Star, and the Purple Heart for injuries sustained in combat. Major Perini is on temporary leave pending separation from the service on full disability. He lives in a rental apartment in Georgetown.

Morgan spots the young man, supporting himself on a cane, moving jerkily toward his table. Anthony Perini is six feet tall, thirty-eight years of age; his close-cropped hair is brown, eyes an unclouded blue, the skin drawn tight across his jaw. *He has the look of an athlete,* observes the general.

"Ah, at last," Morgan says, lumbering to his feet and shaking hands. "Thank you for joining me, Major. The Metropolitan Club has the best beef and the freshest seafood in town."

Tony Perini lowers himself heavily into a chair. The pain in his right leg subsides and he breathes out an audible sigh of relief.

"A drink?" Morgan asks.

"I'll pass. Thank you, sir." Tony studies the man opposite him. The former general's hands are large; the tight fit of his civilian suit suggests powerful muscles. Morgan's lips are broad, cheekbones high, head square, skin quite dark. *A mountain of a man,* thinks Tony.

"How should I address you, sir? Mister Secretary or General?"

The big man grins. "I was christened Preston. That will suffice."

"It's not every day I'm invited by the Assistant Secretary of Defense to have lunch in a posh place like this, and in civilian clothes, yet."

"Well, son, our brother service, the 'Company,' as the CIA is euphemistically called, prefers meetings after midnight near the Lincoln Memorial or in West Potomac Park. I don't like those lonely spots. I'm afraid of being mugged." He laughs hoarsely. "I prefer this location for several reasons: first, they serve the best single malt whiskey, plus a damn good steak, and it's all on the government expense account. Second, if you look around, this club is loaded with important politicians and lobbyists."

Morgan continues, "Remember your classes in military science and tactics at the Point, Perini? Cover and concealment, lad. If you're out in the open, people don't get suspicious. If they recognize me, they'll think you're a wounded veteran and I'm an appreciative Pentagon honcho, which incidentally, I am. Or maybe you're a defense contractor and I'm being entertained and bribed."

As the waiter hovers over them, Morgan says, "Let's order. I recommend the prime rib."

Tony nods his agreement.

"How's the leg coming along?"

"I was discharged from Walter Reed last week. The doctors make no promises; they say I'll need physical therapy for years. So, no more lacrosse or marathons. I'm lucky, I guess, compared to all of those young amputees in my ward. What a waste."

"Tony. You're something of a hero. The Silver Star awarded you in Afghanistan would have been the Medal of Honor in Vietnam or World War II."

"How's that?"

"The Pentagon's asshole lawyers argue that Iraq and Afghanistan had exponentially fewer troops on the ground than World War II, which had millions of Americans in combat. I know it sounds stupid, but acts of bravery like yours were once slam-dunks for the big medal. Now such heroism is going unrecorded or delayed by years of investigation."

Tony puts down his fork. "May I speak frankly, sir?"

"By all means, son."

"What's going on? Why me, and why here in this fancy club?"

"All in good time. Aren't you on medical leave?"

"Yes, sir."

"Well, consider this sort of a job interview. Even with your disability, Major, Uncle Sam may have an important mission for you, if you're interested. First, I need more information before proceeding further with this conversation. And, just so we are on the same page, I wasn't always a desk jockey. I also have *beaucoup* fruit salad decorations, courtesy Vietnam, so I know it's no fun telling war stories. Most people don't give a shit. But I need to know what was in your head when you jumped on that grenade."

"Sorry. It's personal, and I don't know you well enough."

"This isn't a social tea, and you're smart enough to know it, Major. If I conclude that you're an impulsive hothead or a crazy wide-eyed-patriot—then finish your lunch, take your disability payments and get a life outside the military."

Perini's eyes harden. He remains silent, trying to hold down his rage, shifting uncomfortably in his chair. "You're paying for the meal, General—I'm listening."

"No. The U.S. taxpayers are paying for your meal, and I represent them. If I think your head is screwed on straight, and with your outstanding military record, the Army may have an important assignment for you. Tell me about the grenade incident."

Tony Perini looks at the ceiling and draws in a deep breath. "Okay, but you may not like hearing the truth. When I was in Afghanistan, I got a double whammy. My mom went into the hospital for a lymphoma cancer operation. They told my stepfather that Johns Hopkins was the best in the country and Mom didn't need private nurses. The night after the operation, my mother had a respiratory arrest... By the time they got to her, she was brain dead. I was half-way across the world. After three days, my stepfather 'pulled the plug,' or as they politely called it, 'ceased all aggressive treatment.' "

Tony Perini pauses to settle his emotions. "One week after they buried my mother, Joyce, my fiancée, sent me a 'Dear John' letter. She read that the Army was sending troops back to Iraq and Afghanistan for three or four tours, so she decided to get married—but not to me.

"I was bitter and I did something stupid." Tony laughs. "I collected pictures of all my buddies' girlfriends. Then I wrote to Joyce and said I had received her letter, but had a hard time remembering which one she was. I asked her to take her photo and return all the rest to me.

"After I lost my mom and Joyce, I didn't give a shit about anything. Jumping on that grenade wasn't just 'looking after my people,' it was also not caring much about living." He takes a drink of water. "Thanks for the meal, General. I'm not your man."

The waiter returns with coffee. Morgan waves him away and leans forward, his voice pitched down so nearby diners can't hear. "I know you're in a world of hurt, son; but taking on a new assignment might be just what you need at this difficult time in your life."

Tony shrugs. "I'm listening."

"We have a secret unit at the Pentagon devoted to gathering intelligence. We are quietly expanding into the CIA's sacred bailiwick —clandestine operations abroad."

The Assistant Secretary looks warily around before continuing. "This country has an insoluble problem: the war on drugs. And the drugs are winning. On a global level, heroin consumption is now the greatest drug problem. Worldwide production of opium has more than doubled in the last five years. What that means is there is twice as much heroin out there looking for customers.

"Our concern is not just about drugs, as bad as that is; it also concerns the channel of drug money funneling back to terrorists to buy arms, ammunition and weapons for insurgency operations in Afghanistan and elsewhere. What I'm telling you is simply this: the poppy fields of Afghanistan are producing in excess of 3000 tons of raw opium a year—most of it for export. We estimate 14,000 kilograms of heroin is shipped into the country each year. Florida is turning into a heroin warehouse.

"In Iraq," Morgan continues, "our failure to effectively plan long-range cost us blood and lucre. The United States cannot afford to lose in Afghanistan. The old leader of the Taliban was Mullah Omar. He said the use of opium by Muslims was wrong, but selling to the West was not, according to Islamic law."

Tony listens to the rambling outpouring of information, doing his best to digest it.

Morgan continues, "The facts on the ground are that a large drug cartel is attempting to increase their share of the American market by transshipping drugs from Afghanistan to a port in the Adriatic, near Venice. The heroin is then shipped into the U.S. It's a double whammy: first, the imported drugs addict American civilians, and second, the heroin-financed weaponry kills American soldiers. And what is even scarier," Morgan says, "is that this cartel is trying to unify the major Al Queda, Taliban, Haqqani Network and Hezbi-Islamic factions of Pakistan, Mongolia and Afghanistan into a confederation."

Tony shakes his head. "My outfit hunted terrorists in the mountains of the Hindu Kush in Afghanistan, in Pakistan and the no-man's-land border that separates the two. With their political and ethnic differences, I doubt they can be unified."

"It's happened before," Morgan explains. "In 1206, an enterprising Mongol, Genghis Khan, joined his clan with the Tatars, Turks, Kerait, Merkit and Naiman tribes, forming a military juggernaut which swept across the Asian continent to the fringes of Europe. In terms of square miles conquered, Genghis Khan was the greatest conqueror of all time. Mongols believe that Genghis Khan was the greatest man of all time, a man sent from heaven, and one day Genghis Khan will rise again and lead his people to new victories."

Perini chuckles. "Excuse me, sir, but I think you've had too much to drink."

The general's angry stare is unnerving, almost physically penetrative. "God dammit, that's the second time in twenty-four hours

I've been accused of talking through my alcohol. I learned about this cartel from my most experienced agent, a man called the Venetian."

"The Venetian?"

"His real name was Nicolo Polo. The Venetian's feats are still whispered about in the halls of the Pentagon and the conference rooms of the CIA. He was a descendent of Marco Polo and a legend in the intelligence community. Nicolo was an Italian partisan-hero in the war. Bill Donovan recruited him to join our first intelligence organization during World War II."

"The OSS?"

"That's right. The forerunner of the CIA. Nicolo Polo was an important CIA asset for years, but he became disenchanted. He said that apart from some old warriors serving out their time, the CIA was staffed with wall-to-wall bureaucrats and incompetents who he didn't trust. Fortunately for Nicolo, he anticipated something like the Aldrich Ames mess happening, and left before he could be exposed by Ames. When Polo resigned from the Company, we picked him up." Morgan gulps down his drink and signals for a refill.

"The Venetian uncovered who was smuggling drugs into Fort Pierce, Florida. He insisted on an immediate meeting in person; he didn't trust telephone conversations. I was too naive to listen and react, and I will carry that miscalculation to my grave. Nicolo Polo's dead body was found floating in the Fort Pierce inlet yesterday morning."

Tony's attention wanders. His leg throbs where the nerves were damaged. The doctors said it would take time. They also said it might never get better. "What does all this have to do with me?" he asks.

"Your old man is police chief in Fort Pierce, right?"

"Dad and I don't get on very well. He and Mom divorced when I was young, and I lived with my mother in Baltimore. My father went to Florida. I don't hate him, it's just that we've been out of touch so long that we're strangers."

"I hear that your father can be a stubborn mule when it comes to his local turf. I want you to go see him and convince your dad that there are larger national interests involved. As much as I would like him to, he's not to pursue Nicolo Polo's killers. We don't want the drug cartel evaporating before we can identify their European sources. Go and make nice-nice to your papa and reestablish your relationship.

"After you help shut down your father's investigation, I want you to go to Venice. I read your 201 file and know you're fluent in Italian. We think the Venice area is where drugs are being shipped from. Reservations have been made at the Hotel Marconi, near the Rialto Bridge. We will arrange to delay shipping Polo's body for a few days until you are in place to attend the funeral. Use your cell phone to take pictures of the attendees. Then e-mail them to me. Somebody interesting might show up."

"You can't be serious. If this is mission is important, why send me? I can barely walk."

"The Venetian proved to me time and again that a competent agent operating under the radar can get better results than a whole crew of spooks. Your mission is to determine how the drugs get to Venice and who arranges the transshipments to America. If you are successful, we then work with Italian authorities to interdict the drug flow and indict the major operators."

Morgan reaches under the table and lifts a walnut cane with a curved marble handle. "Our research department wants me to exchange this model for your cane. It has an extra feature." Holding the cane below the table level, so only Tony can see it, the general clicks a button and a twelve-inch stiletto snaps outward.

"Ceramic," he says. "Harder than anything except a diamond, and sharper than steel. It doesn't trigger airport metal detectors." Morgan smiles, but his eyes are steely. He hands Tony a Neiman Marcus tote bag. "This is the newest MacBook Air laptop. It weighs three pounds and has a WiFi connection that will operate anywhere in Europe."

Morgan withdraws a folder from his coat jacket pocket. "This contains my private phone number and your plane ticket for the 8 A.M. flight tomorrow to Melbourne, Florida. Rent a car, drive to Fort Pierce and connect with your father. I have established an e-mail address just for this operation. Memorize it.

"This folder includes your ticket for Venice out of Orlando. You will be operating in the wilderness of mirrors." Morgan continues, "The greatest enemy any agent has is the UCU. The 'unforeseen cock-up' has disrupted more covert operations than incompetence, treachery, or brilliant counterintelligence from our enemies. So be careful, very careful. The Venetian was not only my dear friend, but the most experienced operative I ever worked with."

Tony listens with a tight, polite smile. "General, when do I get to say if I accept this assignment or not?"

"I don't hear so good, Major. It's middle-ear deafness from being around artillery in 'Nam. Have a good trip and don't end up floating in a canal in Venice, *capisce*? It's good to have you on board," Morgan says, putting his hand on Perini's shoulder.

Across the resplendent, high-ceilinged dining room, a man in a blue blazer studies his *New York Times*. He is very tall and blond with a deep tan, wearing blue-tinted aviator glasses. The man appears not to notice the departure of Morgan and his guest. He palms the miniaturized recording device and places two hundred dollars in cash on the table.

Outside the Metropolitan Club, he punches in a private number on his cell phone. The American Secretary of Defense picks up. "Cody here."

"All's well."

"Did you hear their conversation?"

"Morgan's sending a cripple with no experience. I don't foresee a problem."

"Don't underestimate the general," Cody warns. "He's been around a long time. I want his man followed and all communications intercepted."

"Morgan mentioned the Marconi Hotel in Venice. I'll bug the room."

"No slip-ups, Brad. Too much at stake. If Tiny Tim becomes a problem—kill him. No excuses; just do it. And I don't need to know the details."

...10

"THE EAGLES LANDED ON INDRIO. What the hell does that mean?" Perini says to Detective Unger. "The drug dealer's making a pickup because 'the eagles landed on Indrio.' "

Perini shrugs as he drives down Indrio Road beneath a leafy canopy of grayish-green Spanish moss hanging from the roadside trees in thick masses reaching 20 feet in length.

"Indrio looks like it did before the hurricane," Unger observes.

"There's serious pressure to shut down this investigation, Connie. The feds say that Lou Brumberg's working with them. I find that hard to believe, but Lou may see it as his ticket for promotion; best be careful what you tell him."

"Did you find anything in Mr. Polo's post office box?" Unger asks.

"It could be a treasure trove of drug dealer license tags." Perini turns into the Indrio Crossing Shopping Center and cruises slowly along the storefronts. "I used to work out at the Indrio Gym," he says, pointing. "Other than the shopping center, there's nothing but a few scattered homes along Indrio Road between here and I-95. So this is the likely pickup location. I'll begin at the far right at the dry cleaner's. You drive past Winn-Dixie and start on the other side, but don't get lost shopping in Bealls. We're looking for some kind of eagles."

"If I'm late," she says, giving a quick wink, "you're a detective, you'll know where to find me."

Perini peers into the open doors of the Indrio Gym. He waves to the owner, Tom, and flexes his biceps. Tom laughs and gives him a two-thumbs-down sign.

Next door is a Spanish restaurant, El Cid. Perini walks in and orders an espresso with two sugars. At 10 A.M., the place is empty. An overweight man wearing a spotless white apron sits dejectedly reading the paper.

"You the owner?"

"Whatever you're selling, I don't need any. Since the snowbirds left, this is a morgue."

Perini flashes his gold badge. "Just a couple of questions, friend."

The owner frowns, excuse himself and goes into the kitchen. Perini hears whispered mutterings in Spanish; a door slams. The man returns. "How can I help you, Captain?"

"Noticed anything unusual going on in this center lately?"

"More unusual than half the stores going out of business?"

"Yeah, I know the economy sucks. Anything else strange?"

"The summer months are always rough. Winn-Dixie has a steady stream of traffic because people have to eat. Bealls is an outlet store, so, dependent on gas prices, people drive from Vero and Fort Pierce looking for bargains. The rest of us are holding on till October."

"Does the word 'eagles' mean anything to you?"

"The Eagles are my team. I never should have left Philadelphia to come down to the beautiful Sunshine State. With the hurricanes and real estate taxes—"

"Spare me, pal," Perini says, holding up his hands. "We all have our crosses to bear. The next time I'm in the area, I'll stop in and eat. What do I owe you for the coffee?"

"On the house, Captain." He smiles. "Thanks for not hassling my help."

Perini drops a five-dollar bill on the table.

"There *is* one thing that strikes me odd," the owner says. "For a gift shop, the Treasure Box next door gets a rough-looking trade."

THE TREASURE BOX display window features a crowded assortment of artificial flowers, candles, a hand-painted ceramic vase, and a multicolored porcelain pasta serving bowl. Perini also notes the sign in the window: "We Pack, Mail and Ship All Around the World. Fully Insured."

He pushes open the entrance door and is hit with strong scents from flowery potpourri and candles. Glassware and artificial flowers line the walls and center aisle. Perini spots the checkout counter in the middle of the store. To the right of the checkout area are shelves of books from floor to ceiling. On the left are displays of decorative glassware and figurines. To the rear of the store is a door leading to an office or storage area.

"How may I help you, sir?" says a short, middle-aged lady with a round face and beaming smile. "Aren't these scented candles wonderful? They're individually hand poured; this ensures the perfect wick placement and the right fragrance concentration. Are you looking for a gift for someone special?"

"Are you the owner?"

"Oh, my goodness, no. My name is Jackie. I open the store at ten and work until two, when Mr. B comes in."

"What's the owner's full name?"

She giggles. "It's too hard to pronounce. He said to call him Mr. B. And that's what I've called him since the shop opened four months ago."

Perini nods. "Isn't his name on your paycheck?"

"Mr. B pays me in cash." Jackie winks. "Don't tell Uncle Sam."

In the book area near the back office, the aroma is different. Perini sniffs a familiar aroma. *Smells like garlic.*

"I notice you only carry hardcover books. No paperbacks?"

"Mr. B only handles hardcover fiction; no fancy coffee table books or paperbacks. He prefers large novels from the *New York Times* best seller list, authors like P.D. James, Michael Connelly, or John Le Carré. Every four weeks Mr. B orders a full pallet load from our distributor, Ingram Book Group."

"For a small gift shop, you must sell a lot of books to bring in a pallet every month."

"We get twenty-seven cases on a pallet; that's eight hundred books each shipment, but we don't sell them all. Some are shrink-wrapped and reshipped to our branch store."

Perini eyes a ceramic piece with a large eagle landing on a snow-capped perch. The figurine measures two feet tall and another two feet wing tip to wing tip.

"Where is your branch store?"

"Mr. B's cousin runs the Treasure Box over in Grand Cayman Island," she says, then points at the eagle. "This is Hugh DeCapoli's traditional American eagle figurine. If you are into eagles, this is definitely the piece for you. We are discounting it for $149.75. The de-tail is just magnificent, which is always true on any DeCapoli figure. And the eagle is the symbol of our great American heritage. Are you interested in purchasing it?"

"I'm interested in eagles, but this one's a little large. Do you have any smaller ones?"

The woman scowls. Her lips form a tight line. "I wouldn't know about that," she stammers. "You'll have to talk to Mr. B."

Perini leaves the store and calls Unger on his cell phone. "Connie. Contact the Florida Department of State, Division of Corporations. Get me the name and home address of the owner of the Treasure Box at 4880 N. Kings Highway. I'm going to check around a little more."

Perini walks to the rear of the shopping center. He notices a large dumpster that services the gym, restaurant and Treasure Coast Gift Shop. On a whim, he raises one of the dumpster's lids. The offensive odor from the restaurant's refuse is pungent. Perini notices that the bottom half of the dumpster is jammed with piles of printed paper.

Searching around, he locates a wooden branch and sticks it deep into the dumpster. Two foul-smelling pages come out on the tip of the branch. Peering closely, he sees they have been razor cut from a book. At the top of the sheet it reads *Page 170 Michael Connelly.*

"NOW WE KNOW how the money is transferred to the Cayman Islands," Perini tells Unger, driving back to the station house. "Damn clever. They buy large books, hollow them out, shrink wrap the drug money into airtight stacks, then ship the books by Federal Express to their Grand Cayman store, where they disappear into numbered accounts. Whew, it's hot," Perini grouses. "I could use a Guinness about now. What did you find on the store owner?"

Unger opens her notepad. "The Treasure Box is owned by Mr. Chuluun Bagabandi. His home address is listed as 2345 Affuso Avenue in Fort Pierce."

They pull up in the police headquarters parking lot. Perini takes out Polo's list and reviews the last few entries:

04-04-0215-BJU495
04-04-0445-VGH556
04-05-0315-RGU023
04-05-0445-MCT424

He says, "Today is May 4th. Polo's list was for April. If they keep to the same monthly schedule, then three-fifteen tomorrow morning is the time for another pickup. I'll check it out. If any of these license plates shows, we're in business."

Perini enters his office and checks his answering machine.

"Hello, Dad," the first message says. "This is your son, Tony. Remember? I'm coming to Fort Pierce. I have to talk to you. It's important."

Perini closes his eyes and sighs deeply.

The second call is from Spence Hartman, the head of the Martin-St. Lucie-Indian River Tri-County Narcotic Task Force. "Got your message, Perini. Give me a buzz back."

Perini returns the call. "Hartman, I've got a problem. Off the record. OK?"

"I'm listening."

"There's a major drug network operating out of a gift shop in Indrio Crossing; it's called the Treasure Box. I have reason to believe they are receiving and distributing large quantities of heroin. The owner's name is Bagabandi; home address: 2345 Affuso Avenue in Fort Pierce, off Virginia Avenue. Got that? I figure the drugs are stored either in the guy's store or his house. Write down these license numbers. I think they may be owned by drug dealers. Have your people check the addresses with DMV."

"Since when are you doing us a favor, Perini? It's your turf."

"There's pressure from the Feds for me to stand down. In the meantime, heroin is being pushed all over the tri-state area."

"So, it's *my* ass on the line. Is that the story?"

"Look, Hartman, you're just following up on a lead. Have your guys raid the store and the owner's house, and check with the DMV for the drug dealers' addresses. Look for heroin packed in glass eagles. Also, alert your counterparts in the Islands to check out the Treasure Box branch on Grand Cayman. The money is shrink-wrapped, hidden inside dummy hardcover books, shipped to the Caymans and then transferred to offshore banks. "

"If this goes bad, Perini, you'll be hearing from me and—"

"I'm pissing in my pants, Hartman." He hangs up.

...11

IN VENICE, Director Dante Foscari sits behind his desk at the Correr Museum. Foscari has a kindly, lined face and a shock of fine white hair.

"The Foreign Ministry in Rome is on the line for you, sir," his secretary announces.

"*Doctore* Foscari," says the flat, impassive, bureaucratic voice on the phone.

"*Si*," Foscari replies.

"Bad news, I'm afraid, *Doctore*."

Foscari's stomach tightens. "Tell me."

"Our Washington embassy has received word of the untimely death of Nicolo Polo."

Foscari inhales deeply. *Nicco, you were too old to play the spy game anymore.*

"The Americans have arranged to fly *Siro* Polo's body to Marco Polo Airport for burial in Venice," the ministry man continues. "As his friend, will you handle the arrangements?"

"Of course."

"Did *Signor* Polo appoint an executor or attorney to probate his estate?"

"Estate!" Foscari snorts. "Nicco accumulated nothing in his life excepting scars and medals. The medals are rusted and the scars will soon be covered with the soil of San Michele. As for money, his ancestor's fortune, which may have been over-exaggerated to begin with, was dissipated in family haggling and lawsuits centuries ago. When Nicco joined the partisans, he took nothing but the clothes on his back and his family ring." Dante Foscari laughs mirthlessly. "And Nicco even gave away the ring to a farm girl who hid him from the Nazis."

"Good, good," the functionary answers absently. "The government will send a representative to the funeral."

...12

AT MIDNIGHT, Perini slouches in his car in rear of the Indrio Shopping Center. He drinks cold black coffee and watches the gift shop's back entrance through Steiner 8x30 Marine binoculars.

The shopping center's security guard makes sweeps of the area every half hour, so Perini has to duck his head down. By 2:30, his kidneys are overflowing. After the guard makes his rounds on schedule, Perini troops into the nearby woods. Walking back to the car and zippering up, he realizes how predictable the security guard's rounds are every half hour. Perini rereads Polo's list. All listed pickup times have been scheduled to avoid the security guards. At 3 A.M. Perini sees the guard's lights reappear. *Right on schedule*, he muses.

Fifteen minutes later, a large, dark Humvee without headlights on slips silently into the area behind the gift shop. Two black men get out, peer around, then move quickly to the rear entrance of the store. Perini watches through the glasses. The back entrance is opened by a broad-shouldered, swarthy-looking man.

Perini can't read the license numbers in the dark. "Shit," he says, unscrewing his car's interior light so it won't operate. He creeps up to the Humvee. In the pale light from the rear of the store he jots down the tag number and scampers back to his car, just as the store door opens. Each man carries two cartons. Within seconds the dark vehicle drifts off—without headlights.

With a pen flashlight, Perini compares the tag numbers to his list. "Gotcha!" he mouths silently, temporarily losing sight of the departing Humvee in the pitch black parking area. The Humvee's lights suddenly flash on as it turns east on Indrio Road. Perini quickly takes up the chase. A second car remains parked in the dark shadows of the shopping center.

As the Humvee turns right onto US 1, Perini radios headquarters. "This is Captain Perini. Send this out to all cars in the area of the courthouse. A dark-colored Humvee is proceeding south on US1. The license number is PBY565. It should pass Georgia Avenue in a few minutes. I want the vehicle stopped for probable cause and held until I arrive. Be advised the occupants are suspected drug dealers and may be armed and dangerous."

At this hour, traffic is sparse. At Delaware Avenue, Perini sees that police have formed a barricade. The Humvee is directed at gunpoint into the Kentucky Fried Chicken parking lot. Uniformed police drag a young black woman from the driver's seat. She looks angry and agitated. Perini grabs his Mag-lite from the glove compartment and inspects the vehicle, finding it empty. He rechecks the license number. It is correct.

"Captain," says an officer. "There's only one occupant in the car, and she's unarmed."

Perini faces the girl. "What are you doing driving around alone at four o'clock in the morning?"

"Ain't this still a free country?" she snaps at him. "I done nothing wrong. I should call my lawyer; you're harassing me."

Perini hears snickering from the policemen.

"Let her go," he says. "The bastards switched cars on me in the parking lot. Fuck."

HARTMAN'S NARCOTICS SWAT TEAM ARRIVES at the Indrio Crossing Center in two groups: a blocking group at the Treasure Box's rear entrance and one at the front. The men move quietly along the mall, past the closed gym and the El Cid Restaurant. On signal, both doors are kicked in and the narcotics squad storms the building. The store is searched thoroughly. All the books and the store's cash register are missing; the back room has been hastily vacated.

Spencer Hartman radios the SWAT team that simultaneously is raiding the owner's home. "What have you got?" he barks.

"Empty," comes back the second SWAT team leader. "Whoever was here split. And they left in a hurry. Nothing incriminating, but we're checking the house over."

* * *

THE ALARM CLOCK AWAKENS PERINI. *I'm too old to operate on three hours' sleep.* He takes a hot shower, fixes coffee, and checks his e-mail messages.

HI DOM:
GREETINGS FROM BAGRAM AIR BASE, AFGHANISTAN. I DISCUSSED THE 'BROKEN NECK' INCIDENT WITH AN AFGHAN DOCTOR. HE SAYS THE RITUAL OF KILLING A RESPECTED RIVAL BY THE BREAKING OF THE NECK WAS STARTED BY GENGHIS KHAN. MY FRIEND SAYS SOME MONGOLIANS STILL TAKE THIS TRADITION SERIOUSLY. UGH!
SAY HI TO MISS BESSIE AND MY BIKER FRIEND. AND PLEASE BE CAREFUL.
LOVE, MIRIAM.

PERINI'S CELL PHONE JANGLES. "Perini, Spence Hartman here. My people raided the store and house. We found shrink wrap equipment in the store, but it could have been used to pack anything. Both places were vacated. The bad guys were warned off."

Perini sighs. "I'm sorry, Spence. I personally eyewitnessed the drug transfer last night. Beats me how things went so wrong so fast."

"Not to worry, pal," Hartman chuckles. "Thanks to your license numbers, we nailed ten dealers and bagged a ton of shit. Watch me on the news, Perini. I'm a hero."

...13

"I'M GLAD TO SEE YOU, TONY," Perini says, experiencing a tightening in his chest as he watches his son limp across his office and lower himself heavily into the chair. "Is that leg a war souvenir?"

Tony nods.

"Temporary or permanent?"

His son shrugs.

"Are you discharged from the Army?"

Tony studies Perini without replying. The man behind the desk looks different than he remembers him. The same blue eyes and thick jaw, but the face is lined and the thick black hair is receding and turning gray. The father he had idolized, the tough hero cop from Baltimore with a box full of decorations, is now a tired-looking man with a paunch and slumping shoulders. Tony inhales and says, "I'm on special assignment."

Dominick clears his throat. "I'm sorry we've been out of touch. The first few years I came to Florida, I wrote and sent birthday and Christmas gifts but never heard anything back; then, when your mother remarried, I figured you bonded with the new guy."

"Mom invited you to my West Point graduation. I told her not to, but she did anyway, and, of course, you never showed."

Perini feels his cheeks flare hot. He understands that apologies are too late and useless. "You have every right to be pissed. We had half-drowned Haitians landing on Fort Pierce beaches, and after the Rodney King beating, there was looting and arson. I couldn't break away—"

"Face it, Dad. Your job came first. It always did—ahead of your family. That's why Mom left you."

"I know I blew it. The happiest moments of my life were spent with you and your mother in Ocean City. I couldn't wait for you to be old enough for me to teach you to surf. It didn't happen. Instead I drank my way out of my marriage and the police department. Life doesn't always turn out like we expect."

Tony massages his tingling knee. "Yeah. Tell me about it."

"What I'll tell you about is that I've learned in this business that there is no such thing as coincidence. It's no coincidence that you just happened to show up to visit your old dad."

Tony wills himself to stay calm. "Let me make something clear, Dad. There's a piece of grenade fragment sitting behind what's left of my knee. It's so far in, the doctors don't even want to try to get it out. But, if the Army has something they think I can handle, I'll try and do it. Right now, they want me to convince you to back off from investigating the death of some old guy who drowned in your inlet; let Codling's people handle it. You have never done me any past favors. Is dropping this case too much to ask for?"

Perini stares at his son. "Since we are putting our cards on the table, Tony, I'll tell you this: be careful of Mr. James S. Codling. I know his type; he's a snake. The government is putting pressure on me to turn my back and ignore heroin trafficking and the bottom-feeding drug dealing in Fort Pierce."

Dom continues, "I've spent half of my life trying to erase the stigma of drugs and crime in this city. People feel safe walking around the harbor at night. I don't want Fort Pierce to become the Bangkok of the Treasure Coast. This is a great town; maybe not as sophisticated as Vero Beach and not as posh as Palm Beach, but it's laid back and a good place to live. I intend to keep it that way. I love you, son, I'm proud of you, and I can see you're in pain, so I surely don't mean to spoil your visit by arguing. Can we change the subject? How long do you plan to be in town?"

"A day or so, then I'm going to Europe."

"That's nice. You'll like Venice."

"How did you—?"

"I'm a detective, remember? An old Haitian lady once told me that 'All is not butter that comes from the cow.' That's how I feel about this inlet murder case."

"And I'm an Army officer, remember? Since we're sharing homilies, have you heard the one about the son complaining to his father,

'You messed up my childhood!' And the father says, 'How could I, son? I wasn't even there.' "

Perini tried to keep emotion out of his voice and avoid further confrontation. "I have family in the Veneto area, a cousin, Joey Cullotta. He's in the water taxi business. Call him. Joey may be of help to you. This is probably as good a time as any to let you in on my dirty little family secret."

Perini continues, "After your grandmother died five years ago, I was clearing her things and found her passport and naturalization papers. It seems my mother emigrated to Baltimore in July 1944 from a village called Vigorovea, not far from Venice."

"So?"

"So, I was born on February 11th, 1945. Count on your fingers —that's seven months. The man I thought was my father, Salvadore Perini, owned a dry goods store in Baltimore. He had never been to Italy. I have always wanted to go back to Vigorovea and find out who my real father was."

Tony stands, balancing the cane in his right hand. "For the last time, will you help me out and back off of this investigation?"

"I'm sorry, son. You know I can't do that."

"At least I know who *my* real father is; he's a stubborn Italian bastard who has always disappointed me." Tony slams the office door as he hobbles out.

JESSIE CALLS ON THE INTERCOM. "Turn on CNN, Captain, quick!"

Perini flips on the small television set in his office in time to hear Wolf Blitzer say, "We have a special bulletin from St. Lucie County, Florida. The Martin-St. Lucie-Indian River Tri-County Narcotic Task Force broke up a major heroin network last night. This is the largest drug bust in Florida's history. We have with us Spencer Hartman, Resident Agent of the Florida Department of Law Enforcement. Mr. Hartman was the man in charge of running this successful operation. Welcome, Spencer, and congratulations to you and your team."

"Thank you, Wolf. We were just doing our duty."

"What is the estimated value of the drugs you confiscated in to-day's raid, Mr. Hartman?"

"My SWAT teams hit ten dealers and recovered forty dozen glass containers in the shape of eagles. Each glass container was packed with a half kilo, or 1.1 pounds, of heroin. At a street value of $35,000 per kilo, that's $8.4 million dollars in street sales—every month."

"Did you say 'glass eagles'?"

"That's correct. The heroin was wrapped in plastic, then placed in glass figurines in the shape of eagles."

"I'm confused, Spencer. Doesn't glass have to be heated up to 1000 degrees centigrade and then take many hours to cool? Wouldn't that intense heat destroy any organic material packed inside a glass container?"

"Uh... we're trying to figure that out," Hartman says, looking befuddled.

"Wow. That is some story coming to us from St. Lucie County, Florida. To think that drug smugglers would use the American eagle, our national emblem, to perpetuate their nefarious scheme. A final thank-you to Spencer Hartman and his narcotics Tri-County task force. This is Wolf Blitzer reporting for CNN."

PERINI'S PHONE RINGS. Chief Billy Ray Thompkins yells, "Perini, you'll pay for this stunt!" He hangs up.

Jessie pipes in, "Pick up on line two."

"Captain," says Detective Brumberg. "I've rechecked the entry logs from the Ocean Village gate house for May 2nd and 3rd, and—"

"What is it, Lou? I'm busy," Perini interrupts brusquely, still pissed over what Codling had said about Brumberg cooperating with the Feds.

"I found out something strange, boss. Those gatehouse guards aren't rocket scientists, but they do follow orders and register every vehicle passing through without a resident sticker. At 3 A.M. on May 3rd, a car was waved through because the driver flashed a Homeland Security ID. He said they were making a routine inspection. The guard on duty that night remembers two guys in suits were in front and a woman was in back."

"Can he describe them?"

"No," Brumberg reports. "The guard sees hundreds of people passing through the gate every day, and I think he works a day job somewhere else. At three in the morning he's groggy. I'll check the license number with DMV and get back to you."

"WE'VE GOT A SERIOUS PROBLEM ON AVENUE D, Captain," Perini hears over the intercom. "Bessie's Bar and Grill was fire-bombed."

Dominick's body tenses involuntarily. "Anyone injured?" he snaps.

"I don't know, sir," Jessie answers.

"I WAS EXPECTING YOU, DOMINICK," Bessie Carter says. "I knew you would come."

The smoke is acrid-smelling. Perini's eyes water as studies the blackened shell of Bessie's restaurant. Chairs and tables are heaped on the sidewalk next to broken china, glassware and garbage. Willie sweeps debris into neat piles. The fire trucks have left. A yellow and black crime tape stretches across from the tall blue lamppost on the corner to the palm tree standing in front of the restaurant entrance.

"Bessie, people tried to get me to leave this case alone, but I was too pigheaded. As a result, I've driven off my son and caused hurt to people I care about. I'm sorry, really sorry."

"Take my arm and let's walk, Dominick," Bessie says. "A famous lady, a writer I once knew named Zora Hurston, lived right here in Fort Pierce. In fact, I took care of Zora in her old age. She had a hard life. One day she said to me, 'Bessie, I have been in Sorrow's Kitchen and licked out all the pots. Then I have stood on the peaky mountain wrapped in rainbows, with a harp and a sword in my hands.'

"I never forgot Zora's words, Dominick. You did good. Willie told me about the drug dealers that were arrested. I know you had something to do with it. We have a whole new generation of young drug users today. They're not sticking needles in their arms, they're smoking crack and snorting powdered heroin. And once it gets them, they've got about as much chance of kicking the habit as they would beating a major cancer. If people like me and you don't try and stop it, who will? The government never cared what happens to poor black kids."

"What are you going to do about your restaurant, Bessie?"

"I don't think I can reopen. My heart is giving me a fit, and the insurance don't cover the costs of remodeling the way I want. Willie never liked the job. He did it for me. A Haitian lady has been after me to lease her the place; maybe that's what I'll do. I own the building, so I'll fix it up some; then with Social Security and the rental income I can manage."

"And Willie?"

Bessie laughs. "Willie loves baseball. He played for the Dodgers AA farm team, the Jacksonville Suns, until he hurt his shoulder. Fort Pierce Central High School has been after him for years to coach their team.

"I told Willie this morning to go and have a life. And I tell you too, Dominick. Right now you think you licked all the pots in Sorrow's Kitchen, but you did what you thought was right. Nobody can ask for more than that."

She took his head in both hands, stood up on her toes and kissed his forehead. "We need you in this town. Now go stand on some peaky mountain wrapped in rainbows, with a harp and a sword in your hands. You hear me?"

...14

PERINI LIVES IN A SMALL A-FRAME HOUSE situated on a rise overlooking the Indian River on North Hutchinson Island. The lawn has lost its struggle against the brutal summer Florida heat, but three cabbage palms and a brace of blue-purple jacaranda blooms survive and surround the front entrance.

Dom lies on his couch in the dark, quiet living room. He worries that his relationship with Bessie Carter possibly caused the fire-bombing of her restaurant. He wonders why his son and the Feds are pressuring him so insistently to let go of the Polo murder case.

No matter how many angles he comes at it from, none make any sense. *How does an experienced operative like Nicolo Polo get bushwhacked in the middle of the night—in a locked apartment in a gated community? And why is the government pushing so hard to protect a drug network that is causing pain and death to American soldiers? It makes no sense, not even for Feds.*

Perini hears a car pull up and park. Footsteps sound on the front path. The doorbell rings. It is half past midnight, and he has no friends that come calling this late. The hair prickles on the back of his neck. Perini slips off his shoes, unholsters his five-shot .38 Special Smith and Wesson, and walks quietly to the front door. He peers through the peephole.

Detective Connie Unger stares back at him, her pretty face distorted by the fisheye lens. He can see a six pack of Guinness beer held up in her hand. Perini exhales, holsters his gun and unlatches the door.

"I know you had a tough day, boss. I thought you could use these."

"Good idea, Unger. Thanks."

She smiles and says, "Sit down and relax, Captain. The beer's cold. I'll find glasses."

Dominick repositions himself on the sofa. As his mind clears, he suddenly has a realization. *Why would a lonely old man like Polo open his door in the middle of the night?* Without turning his head, he moves his right hand slowly across his chest towards his pistol.

"Here we are, Captain," he hears Unger say; then he feels a prick in the base of his neck. A light show of stars appears in front of his eyes. White noise echoes in his brain.

"You won't need this anymore," she whispers, removing the gun from his hand. Perini hears Unger's voice drifting off as she unlatches the door to admit agents Codling and Fischer.

"Everything cool?" asks Codling.

"Went perfect," Unger replies.

"How you doing, Sherlock?" Codling says in a snide voice, peering over at the sofa. "Cat got your tongue, big fellow?"

Dominick can't respond, feeling disoriented, dizzy; bordering on delusional. The walls are spinning. He collapses heavily on the sofa. It's a struggle just to cling to consciousness. He can hardly move. His body feels like lead. By habit and reflex, the old street cop struggles to reach his ankle holster and his spare Glock 26.

Codling continues, "Some assholes can never get with the program. Right, Sherlock?"

In a daze, Perini raises the pistol, firing in the direction of the wheedling voice above him. A blood red hole appears between James Codling's eyes. His mouth opens in surprise, then he drops like a stone onto the hardwood floor.

Connie Unger gasps, her face ashen.

Dominick Perini never sees the muzzle flash or hears his gun bark. Everything dissolves in a thick black fog. An illusion appears: an old man with blue eyes, white hair and a livid scar across his forehead. The apparition hovers, beckons and extends his hand. Dominick Perini is very tired. He closes his eyes.

"I guess I've been promoted," says Karl Fischer, opening his cell phone and punching in a number. "We will need an extra cleanup crew in Fort Pierce." Then Fischer puts on gloves and attaches a suppressor to Dominick's .38 Special Smith and Wesson. He places the gun against Dominick's temple and squeezes the trigger.

...15

CHIEF OF DETECTIVES PERINI COMMITS SUICIDE

FORT PIERCE GAZETTE, May 6—Residents of Fort Pierce were shocked and saddened at the news today that Chief of Detectives Dominick Perini died of a self-inflicted gunshot wound to the head.

Police Chief Billy Ray Thompkins was quoted as saying Captain Perini recently showed signs of stress and depression. The police chief also announced that Lieutenant Connie Unger has been promoted to the position of Captain of Detectives, making her the first woman on the Treasure Coast to achieve this rank.

The body was cremated. A memorial service will be held on Sunday at the Fort Pierce Community center.

Captain Perini is survived by a son, U.S. Army Major Anthony Perini.

Book II

When the Tartar barbarians (Mongols) invaded China, dragons cried for the people. When the tears came to Earth, they changed to jade.

—Wai Yee Wang Choi

...16

THE HEAD OF MSS, the Chinese Ministry of State Security, stubs out his cigarette and orders another glass of rice wine. General Li Hu Jengh is a short man, heavyset, with a broad chest sloping into a heavy body. He scrutinizes the attractive, leggy woman entering the revolving door of Shanghai's Pudong Shangri-La Hotel. As instructed, the woman is dressed in a black linen suit with an open white collar. She carries a leather briefcase under her arm and tows an overnight suitcase on wheels.

"*Kne How*," says the pretty hostess at the door, dressed in a traditional Chinese embroidered figure-hugging white *qipao* dress with a high mandarin collar and side slits.

The woman enters and pauses, taking in the breathtaking view of the palatial marble and glass lobby and across the Huangpu River to Shanghai's legendary riverfront promenade. As dust begins to fall, she sees the Bund's blue, red and green lights illuminating the art-deco buildings, the skyline and the famous clock tower. The red flag of the People's Republic flaps in the evening wind in front of the tower.

Scanning the lobby, she spots the heavyset man, recognizing him from newspaper photographs. He looks less intimidating in civilian clothes.

"I took the liberty of registering you, Captain Cheng Lu Yao," the general explains. "How was your trip?"

"Excellent, thank you, sir."

"Would you like rice wine, tea, beer, or do you drink coffee?"

"Tea, thank you," she replies. "Forgive me, General, but I am curious why my superior would order me to suspend my regular duties at the ministry in Beijing and direct me to fly to Shanghai and meet the illustrious General Li Hu Jehng. Why me, and why here?"

"All in good time, my dear. How long is it now that you have worked at the Ministry of State Security?"

"Five years, General."

"Five years," he mutters. "I've been in the intelligence business since before you were born—in Hangzhou, right?"

The woman's mouth opens in surprise. "Yes sir. Why do you mention Hangzhou?"

"We will get to that. Now to your first question: why do two active-duty military officers meet in a plush tourist hotel and not in my office? I've learned that the less secretively one conducts business, the less suspicion. In our line of work, secrecy is the mother's milk.

"I am attending a conference in Shanghai this week," he continues, "so if people recognize me here at the hotel, after work, drinking with a beautiful young woman, they will believe what their eyes tell them: a senior PLA officer is relaxing and taking his pleasure."

Lu Yao's face reddens. She remains silent.

"After all," the general says, "is that such an unattractive proposition?"

Her lips compress and she smiles. "You flatter me. But Shanghai is known to have the most beautiful women in all of China. The Chief of Military Intelligence doesn't need to fly a weary, rumpled PLA officer 1500 kilometers for a sexual liaison. So, why am I really here?"

Li Hu Jengh claps his hands in delight. "Ah. I knew you would be a good choice. Now to business. Have you ever heard of a man called the Venetian?"

"The Venetian? No, sir."

The general's eyes harden. "Are you certain?"

Lu Yao uncrosses her legs and gazes steadily at the general. "Quite certain."

The general raises his hand to gain the attention of a waitress. "Oolong tea," he orders.

"The Venetian was an Italian partisan in the Second World War. Then he joined the American OSS, which became the CIA. When it was in our mutual interests, we shared information. I first met the Venetian during the Cold War in Xinjiang while setting up a monitoring station that we operated jointly with the CIA—aimed at Russia."

"Was he a double agent?"

"Would that he were. The Venetian had his own code of honor. He was a pragmatist, interested in results, not money or promotion."

Cheng lights a cigarette, sucking smoke into his mouth. "Why am I telling you about an American agent? Because the Venetian was murdered yesterday in an East Coast Florida city. We picked it up from the Third Department's tracking of Pentagon dispatches. It is no secret that we probe the U.S. intelligence networks; they also conduct hacking and scanning into our systems."

Lu Yao says, "Why is this American's death important?"

"He was tracing heroin smuggling into the United States. The man controlling the flow of drugs is named Gianpietro Scarlatti, headquartered in Venice. Scarlatti uses the drug profits to buy arms and unify tribes in Mongolia, Pakistan and Afghanistan. This could pose a serious problem for China—not the drugs, but modern weaponry in the hands of Mongolian terrorists.

"Some Mongols are upset because China is economically expanding steadily north beyond the Great Wall, beyond the Yellow River, up to the Mongolian grasslands. Mongolia has valuable resources, especially oil in the Gobi. These resources will find a natural outlet when Mongolia becomes an economic colony of China— and mind you, I don't speak of a military takeover—for Inner Mongolia is already more Chinese than Mongol. We shall point out to the world that Mongols have been members of the great family of China for centuries. We are merely returning to the status quo as established by Genghis, the founder of China's Yuan dynasty, and that dynasty's great Chinese leader, Kubla Khan.

"The Venetian alerted me to the threat of a Mongolian conspiracy rising to our north. Scarlatti is interfering in our oil leasing and is rumored to be negotiating for weapons, possibly even nuclear, from Pakistan. He must be stopped, and you have been chosen for the task."

"Sir, I am confused. At the ministry, my title is senior researcher. I am a glorified clerk. Mostly, I translate European-American transmissions that are intercepted by our monitoring stations. I am not a trained field agent."

"You are fluent in Italian and English. You were first in your class at the PLA Institute of International Relations at Nanjing; you have a black belt in martial arts; you swam for our Olympic team, and you have an expert rating with a pistol. There is one last reason. The Venetian's family had a long relationship with China, tracing back to the days of Marco Polo."

Lu Yao's face pales.

"Now I have your full attention, eh? As you know, the people of your birth city, Hangzhou, once called Kinsai, have an ancient custom. As soon as a child is born, they write down the day and hour and the planet and sign under which its birth has taken place, so that everyone among them knows the day of his birth. This was reported by Marco Polo himself when he was governor of Kinsai; we Chinese are good at keeping our records."

"I'm familiar with my *Jia Pu* family list," Lu Yao says.

"Then you know that Polo had a child by his mistress."

"And why is that relevant, may I inquire?"

Under his heavy eyebrows, his eyes sparkle. "With the death of the Venetian in America, *you,* my dear, are the last living descendant of Marco Polo."

BEHIND THE CONCIERGE DESK, a slender man in his forties with large glasses and straight black hair reaches for his cell phone and depresses a button. "*Apart from our shadows we have no friends,*" he whispers into the phone.

"*And apart from our horsetails we have no whips,*" comes the reply.

"I wish to report that General Li Hu Jengh is in the Pudong Shangri-La lobby meeting with a woman agent."

"How do you know she's an agent?"

"They have been conversing seriously for an hour. She's a young, attractive girl, dressed in a conservative black suit, not the consort type. Her manner and posture look military."

"Could she not be a relative?"

"Perhaps so. General Jengh signed for the room himself—for one night. Only his name appears on the room registry. Also, the general ordered a car to drive the lady to Hangzhou tomorrow morning."

"The old fox may be up to something. Have someone photograph the woman, e-mail it to me, and have her followed to Hangzhou. Li Hu Jengh has taken an unwelcome interest in our ventures. He and his friend need to be watched carefully." The call ends.

"DID YOU BRING A PASSPORT as requested?" General Jengh asks. Lu Yao nods.

"Good. Now if a tourist comes by and snaps your picture, smile and act natural."

"But what—"

Jehng interrupts. "I've reserved a room here at the Shangri-La until tomorrow," he says, handing her a white plastic card-key. "Go shower and change. I'm going to the second floor for dinner. In an hour, a maid will knock three times at your door. She will take your suitcase and lead you down to the employee's entrance. A car will take you to the Hongqiao International Airport. The driver will have your travel documents—"

"Hongqiao Airport?" she cuts in.

Jehng shoots her a hard look. "Do not interrupt me, Captain, time is short. You are booked on the 11 P.M. flight to Venice. Reservations have been made in your name at the Hotel Marconi in the Rialto area."

"Is this some kind of test or joke, General? I am tired from traveling all day and—"

A plump Pakistani tourist, wearing an open neck orange sport shirt and black cap reading 'Beijing Olympics,' asks timidly, "Pardon, may I take your picture against the magnificent backdrop of the river and the Bund fully lit at night?"

Without waiting for their reply, he snaps the photo as the light bulb flashes.

"Thank you so very much," the man says, and quickly exits the hotel. Lu Yao stares after the departing stranger.

General Jehng moves closer, touching her arm. His smile is genuine. "Have you never wondered how you achieved the scholarship to Zhejiang University, or how you were chosen by the Ministry of State Security even before you graduated?"

Words hung heavily in her throat. "I thought it had to do with my swimming medals."

Jehng pours another glass of rice wine. "What it had to do with, Lu Yao, was my repaying a debt to your father." He holds up a hand. "Allow me to tell my story. Before the Cultural Revolution, your father, Middle General Cheng, was my commanding officer and a loyal Communist. General Cheng didn't trust the government and often disagreed with Mao. Challenging the chairman was not an intelligent thing to do. A few years before Mao's death, General Cheng was condemned as an enemy of the state and a traitor. He was executed, along with your mother.

"The official account was that they died in prison. Lu Yao, in those days there was no room for morality. We survived at any cost. Young people can't understand how it was. Your father was a man of courage and integrity. I revered him. For that reason, I have kept track of you for years, and arranged for you to be employed in the ministry. Are you all right?"

"I'm fine," she lies.

"I know your bloodlines, and I need someone I can trust for this mission. The Mongolian conspiracy has tentacles in Shanghai. My people will follow that man with the camera to see where the trail leads. This is serious business, Lu Yao. There are high-ranking Chinese military officers of Mongolian ancestry in our People's Liberation Army. Just last week a general staff officer held talks at the Khan Palace Hotel in Ulaanbaatar with Besmillah Mohammadi, head of the Afghan National Army.

"Something unsavory is happening, and we need to know before it comes to a boil. Venice is the crossroads of the drug money trail, and also where the Venetian is to be buried. Go and observe the funeral attendees. Perhaps the murderers will be present, like in the American movies. Also, we know the heroin is being transshipped from that area, so Venice is where we need you. Your cover will be as a writer for the Guangzhou-based *Southern Metropolis Daily*. You are doing research for a book you are writing about Marco Polo, a subject about which I am certain you are familiar. In the world of agents, it is best to skate near the truth as much as possible. I have prepared letters of introduction from your paper and business cards."

"How do I communicate with you?"

"A short distance from the Rialto Bridge, near your hotel, is a Chinese restaurant called SunWuKong. The restaurant is our Venice base station. I will not write it down, so memorize the name. It will appear natural for you to dine there. Under no circumstances talk to the owner; the restaurant may be bugged. I don't want to appear melodramatic, but in the ladies' room you will find a jar of lavender potpourri. The bottom unscrews. There you leave and retrieve messages which will be immediately forwarded to me by e-mail. If, instead of lavender, the potpourri aroma is geranium, you are in danger and must leave Venice."

Jehng continues, "The Chinese embassy is on Via Bruxelles in Rome. They are an hour away. Contact them only in an emergency. I have included the embassy address, telephone, e-mail and fax numbers in this packet with cash, your visa and tickets. There is also an active triad organization in Venice—"

"Are they not criminals?"

The general grimaces. "The triads are what they are. But first, they are Chinese and they have been alerted to watch over you. I can only handle so many Chengs on my conscience."

"And my mission?"

"We have a saying, 'A fish rots from the head.' Your mission is to locate Scarlatti and to cut off the fish's head—terminate him. Tibet is giving us enough of a headache. China cannot tolerate interference in our oil supplies or tribal uprisings taking root on our northern border, especially if they are potentially armed with nuclear weapons. Captain Cheng, make effective use of your training and pleasing physical attributes. Do *whatever* it takes to abort this Mongolian conspiracy. Do I make myself absolutely clear?"

Lu Yao nods in silent agreement. She gazes across the glassed-in lobby to the Huangpu River and the glittering colored lights of the Bund. Now, however, the scene appears garish instead of glorious. She feels the cold claws of dread in the pit of her stomach.

LATER THAT EVENING, Lu Yao boards her Alitalia flight to Venice wearing a pea-green coat belted over a black turtleneck sweater and black trousers. Around her neck she wears an etched white jade pendant on a gold chain. People noticing her trim, athletic body, high cheekbones and black hair pinned up in a French twist might take her for a model.

She collapses into a window seat, fastens her seat belt, closes her eyes and draws in a few practiced meditational breaths. Almost immediately she is asleep.

"I'm sorry to disturb you," apologizes the Alitalia flight attendant, gently touching her shoulder. "Would you care for a hot or cold beverage?"

"Tea, thank you."

Looking out the window of the airplane as it gains altitude, she wonders how her life has suddenly become tangled up in a web too confusing to understand. Then the ever-recurring dark shadow crosses her consciousness: the haunting image of her parents being dragged out of their big house in Hangzhou at gunpoint by Red Guard hoodlums as their neighbors watch fearfully and five-year-old Lu Yao screams and screams.

Her father, Middle General Cheng Jintao, was a heavyset man dressed in his gray military winter coat. He spit and cursed at the Red Guard barbarians as her parents were herded into the back of an old truck, like migrant workers from the provinces.

"Papa. Don't leave me alone! Take me with you! Please... Please!" Lu Yao sobs and pleads as she is restrained and consoled in the arms of her thin-limbed Little Auntie. Lu Yao never sees her parents again. Revisiting the scene of the worst nightmare of her life causes a momentary shortness of breath. Tears slowly stream down Lu Yao's face.

Shanghai's Airport sinks beneath them. The jet turns east, crossing central China. The two seats next to her in coach class are unoccupied. Lu Yao stretches out, covers herself with the thin airline blanket and tries to sleep. After shifting positions, she realizes that the events of the day have conspired to pump adrenaline into her blood— or it was the caffeine in the tea? She's wide awake.

Fingering her jade locket, Lu Yao remembers her 21st birthday when Big Auntie presented the white jade pendant to her. The old woman's face was weathered from a lifetime of working in the outdoor Dongtau Lu Antiques Market.

"Lu Yao," Big Auntie says. "Not good you live alone."

"I have no people luck, Big Auntie. After losing my parents, I shy from commitments for fear that I will be vulnerable to losing anyone I love too much. I guess that is my *Yuan fen.*"

"My darling Lu Yao," replies Big Auntie. "Having no children of my own, it was *yin* and *yang* for me when I lost my dear brother and sister-in-law. Then, I was gifted with the precious light of my life—you."

Lu Yao is silent.

Big Auntie leaves the room and returns holding an old jewelry box. "You are of age for me to tell you important story. I feel like relating it today. Our legend tellers are old people who tell family histories and write down our ancestors in *Jia Pu*—the family lists."

The old woman continues, "Many years ago, in the time of the emperor of the Yuan Dynasty, Kubla Khan——"

"Are you giving me a history lesson, Big Auntie?" grins Lu Yao.

"No, my dear, it is your lineage. In that time of Kubla Khan, a white-skinned traveler came from across the water. He was an important man, appointed by the great Kubla Khan to be governor of Kinsai province. He took as a mistress a beautiful lady of the city and they lived in a big house on West Lake, which was called 'Upper Lake' in ancient times.

"According the *Jia Pu*, in the Year of the Dragon, a baby girl was born to the man called by the name Marco Polo and to his mistress, Mei Li. Legend tellers relate that the traveler wished to take Mei Li and the child home to his native land and marry her in accordance with the custom of his people. But Kubla Khan resisted giving permission to leave, for Marco Polo was a valuable servant of the Great Khan. Then, in the Year of the Horse, Kubla Khan allowed Polo to return to their home in return for escorting a princess-bride on a long trip to one of the Khan's important allies. During the trip preparations, Mei Li contacted a serious illness, maybe the bird sickness... and she died."

"And the child?" Lu Yao asks.

"The journey to their home in Italy would have taken three years. The man, Polo, knew that without her mother, the infant might not survive the trip."

"Just like a man," Lu Yao grumbles.

"Marco Polo left his child in the care of the Cheng family in Hangzhou, who raised her."

Lu Yao bolts upright on the sofa, staring at Big Auntie.

The old woman opens the jewelry box. Inside, Lu Yao eyes a white jade pendant and a gold chain.

"The baby's name was Lu Yao, meaning 'Beautiful Jade.' " Big Auntie continues, "Yes. You are the direct descendant of Mei Li and the man, Marco Polo. Their blood runs through your veins. You were also born in the Year of the Dragon, and as such, you are a strong woman. You needn't be fearful of life. This locket was given by Marco Polo to his child, and has been passed down in our family for over 30 generations. Now it is in your keeping."

Lu Yao takes the stone in her hand and feels the coolness. The creamy white jade glows with clarity. She notices that delicately etched in the jade is a shield with three stars under a knight's helmet and plumage bordered by filigree.

"Last word," warns Big Auntie. "Be careful never attach your-self to white-faced foreigner. For our family, it not good *Yuan fen.*"

...17

THE STEWARDESS GENTLY SHAKES TONY. "Are you all right, sir? You were having a bad dream. Can I get you something to drink? We will be arriving at the Marco Polo International Airport in approximately twenty minutes. It is now 6:30 A.M. Venice time."

Tony mumbles sleepily, "Coffee and a glass of water. Thanks." He massages his aching knee, then gulps an oxycodone pill, a prescribed pain-killing medication and opium derivative that makes him feel better. His dream was eerie and elusive. The psychiatrist at Walter Reed, Dr. Schnaper, had encouraged him to attempt to interpret his dreams.

"Better out than in," Schnaper counseled. "Here's a way to test the validity of your dream interpretation. Your dream will usually be something or someone you were thinking about during the past twenty-four hours. You need to try and focus on the very *first* thing that comes to mind—and no fudging the answer."

Tony gazes out the window at the fluffy cloud bank below. His father's face pops into his mind. In the dream, Tony is a small child sitting alone on a sandy beach fearfully looking at a blood-red sunrise. Clouds gather and the sky darkens, and lightning strikes in the distance. Tony sees his father, Dominick, alone in the ocean, struggling to stay afloat amid huge crashing waves and a rip tide that carries him further out to sea. The beach is deserted. There is no lifeguard or anyone to save his father. Three shark fins circle the weary, struggling man; then there are only two fins. In a horrifying instant, Tony sees his father slip beneath the surface of the waves. A loud clap of thunder follows and the sea turns red. The horizon becomes inky-black. Tony screams in his dream, "Daddy! Daddy!"

* * *

THE DESCENDING PLANE punches through the cloud layer. Tony gazes down at the narrow foggy-gray airport runways far below. To the south he spots Venice.

The stewardess leans over his seat and points out the window. Tony is conscious of her breast brushing intentionally against his shoulder. He enjoys the heat of her proximity and the sweet floral smell of her perfume. He feels his face grow warm.

"Look," she says. "Venice is shaped like a fish swimming east to west. The tail fins are the neighborhoods of Castello and Sant' Elena. The fish's body is where St. Mark's and the Rialto Bridge are located, and the head is the train station. If I can help you with anything," she coos, "please let me know."

Tony stands, stretches, removes his carry-on bag from the overhead rack, and withdraws his shaving kit. He heads to the bathroom. Returning to his seat, he notices a tall, blond passenger standing in the aisle. The man is wearing blue tinted aviator glasses and a tan suede jacket over a black crewneck sweater. The passenger gives Tony a quick look before slipping into his seat.

That guy was at the Metropolitan Club. I remember the glasses.

The stewardess is back, replacing his suitcase in the overhead rack. "All bags must be safely stowed before landing," she says with a smile and a wink.

AT THE MARCO POLO INFORMATION COUNTER, Tony asks directions to the Rialto. A short, round figure of a man with pitch black curly hair sits behind the counter, silently observing the clean-shaven young man with a carry-on bag, leaning heavily on a cane.

With a practiced smile, the man advises, "It is a long walk, *signor*, from our terminal to the boat dock. I advise you avail yourself of a baggage cart. As to transportation, there are two choices. One is the *vaporetto*, a water bus which will deposit you at St. Mark's Square. From there you transfer to the number 82 boat, which goes to your Rialto stop." He sighs. "But the *vaporetto* is a long and unsteady boat ride. If you can afford it, I offer the suggestion that you take a private water-taxi directly to your hotel."

"How expensive is the water taxi?"

"Approximately 100 dollars U.S."

Using the baggage cart as walker, Tony maneuvers the long passageway connecting the airport to the boat pier. Next to the *vaporetto* waiting area, five sleek water-taxis are tied up to the pier, their pilots smoking and gesticulating furiously. He motions to one of the boatmen, a smiling, ruddy-faced man with dark, curly hair. Tony says in American-accented Italian, "*Scuzi, Rialto.*"

"*Va bene!* Good! An American?" the man laughs, reaching up to help steady Tony as he steps on to the bobbing boat. "Which hotel, *signor?*"

"Marconi."

"*Si.* No problem." He crushes out the cigarette and says, "We go."

The motorboat's prow slices through the morning mist. The wind coming in from the east stirs up whitecaps that knock and bounce the boat. Tony starts to step down to the cabin, but pauses as the boat swings out of the airport channel into the flat expanse of the Venetian lagoon. On the horizon, rising from the sea, he can make out the gorgeous pink and gold outline of Venice, with gilded spires, domes and bell towers partially obscured by the fog. The brine-scented air revives him as the boat picks up speed. In the distance rusty tankers head for Maestrae.

Tony sniffs the odors of salt, fish and diesel oil. On the port side he sees the red brick outline of the island of Murano, with its dusty glass furnaces puffing blue-gray smoke from their chimneys—looking like a ghostly, rundown Pennsylvania mill town.

"Is that Murano?" he asks.

The water-taxi driver nods and shrugs. "Things not good on Murano. I have cousins who work in the *fornaci*. Everybody knows everybody's business."

"What's the problem?"

The pilot turns his palms up in a gesture of helplessness. "Since my grandfather's time, Murano men earn living by fishing or glass blowing. No more. Now, glass business stinks like the lagoon. The damn Chinese sell glass cheap, and the high euro rate keeps away American buyers. Master glass blowers only working part time. Murano is dying." He spits over the side. "The lagoon is polluted; nitrates and phosphates from the agriculture, and chemical wastes from industries in Porto Marghera—so no more fishing either."

The island is swathed in a bluish light. Tony points. "Smoke's coming from those chimneys. Somebody is working."

The boatman doesn't respond.

"Are drugs a problem here, like in America?" Tony inquires.

"For a tourist, you ask too many questions." The man gives his passenger a hard stare.

The boat shoots out into the *laguna*. Through the dissipating mist appears a cemetery shrouded in a pearl-colored haze.

"*San Michele Cimitero*," the pilot volunteers.

On the starboard side, Tony sees dark spears of cypresses rising above the apricot-orange brick wall that surrounds the island. He hears the Campanile bell tower toll eight times. The taxi pilot returns to his stony silence.

"I have family here," Tony says, trying to remember the name of the cousin his father had mentioned. "He's also in the water-taxi business. His name is Joey Cullotta, do you know him?"

The boatman blanches and blows through his lips. "Giuseppe Cullotta is your cousin? Forgive me, *signor*, if I have offended you in any way. It is a great honor to have you on my water-taxi. My name is Mario Belotti." He reaches under the console and withdraws a business card. "Telephone me anytime you wish transportation. I am at your disposal."

"You know my cousin?"

"The people who wield the power in Venice are not the tourists or politicians. No, it is the water-taxi drivers, the gondoliers, the garbage collectors, the freight boat pilots and the hotels and restaurant owners. They run Venice, and do you know who runs them? The *Mala del Brenta*. And do you know who runs the Mafia in Venice?"

"I think I can guess."

"*Si, signor.*"

...18

THE MARCONI is situated on the Grand Canal facing the Rialto Bridge. In front of the hotel, idle gondolas lie tethered to poles, covered in blue tarpaulins. Construction workers noisily unload wheelbarrows full of broken concrete onto colorful barges. Tony limps into the lobby.

"*Buon giorno,*" says the desk clerk. "You are—?"

"Perini, Anthony Perini. I have a reservation."

The clerk thumbs through a ledger and glances at Tony's cane. "I am so sorry, but we have no lift in this hotel. Your room is on the second floor, *Signor* Perini. It is a little roundabout getting to the room, as you must traverse up to the first floor, all the way down the hall. Will you require a porter?"

"No thank you."

"My name is Carlos, sir. Here is your key. Allow me to retrieve your *telefono* message." He hands Tony a slip of paper. "A gentleman called from America. He says it is urgent that you contact him. Also, *Signor* Perini, if you are interested, the glass factories on Murano offer a courtesy water taxi ride for a short demonstration of glass blowing."

Tony glances at the message. "Call immediately. Morgan."

He nods to Carlos and labors up the stairs and down a long corridor. The room is not facing the canal, and it smells a bit smoky. But it's clean, and Tony is too exhausted to care.

He looks at his watch. *3 A.M. Washington time*, he muses, punching in Morgan's number. The phone is picked up on the first ring.

"Tony?"

"Yes, sir. It's late and I was hesitant to call—"

"Bad news, I'm afraid," Morgan interrupts. "It's your father... he committed suicide."

85

Tony can't breathe. His chest tightens. He takes deep rasping breaths and breaks out in a cold sweat. "Dad's dead?" he mumbles, in shock.

Death is no stranger. In Afghanistan, Tony eyewitnessed soldiers under his command shot by snipers while on patrol or killed by remote-controlled roadside explosives. As brigade commander, he wrote the painful, obligatory letters to families of his men and women killed in action. But the untimely death of both of his parents in the same year is heart-wrenchingly hard. Tony doesn't trust himself to speak. He squeezes his eyes closed and grits his teeth.

"Are you still there, Major Perini?"

Tony inhales deeply. "What happened?" he asks in a muted voice.

"All I know," answers Morgan, "is what the local paper reports. I didn't want you to hear it from someone else. It's been a rough day all around. My assistant, James Codling, died of a heart attack in Fort Pierce last night also."

Something doesn't feel right. Growing up, Tony had heard accounts from family friends and relatives about Dominick Perini, the multi-medaled legend on the Baltimore police force, a detective with a reputation for honesty, toughness, and heroism—before getting into the bottle. Tony remembers fingering his dad's medals. Dominick Perini being suicidal doesn't compute.

"What was the exact time of my dad's death?" Tony asks, recalling his nightmare on the flight and the stewardess awakening him, then announcing, "It's 6:30 A.M. Venice time."

"I don't have that info—"

Tony clears his throat. "Find out who is in charge of the investigation, and who my dad's lawyer is... and the time of death. I'll call you back." He hangs up.

MILITARY TRAINING takes over. Tony's mind is calmer with a task to focus on. He unzips his carry-on bag. Pushing aside clothing, he notices the laptop computer is missing. He mumbles, "Damn. This bag was never out of my sight." Then he remembers the sexy stewardess replacing his suitcase in the overhead rack.

The stress from Morgan's call and the long hours of travel are taking a toll. He lies down exhausted on the bed, inert and utterly deprived of will. Finally he dozes off. One hour later, a church bell starts ringing close by, forcing him back to consciousness. He sprinkles cold water on his face and telephones Morgan.

"Are you OK?" Morgan asks anxiously.

"If you can call learning that your father committed suicide, having jet lag, my laptop being stolen, and an aching leg *okay*, then I'm okay."

"Have you checked your room for bugs—listening devices?"

"General, my experience is with mines and booby traps, not this James Bond shit."

"Easy, Major," Morgan cautions. "Leave your room and call me from outside the hotel."

"YOU SENT THE WRONG MAN, GENERAL," Tony gasps after climbing the stairs of the Rialto Bridge. "This isn't working out. I should never have allowed myself to be talked into a mission that I am so uniquely unequipped to handle——"

"Slow down, son," Morgan says calmly. "The Florida narcotics squad made a major drug bust, and according to the grapevine, your father played a key role. The smugglers got away, but a lot of bad guys were taken down. It even made CNN. Your dad was a stubborn man, but a dedicated police officer. He wouldn't have wanted you to back out of an important assignment just because it was uncomfortable——"

"It's not my comfort level, sir. I'm fucking everything up. I was careless on the flight over and my computer was stolen. Fortunately, it isn't compromised because there's nothing on it yet. I think some guy is following me, but maybe I'm paranoid. I made a taxi boat pilot suspicious when I questioned him about drugs. I've only been in Venice a few hours. Give me a whole week and this town will be six feet under water."

"*Aqua alta,*" Morgan laughs. "Not to worry. Your cover sounds perfect. No one as incompetent as you describe will raise any eyebrows. I'll arrange for people to come down from our air base in

Aviano. It's an hour away. They'll sweep your room for surveillance equipment. Tell the concierge you're expecting some Army buddies, and that if you are out, let them into your room. Also, I'll have them drop off a new laptop. I want you to be able to e-mail me pictures from the Venetian's funeral——"

Tony cuts in, "Frankly, I'm more concerned about my dad's burial than the Venetian's. When is the funeral? I'm flying home."

"Your dad has already been cremated, Tony. And, as I understand it, the department is planning a memorial service today."

Tony swallows hard. "And his ashes?"

"Sorry, I don't know."

"How about the time of death?"

"According to the papers it was about 12:30 A.M."

Tony calculates, *12:30 with six hours' time difference makes it 6:30 Venice time... that's while I was on the plane.* He remembers his father's fateful words uttered a few days earlier: "I've learned in this business, son, that there is no such thing as coincidence."

If it wasn't a suicide, who stood to benefit from your death, Dad? Tony ponders as the *vaporettis*, water taxis and produce-laden boats ply their way past the Venetian-Byzantine architecture and the grand *palazzi* on either side of the canal. He fails to notice a blond man in blue sunglasses observing him from deep shadows on the bridge.

THE BAR AT THE FOOT OF THE RIALTO offers coffee and fresh pastries. Tony orders a *panino* with an espresso. He lifts his cup, inhales the rich coffee aroma and gazes at the water. The mosaic facades of the *palazzi* on the other side of the Grand Canal are partially obscured by milling tourists snapping pictures and local housewives returning from the *pescheria* nearby.

A heavyset man in his early forties strides over, smiling broadly. "Antonio?" The man has the ruddy, weather-worn face of a farmer or fisherman. He wears a faded denim shirt and jeans of a similar color. "You my American cousin, eh?" he inquires. "My English not so good."

Tony rises and shakes hands, ignoring the painful pressure on his leg. "And you must be dad's cousin Giuseppe? How did you know I was in Venice?"

Cullotta flops down heavily and orders a glass of wine. "Call me Joey. We're family." He says with an abrupt laugh, "It is my business to know who and what comes and goes in Venice."

"Mario, the pilot?" Tony guesses aloud.

"You a detective like your father, of blessed memory?"

Tony stiffens. "How did you know?"

"Good news travels fast; bad news—faster. I have connections in America."

"My father's death was no suicide. When I get back, I'll find the truth and deal with whoever is responsible. I promise you that." He rubs the sore knee.

"*Bravo*! Spoken like a true Italian. You let me know how I help, okay?" Cullotta glances at the cane and his leg. "Is that a war souvenir?"

Tears pool in Tony's eyes. "Dad asked the same question the last time I saw him."

"What brings you to Venice? A vacation? No. I think not."

"I'm sorry. I can't discuss it—"

Cullotta raises both hands. "No problem, here we all have private business. Your poppa would want me to look out for you. Do not turn your head," Cullotta warns. "There is a man on the bridge who has been watching since I sit down. In my business you need to notice."

"Does he have blond hair?"

"It's hard to tell."

"Blue sunglasses, aviator style?"

"*Si*." Cullotta withdraws a cell phone. "You want I handle this?"

"No. The guy was on my flight. For all I know he was dispatched to protect me."

"As you wish," Cullotta replies. "My mother, she is crazy to meet you. You will come to Vigorovea and see her. Yes?"

Tony nods. "How are—how were you and dad related?"

"Your grandmother, Nonna Marisa, was my momma's older sister. She moved to America; Momma stayed on the farm in Vigorovea. I will tell her we visit this weekend. She has something she save for your poppa. Now, she give it you."

"I have to attend a funeral at St. Michael first," says Tony.

"Of course," replies Cullotta, "Nicolo Polo's."

"WHAT THE HELL'S GOING ON?" bellows Secretary of Defense Cody. "How is it possible Morgan's man meets with the boss of the Venetian Mafia the first day he arrives?"

"I don't know, Mr. Secretary," Bradford Schmidt answers. "The guy's computer is clean; his hotel room is bugged, and he hasn't gone anywhere."

"He and Morgan are cooking up something. I don't like it. You better get rid of that cripple and keep a close watch to see that nothing disrupts our interests."

"MAJOR PERINI, this is Captain Meadows from the U.S. air base in Aviano. General Morgan said to reach you on your cell phone."

"Good, I'm near the hotel."

"Your room has been swept clean, sir. But whoever wants to eavesdrop is using state-of-the-art electronics. We can't sweep every day, so it's unsafe to speak on the phone. If you have anyone in your room, please communicate in writing."

"Or use semaphore, right, Captain?" says Tony, trying to suppress his annoyance at having his privacy violated and feeling irritable from lack of sleep. He re-enters the hotel, nods at Carlos, picks up his room key and hauls himself up the flight of stairs. On his desk, Tony spies a new laptop. Afghanistan has taught him that exhaustion and sleep loss can lead to costly mistakes. He ignores the computer and grabs a nap.

"WHERE CAN I GET SOMETHING TO EAT?" Tony asks the preoccupied night clerk.

The man lifts his nose from a book. "At this hour, most restaurants are closed, sir, but if you walk to your left, past the bridge, along the canal, you will see the fish market. In the next block is the Sapori Trattoria that caters to college students. It stays open late."

"That shouldn't be hard to find."

The clerk shrugs. "Your Mr. Hemingway describes Venice as a 'strange tricky town.' He writes that walking in Venice is better than doing crossword puzzles."

Tony leaves the hotel, passing the empty Rialto bridge on his right and a labyrinth of shuttered stalls and dark passageways on his left. The scurrying of two large rats startles him and makes his skin crawl.

Tony stares at the water. Not a ripple stirs the surface; no boats pass, not even a gondola. He stands transfixed, looking at the heartbreaking beauty of the Grand Canal at night, too preoccupied to be aware that he is not alone.

"Hi there," says the blond-headed stranger, giving him an easy smile. "Weren't you on the flight from Orlando?"

Tony is caught off guard. Beads of sweat crawl across his scalp. "Why are you following me?" he asks, trying to keep his voice neutral.

In the moonlight, Tony can see the man's calm gray eyes. He is still wearing the tan suede jacket and black crewneck sweater.

Bradford Schmidt removes his right hand from his pocket with a smooth, practiced gesture that calls no attention to itself. In his palm is a black revolver. "I'll ask the questions, Perini," the man snaps, aiming his gun at Tony's damaged knee. "How do you know the head of the local Mafia, and what are you and Morgan trying to pull?"

Tony hears the drone of a boat's motor puttering in the canal. He inhales slowly, feeling a rush of adrenaline and aware that his life could depend upon striking first and hitting hard. Tony twirls his walnut cane in both hands like an attackman's lacrosse stick. With the lightning speed that earned him an All-American reputation, he slashes down on the gun hand with the curved marble handle. Then Tony reverses the cane and spins it around, swinging it hard and level across his assailant's face, breaking the man's nose with a crack. The gun clatters to the concrete sidewalk. Perini kicks it away.

The blond-haired man stumbles backwards, but quickly rights himself, wipes his bleeding nose with his sleeve and removes a knife from his ankle sheath.

"I'm impressed," the blond man rasps. "I forgot you were some kind of war hero. Now, nice and easy, hand me the cane." He holds his left hand out in front, fingers stiff, keeping his knife hand back, in the thrust position. Tony struggles to remain in control of himself. He knows he is outmatched; his opponent is a pro, ex-Special forces op, maybe Navy SEAL.

Letting his shoulders sag in apparent resignation, Tony proffers the cane to Schmidt. As the blond man allows himself a thin smile of satisfaction and grasps the wooden tip, Tony twists the cane's curved marble head, and in one fluid motion withdraws the hidden, twelve-inch tempered glass stiletto. A guttural growl rises in Tony's throat as he plunges the dagger into Schmidt's chest, piercing his heart. A sticky-looking pool of blood spreads rapidly over the man's black sweater as he opens his mouth in pain and shock, then slumps dead to the ground.

The enormity of the attempted assassination stuns Tony. This isn't Kabul, Afghanistan; this is Venice, Italy. Behind him, he hears noises. Turning, he faces two rough-looking gorillas holding large revolvers in their hands.

Tony looks around for the fallen gun, but can't see it in the darkness. He clenches the cane and turns to face his would-be attackers.

"*Bravo, fantastico*," one of the men says. Then the two men laugh, holster their weapons and clap their hands. "Your cousin Joey sent us to look after you, but it looks like all you need is help getting rid of garbage."

"Jesus!" Tony says, breathing a deep sigh of relief. He kneels beside the body. On the inside of Schmidt's jacket pocket he finds a black leather wallet with a plastic ID. It's too dark to read the card, so Tony stuffs the wallet in his pocket.

The Mafia henchman whistle, and a boat pulls alongside. Tony recognizes the boat pilot in the moonlight. Mario waves. "*Ciao*, Tony, tonight the fishes in the *laguna* will feed on something beside polluted sea grass. Eh?"

...19

THE LAPTOP BOOTS UP and a soft green glow surrounds the screen. Tony enters his code, goes online and checks for e-mail messages from Morgan.

THE INVESTIGATION WAS HANDLED BY FT. PIERCE POLICE CHIEF: BILLY RAY THOMPKINS. (772-461-3820) YOUR FATHER'S ATTORNEY: HAROLD RICHMOND. (772-465-3200)

INFO GATHERED FROM DRUG BUST IN FT. PIERCE.
#1 HEROIN IMPORTED IN EAGLE-SHAPED GLASSWARE .
#2 POINT OF ORIGINATION OF DRUG SHIPMENTS... VENICE AREA.

IMPORTANT... YOUR MISSION... RECONNAISSANCE ONLY... ITALIAN AUTHORITIES MUST HANDLE TAKEDOWN OF DRUG TRAFFICKERS.
REPEAT: YOUR MISSION IS RECONNAISSANCE ONLY!
MORGAN

Tony opens the dead man's wallet, reads his ID, then types an e-mail reply to Morgan:

NEED ANOTHER FAVOR.... FIND OUT ALL YOU CAN ABOUT BRADFORD T. SCHMIDT, HEAD OF SECURITY, CANTON OIL COMPANY. HE TRIED TO MURDER ME TONIGHT. VENICE IS BEAUTIFUL. WISH YOU WERE HERE... AND NOT ME.
TONY

"GOOD MORNING, SIGNOR PERINI," Carlos says. "You would like a glass shopping tour to the island of Murano? No problem. I will arrange a private motor-launch to take you, at no charge, directly from our hotel dock to the famous Glass Museum of Murano, then to visit an example of glassblowing at a well-known—"

"Thank you, Carlos," Tony interrupts. "I would like to wander around Murano and visit the factories without feeling obligated to buy anything. How can I get there by myself?"

"Cross the Rialto Bridge and follow Calle Cantorta. You will see signs to the *vaporetto* stop at Fondamenta Nuove. Then board the number 41 waterbus. It's a ten-minute ride."

Standing in the hotel entrance, Tony eyes the steep steps of the Rialto Bridge. "After the bridge," Tony asks, "how long a walk to the *vaporetto* stop?"

Carlos glances at Tony's cane. "For me, sir," he answers politely, "maybe fifteen minutes."

Tony digs into his pocket and extracts Mario's card. "Carlos, will you place a call for me? And can I get some coffee, please?"

Sitting in front of the Marconi Hotel, Tony opens his cell phone and dials the first number Morgan has provided.

"Fort Pierce Police Department, how may I direct your call?" Jessie says.

"I'd like to speak to Chief Thompkins. This is Dominick Perini's son on the phone."

"Oh. I am so sorry about your dad. I loved that man." There is silence. Tony senses the operator is trying hard not to cry. "Chief Thompkins isn't here right now," she sniffs.

Tony telephones his father's lawyer. "Richmond, Taylor, and White," the receptionist answers.

"Mr. Richmond, please."

"He's in a meeting."

"Tell him Dominick Perini's son is calling from Venice. It's important."

"Hold, please."

Tony waits, sipping his coffee. He spots Mario in the distance waving to him.

"Harold Richmond here," a gravelly voice says. "Is this you, Anthony?"

"Yes, sir."

"My condolences, son. Fort Pierce will miss Dominick. Your father was my friend. I believe that there is something peculiar about his... demise."

"What do you mean, peculiar?"

"For one thing, Dominick set up a meeting with me to review his portfolio and go over his will. Your father didn't have a large estate, by some standards, but he was frugal; it all is assigned to you. What's odd is, I've never had a client commit suicide and be cremated the week before a scheduled appointment to update his will. And Dominick never struck me as the suicide type."

Tony pauses, then asks, "You said 'for one thing.' Was there another thing?"

"There certainly was. When I called the station house to report what I just related to you, I was connected to Chief Thompkins."

Tony signals to Mario that he will be a moment longer.

Richmond adds, "When I told Thompkins about Dominick's appointment, I felt that he blew me off by saying that the case was closed; that he knew your father well and had observed first hand his recent state of despondency. I'm a lawyer, Anthony, not a detective; but the man's attitude doesn't sit right with me. Call when you get back. I've got papers for you to sign."

"Keep Dad's ashes in a safe place until I get home." Tony can't speak further; his voice betrays his emotions.

THE PILOT PULLS THE BOAT to the west side of the canal, flips the motor into reverse, and drifts silently up to the hotel quay. Mario, tow rope in hand, jumps up on the wooden pier and pulls the boat tight to the mooring.

"Where to, *Signor* Tony?"

"Murano, please."

"Sleep well?" the boat pilot asks with a wink as he flips his cigarette over the side.

"Yes. I think it was taking in the night air before bedtime that did it." Tony grins.

The water taxi bobs on the swell from the throng of boats milling on the busy waterway. There is a smell of marine fuel on the water.

"Mario," Tony says. "You mentioned that you had family on Murano who worked in the glass *fornaci*. I am looking for a company that produces figurines in the shape of eagles. Can you inquire around?"

Mario pulls out his cell phone and punches in a number. "My uncle Salvadore is a *maestro* glass blower. He knows everybody and everything on Murano, but sadly, he is only working part-time."

Into the phone he says, "Uncle Sal, this is Mario. A friend of mine is an American and a cousin of Giuseppe Cullotta. He is looking for a *fornace* that produces glass eagles——"

Mario frowns and closes the cell phone. "Uncle Sal tell me this is none of our family business. He says *l'isola dei morti* is bad trouble. I am sorry, *Signor* Tony." The boat pilot wipes his forehead and murmurs, "*Jesu Christô!*"

"*L'isola dei morti.* What the hell is the island of the dead?" Tony asks.

Mario shrugs and says nothing.

"Which *fornace* on Murano is the most famous?"

The boatman takes off his cap and scratches his head with his fingers. "Vetreria Archimede Sagredo, I think," he answers. "But Archimede is dead."

"Is the company still in business?"

"*Si,* his son, Tomasso, runs it."

"How do I get there?"

"I let you off at ACTV *embarcadero.* Follow path on left, along the *laguna,* maybe fifty meters. You see sign: Seguso *fornace.* When you are ready, call me on cell."

Tony eyes the approaching quay and the gray smoke belching from the furnaces of Murano. Mario assists Tony onto the landing, ties his boat to a mooring pole and lights a cigarette.

Tony's phone beeps.

"Anthony Perini?"

"Who is this?"

"Detective Brumberg in Fort Pierce. Jessie gave me your cell number. Your father was my boss. He was a good cop and a decent guy. I know for sure he didn't 'eat his gun.' I'm working this case on my own time. Call me when you get back to Florida."

THE SIGN ON THE BRICK BUILDING is an etched granite slab reading *"Vetreria Archimede Sagredo*: Producers of fine artistic glass, gifts, lampware and chandeliers."

Tony enters through a set of large sliding metal doors. An elderly lady in a black dress sits behind the desk, eyeing him suspiciously.

"I would like to see Signor Sagredo."

"Have you an appointment?"

"No."

"I'm sorry. Signor Tomasso is extremely busy. His father recently died and——"

"I also lost my father," Tony says. "We have something in common."

"You have my sincere sympathy, sir, but—"

"Actually, it was my cousin, Giuseppi Cullotta, who suggested that I drop by."

A tense silence follows. Her hand trembles as she reaches for the phone and whispers.

A short, roly-poly man in a dark smock appears. "What business do I have with the Mafia?" he demands, his voice openly aggressive.

"Can we talk privately?" Tony smiles. "Joey Cullotta is my cousin, but I knew of no other way to get by your praetorian guard. I'm a U.S. Army officer on special assignment."

"Do you have identification?" Segredo asks warily.

Tony hands him his wallet. "You may look through it, be my guest. I'm not a very experienced secret agent, so I had better stick to the truth."

Segredo laughs, handing back the wallet. "What can I do for you, Major?"

"I notice signage in store windows: 'Don't sell Chinese,' and my boat pilot tells me that he has family on the island who are hard pressed because of Chinese competition."

Segredo turns his palms up in a gesture of helplessness. "When you grow up in Murano or Burano, after the obligatory thirteen years of school, you either leave, fish or work in glass. Now the young people must learn something else or leave Murano.

"Times are not good," Segredo continues. "The glass companies cannot afford to pay our top craftsmen their salaries, so they cut their time. We in Italy have been glass blowing for hundreds of years, but the Chinese have been doing it for thousands."

"How do you tell the difference between Murano glass and Chinese glass?"

Segredo laughs. "Unfortunately, by the price."

"Has it affected your company's business?"

"When one of my designs is copied, I delete it from the line and create something new. The Chinese can't do the big pieces, at least not yet. Wait five years and it will all be coming from China. Now, is this what your Pentagon wishes to know?"

Tony decides to risk the truth. "There has been an influx of drug smuggling into East Coast Florida. My superiors believe it emanates from this area. I received word that heroin is being shipped in glass containers in the shape of eagles."

Tony watches Segredo's eyes to see if there is any reaction. There is none.

"You say that heroin is hidden inside a formed glass piece in the form of an eagle? That is unlikely. The glass would have to be dark, probably black. One would have to know about the composition of the glass; how to prepare the *miscela,* the mixture, to get the dark color. And that's just the beginning. The glass must be heated to one thousand degrees centigrade, and then it takes over five hundred hours to cool. The heat would destroy any organic substance inside. I believe your superiors are mistaken."

"Tomasso," Tony says, "I came to your company because I'm told that you are the most important glass maker in Venice and Murano. Hypothetically, if someone wanted to pack one half kilo of powder in plastic and then enclose it in a glass container, how would they do it?"

Segredo steeples his fingers and picks up a pencil and sketch pad. "I have created original glass designs, some even for Tiffany in New York, but nothing quite like this." He roughs out the figure of a bird and he chuckles. "Now then, when the glass is hot we add the dark color and form the eagle shape, leaving a round aperture at the base. Once the glass cools," he pauses and adds with a crafty smile, "it would be possible to insert a package in the cavity—hypothetically."

"But how would you seal the glass?" Tony asks.

Segredo winks and sketches a rectangle. "A wooden platform is glued on the bottom to serve as a base and secure the contents."

"Won't drug-sniffing dogs detect the heroin?"

Segredo laughs. "I hope I don't end up in prison for my newest creation. If we add a little garlic residue to the paint on the pedestal, it will fool the drug-sniffing dogs."

"How do you know about garlic and drug sniffing dogs?"

"I watch your American television."

"Murano is a small island," Tony says. "Who could be producing the glass eagles?"

The glass manufacturer shakes his head vigorously. "If the eagles were being blown on Murano, which I doubt, and being stuffed with heroin on Murano, which I also doubt, then I would surely have heard rumors."

Tony reaches for his cane and rises to leave. He extends his hand. "I sincerely appreciate the time and information you have given me, Tomasso. My father died recently; I know you lost yours as well. At least you had the good fortune to work with your father, Archemede——"

"Wait," Segredo interrupts. "Excuse me, but when you mentioned Archemede, you remind me that we had a master glassblower who my father fired for stealing. After that, the man couldn't get work in any glass factory on Murano. The last I heard was that he opened a small *fornace* on the island of *San Francesco del deserto*."

"Is that near Murano?"

"By *vaporetto*, it lies ten minutes north of Venice, next to Burano."

"What's on the island?" Tony asks.

"It's a scary place; no tourist business or shopping. The island gained some notoriety about one hundred years ago. It inspired a Swiss painter named Bocklin to produce his most famous painting, entitled *The Island of the Dead*."

...20

AT THE SAN MICHELE CEMETERY QUAYSIDE, Tony observes the unloading of straggling mourners. San Michel is a little island sitting between Murano and the northern shore of Venice. Narrow columnar cypress trees dot the cemetery; overhead can be heard the clamor of excited gulls. People are gathering in awkward clusters. Gravediggers linger under a cypress tree, shovels in hand. In the front row are seated a dozen elderly men. It is a day of solemn reunion for the former members of the Veneto partisan force of the Italian resistance movement. "Old men," one of them mutters in a gruff voice, "never forget."

Venetian officials and Italian dignitaries file in to take seats. An elegant motor launch approaches the *cimitero* landing. The boat is twenty feet long, made of rich mahogany trimmed in chrome. Two men in business suits stand on the foredeck behind the pilot. Other men huddle around. Tony recognizes the tall, white-haired man in sunglasses as the American Secretary of Defense. Desmond Cody is in deep conversation with a bear of a man with strong features and a regal bearing. The other men on board have the hard, closed faces that mark them as bodyguards.

Looking through the camera lens, Tony traverses the assembly of mourners, pausing as he sights an exquisite Oriental girl with high cheekbones and lustrous black hair. He tries to ignore her beauty and move on, but he lingers, compressing the enlarge button to get a closer look at the woman's exotic face. She is attractive, no doubt about that. He wonders what it would be like to hold her, kiss her. Go to bed with her.

"MY NAME IS DANTE FOSCARI," announces the bespectacled director of the Correr Museum. Foscari is deceptively bland in appearance, with wispy white hair and flaring eyebrows.

In a carefully measured pace he begins, "I am Nicolo Polo's executor, and was, I dare say, his closest friend. I wish to thank you all for coming today to bid farewell to Nicolo, especially the American Defense Secretary, Mr. Desmond Cody, who flew in this morning to represent his government in paying tribute to a brave man who served both Italy and America with honor.

"Also, I wish to welcome Girolamo Gambara, representing the Prime Minister; and former Ambassador Gianpietro Scarlatti, who served with Nicolo in the partisan movement; and Massimo Bonvicini, Mayor of Venice. To all of his friends and comrades, thank you for coming.

"Nicolo Polo was the last descendent of Venice's greatest son, Marco Polo, who one day, these many centuries past, sailed from this Adriatic shore to unknown lands. Out of his epic journey was to come the world's best-selling book of its time, exceeded only by the Bible: Marco Polo's own account of his 25 years of wandering through the length and breadth of Cathay in the service of its emperor. His book inspired generations of Europe's explorers, traders, and men of culture for hundreds of years after his death, and," Foscari pauses for effect, "in return, the intrepid traveler has been neglected and forgotten by his own people and his own city."

Sensing that his words have irritated some Venetians, Foscari smiles and adds, "Had Marco Polo been born in Verona instead of Venice, his birthplace would be a tourist attraction— ahead of Juliet's balcony, the amphitheater, and eating gelato on Via Mazzini."

The audience laughs politely.

"We are here today to pay tribute and lay to final rest a man who carried on the Polo family tradition with courage and honor, but unlike his famous ancestor, Nicolo was modest. He rarely wrote of, nor spoke of, his wartime activities. Many of you are too young to remember the RSI, the *Repubblica Sociale Italiana*, a puppet state of Nazi Germany led by Benito Mussolini. When the Germans announced their plans to annex most of Friuli-Venezia Giulia into the Third Reich, including Venice, Nicolo Polo left his family and joined the partisans operating in the Veneto region. He was only a lad of 17. I can tell you because I was there, along with Ambassador Scarlatti and our comrades in the first row. Nicco's bravery was legendary. He was responsible for derailing trains at Feltre, Chioggia, Concordia, Padua, Treviso, and Verona, and blowing up munitions depots in Milan and Vigorovea. Not content with only sabotage, he single-handedly killed Germans and was wounded many times. He narrowly escaped capture and death, hiding in barns and one time in a hayloft, being secretly cared for by a local farmer's family.

"Nicolo Polo," Foscari says, raising the inflection of his voice, "was the honored recipient of the *Ordine della Corona d'Italia,* awarded by the Italian government as a token of national gratitude for his accomplishments in the partisan movement." He turns to the veterans in the front row and salutes. "Our partisan uprising showed the world that not all Italians agreed with the Fascist rule, and we were prepared to fight against it, sustaining casualties of nearly fifty thousand partisans killed and twenty-five thousand more wounded or disabled.

"When Nicco came back to Venice after the war, his parents were dead and the Polo family home had been sold. Like his ancestor, he craved adventure, so Nicco accepted an offer from the Americans. The fact that Secretary Cody has seen fit to travel this long distance adds testimony to the esteem to which Nicolo Polo was held by his American associates."

Desmond Cody turns in his seat, takes off his glasses, squints and glares at Tony.

"As the executor of his estate," continues Foscari, "I can tell you that Nicolo Polo was no mercenary. He did not work for money. In fact," Foscari laughs, "I think he only owned one suit—of gray silk. The valuable assets Nicco owned, he gave away. To the Correr Museum, he donated a priceless gift: the ivory and gold tablet of Kubla Khan that was one of a pair given to Marco and his uncle Maffeo when they departed China after twenty-five years. One of the two tablets has never been accounted for; fortunately, the one belonging to Maffeo Polo was passed to Marco Polo in his uncle's will and has been handed down for thirty-two generations."

Foscari's voice falters. "Now Nicco is the last Polo to be interred in the dust of Venice."

A prelate rises and intones the service of the dead in a sonorous singsong; when he finishes he nods to Dante Foscari, who motions to those seated in the front row. The old partisans lift the heavy solid mahogany coffin up onto their shoulders. They hold it steady for a second, then set off on a slow march to the open grave, maneuvering the coffin onto the sashes with care.

Excavated earth is piled nearby and covered with a green carpet. The pallbearers pull back the green carpet, and Foscari scoops up a handful of dirt. He weighs it in his palm and throws it down on the coffin lid. The dirt falls on the coffin with a hollow rattle. The dignitaries each take their turn with a small shovel. The old pallbearers clasp their hands in front of them, looking down at the ground.

A man in a black suit approaches Foscari. "Would you like us to lower it now?"

"Yes, please," he responds.

The man turns a crank under the grave apron. Very slowly the casket begins sinking. Tony watches it until it comes to rest in the soil. The man removes the belts, the apron, and the chain, and disappears.

Mourners mingle among the grave, the women talking together in low voices, the men smoking. Then boats begin to arrive for the five-minute return trip to Venice.

Tony approaches the Oriental girl. "Can I give you a ride back?" he asks.

She studies him closely, gives a half smile, shakes her head and walks towards the c*imitero* vaporetto stop.

Tony notices Desmond Cody huddling with Ambassador Scarlatti. Cody glances over, locks eyes with Tony, turns and speaks quietly to the other man. Scarlatti gives Tony a quick look, then nods to the Secretary of Defense before boarding his luxury motorboat.

Once on board, the ambassador takes out his cell phone. "*Apart from our shadows we have no friends,*" says Scarlatti.

"*And apart from our horsetails we have no whips,*" the hoarse voice responds.

"GENERAL MORGAN, did you check out that guy from Canton Oil?" Tony asks.

"Are you in a secure area to be making this call?"

"I'm on my cell phone outside the Marconi Hotel."

"Bradford Schmidt is head of Security for Canton Oil Company. Their business is constructing oil refineries and pipelines in developing countries."

"I just came from the Venetian's funeral, General. Your boss, Cody, was a mourner."

"No way. It's Sunday; Cody is scheduled to be on *Meet the Press* at eleven o'clock."

"Trust me. Cody's in Venice. Have you ever heard of a man named Gianpietro Scarlatti?"

"I don't think so, why?"

"Scarlatti and Cody were chummy at the funeral. I took pictures. Check him out?"

Morgan isn't listening. "Cody didn't know the Venetian," he mutters. "Even when I told him about Nicco's death, he brushed it aside, saying, 'Your people are soldiers in this war against terror. Replace him.' Then Cody skips *Meet the Press* to fly to Nicolo Polo's funeral. What the fuck's going on? E-mail me the goddamn photos." He hangs up.

As Tony enters the hotel lobby, Carlos says, "*Signor* Perini, a message."

Take *vaporetto* to Piazzale Roma. Meet me 2 o'clock. We drive to Vigorovea.

Joey

...21

THE CLANGING, GROANING *VAPORETTO* chugs up to the Rialto stop and smacks the quay. Someone yells, "Forward a bit! Now back up! A little more. Closer, closer! Now wind the rope around. That's right."

A stream of bodies disembarks from the taxi bus, and new passengers crowd on board. Tony leans on his cane for balance as the *vaporetto* glides out into the center of the canal, headed north. He marvels at the buildings passing on both sides, Gothic and Renaissance, Baroque and Neoclassical, a startling cacophony of styles and colors.

After a short ride, he hears and feels the engines being reversed as the *vaporetto* slips into the Piazzale Roma quay. Departing the waterbus, Tony spies his cousin, Joey, smoking a cigar and leaning against a shiny black Alfa Romeo sedan.

"How you like this baby?" Joey boasts. "Only twelve thousand built, thirty years ago. One hundred sixty horsepower, six cylinder, Dellorto carburetors, piston brakes. You don't see this car no more, except in Alfa Romeo museum in Arese."

Cullotta drives on A4, following the highway signs in the direction of Milano/Padova. "Vigorovea is one hundred kilometers away," he says. "Momma is happy you comin' to visit."

"Since we're family, what's the *Mala del Brenta*?"

Joey shrugs. "You're Dominick's son. The Mafia in Venice is different than in America or in Sicily. Killing is for the TV and the movies. It brings *carabinieri* on our heads; who needs that?" He makes a gesture with his finger to his nose to indicate the presence of an evil smell. "Instead, intimidation and bribery are the Venetian way. Our power comes from controlling the unions, janitorial jobs, airport catering, longshoremen and water taxis. We threaten to shut down the city during tourist season—that's our power."

Tony laughs. "Yeah, and what else?"

105

"Maybe a little running of liquor and cigarettes from Croatia on the Istria peninsula, but no smuggling of immigrants and no drugs; the Chinese Triads do that."

Cullotta exits at Padova Est in the direction of Chioggia, stopping at a gas station. "You want coffee or need make piss?" he asks.

"No thanks," Tony answers, noticing in the rearview mirror that a green Fiat sedan has followed them into the station and parked on the far side. No one gets out.

As they head back onto the main road, Tony says, "We're being followed."

"Those are my people; even *paranoicos* have enemies."

"THIS IS MADRE TERESA OF CALCUTTA SQUARE, Vigorovea's town center," Joey explains as he maneuvers the Alfa Romeo through the curving roundabout. In the center of the square Tony notices an altar surrounded by stone benches, candles and a mass of blooming forsythia bushes. He smells the sweet scent of violets in the air. They pass industrial areas and food markets; dingy gray low-rise apartment buildings sprout on either side of the road.

"When I was a boy, trees everywhere," Joey continues. "Vigorovea means 'Village of the Oaks, *Vigo de Rovea*.' After the war people leave farms; work in factories to make money."

Joey pulls into a dirt road leading to an old farmhouse. He honks the horn, and Tony is greeted warmly by an old woman in a long black dress, high-button black shoes, a black shawl and a round apple-cheeked face. Her gray hair is drawn back in a bun.

"Antonio, come let me look at you. I am your aunt Caterina." Holding him at arms' length, she studies Tony's features. "You are his twin; blue eyes, the nose, even the body," she winks.

Turning to Joey, Tony asks, "Who is she talking about?"

Caterina Cullotta answers, "The boy from Venice."

"Momma," Joey says, "let's go in, sit; have some coffee and biscuits."

"You married, Antonio?" Caterina asks, glaring at her son.

Tony shakes his head.

Caterina mutters under her breath, "My Joey—"

"Enough, Momma," Cullotta interrupts sharply. "We don't need to go there."

Caterina shrugs sadly, reaches into a deep fold in her dress and removes a small pouch. "I wait to give this to your poppa, but he never came. Now I give it you."

Tony unfastens the ribbon on the pouch, stretches it open with his fingers and extracts an antique signet ring with a large rough-cut ruby in a beaded setting of pure gold. The etched coat of arms on the sides is too worn to be seen clearly. He stares at Caterina in bewilderment.

"Years ago, Antonio, during the war," Caterina tells him, "many German soldiers stationed nearby in Padua to protect important railroad crossings and airport. Here, in Vigorovea, Germans have big ammunition storage places.

"The boy from Venice fight with partisans. One night he stumble into our yard, bleeding bad from gunshot. Momma bandage him and Papa hide the boy in haystack. My sister Marisa take food after dark. Thank God Nazis have no sniffing dogs, or we all be shot."

Tony looks over to his cousin, who smiles and raises his eyes to the ceiling.

"The boy stay five days in haystack. When no one around, I go and have a peek. He was much handsome, like you. Then one day, he gone. My sister say he have no money to pay, but give her gold ring with red stone. Two months later, I never forget, April 1945, Vigorovea liberated by partisan and British troops." She hesitates.

"Tell him the rest, Momma."

Caterina crosses herself. "The boy from Venice give Marisa another gift: *dell 'infante del bambino.*" She pauses. "My parents afraid Marisa never find husband in Vigorovea. So, marriage arranged through cousins overseas, and your poppa, Dominick, born in America."

Tony flushes and manages a weak smile. "Wow. That's some story. Whatever became of that boy from Venice—my grandfather? What was his name?"

The old woman shrugs and offers a small, humorless smile. "Who knows?"

...22

TONY STUDIES HIS E-MAIL MESSAGES:

USED PENTAGON'S DDI'S DATABASE AND LINUX FACIAL REC-
OGNITION COMPUTER SYSTEM ON YOUR FUNERAL PHOTOS.

PHOTO OF MAN IDENTIFIED AS GIANPIETRO SCARLATTI BORN
VENICE, ITALY 1927. MONGOLIAN HERITAGE. SERVED WITH DIS-
TINCTION IN ITALIAN PARTISAN MOVEMENT 1944-1945.

GRADUATE, UNIVERSITA DI MILANO. JOINED ITALIAN DIPLO-
MATIC CORPS. SERVED AS MINISTER RESIDENT IN PAKISTAN. AP-
POINTED ENVOY TO AFGHANISTAN 1978-1989. DURING RUSSIAN
INVASION, HE SUPERVISED DISTRIBUTION ITALIAN MILITARY
AID TO MUJAHIDEEN.

LAST DIPLOMATIC POST PRIOR, 2003, WAS ITALIAN AMBASSA-
DOR TO PAKISTAN. UPON RETIREMENT SCARLATTI RECEIVED
THE MEDAGLIA D'ORO AL VALOR CIVILE, ITALY'S HIGHEST CI-
VILIAN AWARD.

SCARLATTI CURRENTLY SERVES AS PRESIDENT OF EMA, THE
EUROPEAN-MONGOLIAN INTERNATIONAL ASSOCIATION DE-
VOTED TO INCREASING ECONOMIC COOPERATION BETWEEN
MONGOLIA AND EUROPE. SCARLATTI IS SOLE OWNER OF AN IM-
PORT-EXPORT LICENSING COMPANY IN THE VENICE AREA.

PHOTO OF MAN WITH WHITE STREAK IN HAIR NEXT TO SECRE-
TARY CODY IS KARL FISCHER, FORMER NAVY SEAL. DISHONOR-
ABLY DISCHARGED. CURRENTLY EMPLOYED BY CANTON OIL
COMPANY IN SECURITY CAPACITY.

MORGAN

"CARLOS, CAN YOU RECOMMEND a restaurant?" Tony
queries the concierge.

"Galleria and Casanova Grill by the canal have good Italian dishes," announces Carlos, rubbing his thumb against his fingers. "But steep prices, eh? If you can walk a little, take Ruga degli Orefici in front of Rialto Bridge." He motions to his left. "Maybe five minutes, you come to Ruga Vecchia S. Giovani. Many nice *osterias,* no tourists, not so expensive."

Curiosity and hunger lead Tony to follow Carlo's advice. On Ruga Vecchia S. Giovani, he discovers a Chinese restaurant and slumps gratefully into a booth. Thumbing through the beverage menu, Tony sees that sake is listed, and he orders it. *It's going to rain*, he muses; the soreness in his knee is more pronounced. To lessen the ache, he takes an oxycodone and downs it with sake, pondering, *What's wrong with this picture? I'm an American. drinking Japanese plum brandy in a Chinese restaurant, in an Italian city?*

As he looks around the restaurant, he is startled to see the beautiful Chinese girl from the funeral sitting in the booth directly across from him, writing in a notebook.

The waitress delivers his second sake and moves away. Tony stage-coughs and smiles across at the girl, who looks up. He raises his glass in a silent toast. Her smile is warm as she raises her glass in response, than returns to her writing.

After his second drink, he feels dizzy and disoriented. Tony orders coffee to sober up, but the room keeps spinning. *I have to get to the hotel,* he thinks, as he reaches for his cane and tries to rise to his feet. His legs are wobbly and he breaks out in a cold sweat. He nods to the Chinese girl and struggles to make his way slowly to the door; then total blackness.

TONY OPENS HIS EYES, turns over and gazes up at the worried-looking faces in front of him. He is lying on the floor in front of the cashier's desk.

"Are you okay, sir?" he hears the anxious owner asking in a singsong cadence.

The Chinese girl kneels next to him, feeling his pulse. Tony raises himself unsteadily to his feet, leaning on the girl's arm for support. He brushes himself off and rubs his aching chest.

The owner looks at Lu Yao and whispers, "Captain, shall I call for a boat ambulance?"

"No," she orders sharply. "Get me a chair!" To Tony she says, "Please sit for a minute. My name is Lu Yao. Can you smile for me?"

Tony is confused and embarrassed. He manages a weak smile.

"Good. Now, please try to raise both of your arms?"

He leans his cane against the chair and lifts both arms to shoulder height.

"Very, very good," she smiles. "Next, can you please repeat my name?"

"Lu Yao."

"Correct. One more question only. Speak clearly and make a complete sentence."

"You are the most beautiful woman I have ever seen in my life."

Lu Yao's eyes sparkle; she blushes and confides to the owner, "I performed the three- step diagnosis. It is not a stroke, and I think he is too young for a heart attack. The episode is likely a vaso vagal syncope. Now that he has recovered, I will accompany him to his hotel."

Walking slowly along Ruga degli Orefici, Lu Yao says, "You have an unusual way of striking up an acquaintance."

"Whatever works," he grins. "I took oxycodone on an empty stomach, then had two sakes in the restaurant." He rubs his tender chest again.

"Dangerous side effects can occur when alcohol is combined with narcotic pain medicine." She adds, "I noticed you also had coffee. Caffeine can also aggravate the symptoms that cause light-headedness or fainting."

"Are you a doctor?"

"No. My Big Auntie had fainting spells; I ministered to her."

As they approach the hotel entrance, Tony says, "Thank you. I feel better now."

"Allow me to escort you to your room. It is proper; I am also a guest."

Lu Yao assists him up the stairs and down the long corridor. "Considering your chest discomfort, you would wish to be certain the pain comes from contusions and is not heart related. With your permission, I will inspect your chest to see if it is bruised and turning purple."

"You want to undress me?" he asks with an abrupt laugh.

Her voice tightens. "If you would rather I not..."

"No. No." He turns towards her and lifts up his shirt.

Lu Yao gasps; she brushes her fingers lightly over the fresh scars and unsightly pink incision on his side. The crude reminders of field hospital stitching are still visible.

"You are a soldier?"

"Was. Afghanistan."

"The knee, also?" she inquires with a nod.

"Same grenade, different fragment."

Lu Yao gathers her composure. "The purple color is spreading on your chest. That is good. Your chest pain is, I think, an abrasion, not a heart problem. Get a good night's sleep, and if you experience a tightening in your chest during the night, please notify the desk at once."

Her cool, dry hands touching his chest feel like an electric current. Tony laughs and in a low voice says, "I must confess that when I saw you at the funeral this morning, it was my fantasy to undress you, rather than have you undressing me."

"One must not confuse fantasy with reality," Lu Yao replies, reddening. "What is the expression you Americans use? 'Maybe I take the rain check.' "

THERE IS COMMOTION in the Marconi's dining area, punctuated by the clatter of silverware and the buzz of animated breakfast conversation. A party of German tourists, enjoying their complimentary breakfasts, are conversing noisily between tables; several hold newspapers in one hand and coffee cups in the other.

Tony spots Lu Yao sitting alone in a corner drinking coffee and writing. "Coffee smells great. May I join you?"

"Of course. How is your chest feeling this morning?"

"Sore. Want to look?" He pretends to pull up his shirt.

"You will frighten off the tourists," she says, nodding in the direction of the Germans.

Tony helps himself to coffee and croissants at the sideboard and returns. "What is it you are so busy writing?"

"I am working on a book about the famous Italian explorer, Marco Polo."

"While I was in the hospital, I watched a TV interview with an English author. She claims that Marco Polo never went to China."

Lu Yao's face clouds. A hard edge comes into her voice. "Unfortunately, some people can only attain recognition by scoffing at giants in order that their own small voices be heard." Lu Yao inhales deeply. "Most of these arguments have been aired since the beginning of the 19th century, but have never been taken seriously by scholars. I'm sure the woman argued that Marco Polo failed to mention important aspects of Chinese life, like the Great Wall, the custom of foot binding, the writing system, and, of course, tea drinking. And for each omission, there is a rational reason."

Tony holds up both hands. "Hey," he pleads, "I'm on your side, but isn't it curious that Polo didn't mention the Great Wall? Isn't it one of the wonders of the world?"

"You must understand," Lu Yao answers. "The Great Wall of China is a four-thousand-mile fortification built to protect various dynasties from raids by nomadic tribes coming from the north, which is modern-day Mongolia. When Marco Polo was in China from 1273 to 1293, Kubla Khan was the emperor. Kubla Khan was himself a Mongol, the grandson of the great Genghis Khan. During his reign there was no threat from the north, so the Great Wall was only a stone landmark and not considered to be of great importance."

Tony grins and pretends to count on his fingers. "Polo spent twenty years in China? And I thought my two-year tour in Afghanistan was a long time."

"Twenty years was a long period," Lu Yao continues. "And you must also include four years of travel time. In total, Marco Polo was away from home for twenty-four years. After his return to Venice, Marco fought against the Genoese and was captured. While in prison he met a writer named Rustechello, and they collaborated on the book of Marco Polo's adventures.

"If you are interested, I have a meeting today with Doctore Dante Foscari, director of the Correr Museum. It appears that an old manuscript, a diary of Marco Polo's, has surfaced, and the director has kindly scanned a copy for me to study."

"Count me in."

"I could not help but notice your ring with the ruby stone," Lu Yao remarks. "In China, all women have great interest in jewelry. A ruby such as yours is referred to as a *Pigeon's Blood* or *ko-twe* ruby. It has been compared to the center of a live pigeon's eye."

Tony winces at the name. "Pigeon's blood sounds gory."

Lu Yao lightly touches his arm. "Then let us say that your ruby has the color of the fresh pomegranate seed. Sounds better, eh?"

"WELCOME TO THE CORRER," Director Dante Foscari says in greeting.

Lu Yao nods and introduces Tony. "Mr. Perini is from the United States."

"Good," Foscari comments, his eyes crinkling with pleasure. "My dear Ms. Cheng, regarding that document we discussed. I have no doubt but that the diary is an original manuscript penned by the old traveler, Marco Polo, towards the end of his life."

"*Doctore* Foscari," Lu Yao replies, "I am honored by your kind assistance and—"

Foscari interrupts. "Your indulgence, please. Unfortunately, before we are permitted to publicly display the Polo manuscript, it must be authenticated to satisfy the infernal insurance people and the museum's lawyers. The fundamental responsibilities of any museum director are avoiding copyright infringement, proving provenance, and ensuring true ownership of works in our collections. There are no other copies of the original except the one I prepared for you, for which I believe you have some entitlement. Yes?"

Tony sees Lu Yao's face suddenly redden.

Without waiting for her reply, Foscari continues. "We are also restricted from publishing and marketing copies of the manuscript until the investigations are completed."

"Publishing and marketing?" Lu Yao looks quizzical. "I don't understand."

"I've read the manuscript," Foscari states. "While Marco Polo's original book, the *Description of the World*, can be, at times, tedious and boring, Polo's lost diary is an earthy revelation. It will undoubtedly be a bestseller. If the Correr Museum's ownership is firmly established, we can anticipate a much-welcome source of royalty cash inflow."

Foscari swirls the tumblers on his safe and extracts a folder. "This is a scanned copy," he says to Lu Yao. "I offer it to you on the condition that you keep it secure and publish nothing without first submitting your work for review and obtaining permission rights. Agreed?"

"Agreed," she repeats, encircling his hand with both of hers and smiling broadly. "*Doctore*, we both know that Italian copyright laws do not apply in China. However, I give you my solemn word, I will honor your requests."

"I know you will, my dear." His eyes twinkle knowingly. "It's in your blood."

Lu Yao gives the director a smile and a dismissive nod. "At the funeral, you mentioned that the Correr has been bequested one of the tablets of Kubla Khan. Will it be on display?"

"No. We are constructing a special housing. For now, I keep the tablet in my safe."

"I will be returning to China shortly and may never have another opportunity. Would it be possible to have a quick look? I would be most grateful."

Foscari shrugs and returns to the safe. He withdraws an oblong metal box. "Airtight," he pronounces, unclasping and opening the box to reveal a five-by-twelve-inch ivory and gold tablet engraved with a gyrfalcon—Kubla Khan's imperial golden tablet of authority.

A drop of moisture gathers at the corner of Lu Yao's eye. "So beautiful," she whispers. "In China, we call this fabled tablet of Kubla Khan the *paiza*."

"My dear," Foscari asks, "will you translate the inscription for us?"

Lu Yao borrows Foscari's magnifying visor. " '*By the strength of the eternal Heaven, holy be the Khan's name. Let him that pays him not reverence be killed.*' "

"This tablet," adds Foscari, "was a VIP passport, authorizing the Polos to receive, throughout the Great Khan's dominions, such horses, lodging, food and guides as they required."

"Were there not two tablets?" Lu Yao ventures.

Foscari pauses, a small crease of worry appearing on his brow. He points to the manuscript. "The Polo diary will answer your question, my dear, and the answer may surprise you." Then his gaze shifts to Tony's ring. "That is a very unusual stone; may I have a look?"

Tony slips the signet ring off and places it on Foscari's desk.

Foscari holds the ring to the light. "Yes, indeed," he murmurs to himself. "Pigeon's Blood. I have only seen one like this in my lifetime..." Foscari's voice trails off. "Many years ago." He retrieves the magnifying visor and rotates the ring slowly in his hand. "Ah," he sighs.

"What is it?" Tony asks.

"First, young man, may I inquire as to how you came to be in possession of this ring?"

Tony coughs. "It's a complicated matter, and it's personal."

Foscari raises his eyebrows. "The markings on your ring are well-worn; however, the Polo family crest is decipherable under magnification. My boy, I do not know what brings you to Venice. Maybe it is fortuitous, maybe coincidental, maybe something else... eh?"

Tony chooses to remain silent.

Foscari opens the Polo diary. The director moistens his thumb on his lips and flips through pages. "Yes. Here we have it in section nine," he observes. "Messer Polo describes visiting the island of Zeilan while he was in the service of Kubla Khan. The island he refers to was most likely Ceylon; now it is known as Sri Lanka. The names keep changing. No matter, the island of Zeilan was governed by a king named Sender-naz. Polo notes that both the men and women would go around nearly in a state of nudity, only wrapping a cloth around the middle parts of their bodies."

"Sounds like Club Med," Tony cuts in.

Foscari politely chuckles, but his eyes are devoid of humor. "Permit me to continue, quoting Polo's own words: *Zeilan produces the most beautiful rubies in the world, and the king possesses the grandest ruby that I have ever hoped to see, being the thickness of a man's arm, brilliant beyond description, and without a single flaw. The red jewel has the appearance of a glowing fire and is so precious that no estimate of its value could be made in money. The great Khan Kublai dispatched me to Zeilan to offer King Sender-naz, in return for the ruby, the value of an entire city. The king refused me, saying he would not sell it for all the treasure in the universe nor could he on any terms suffer it to go out of his dominions.*

"'In a gesture of appreciation for my efforts in the Khan's behalf, Sender-naz presented me, at the time of my departure, a ruby as a gift. He called it Padamya, so named, the king said, because the ruby is the color of the first two drops of blood from the nose of a freshly slain Zeilan pigeon. Upon my return to Venice, I had the Padamya embedded into a ruby signet ring etched with our Polo crest: the knight's helmet and three stars."

Tony raises his hand slowly, twisting the ring and squinting to read the inscription.

Foscari stares hard at him. "When you walked in, I immediately recognized the resemblance: the face, the build, the eyes, the nose. In addition, you are in possession of Nicolo Polo's family signet ring. I therefore must presume you are closely related; perhaps Nicco's grandson, eh? And, if that is so, you are the last—" Foscari pauses and turns to Lu Yao. "—*One* of the last descendants of Marco Polo."

Tony listens to the curator in utter disbelief, like the earth is tilting under his feet.

Lu Yao's face goes pale. Her eyes shoot to Tony, regarding him carefully, as if for the first time. She keeps her hands clasped around herself, as though she has taken a hard blow to the stomach. A single tear spills onto her cheek. She brushes it away, rises, locks her copy of the Polo diary in her briefcase, bows respectfully to Foscari, and rushes blindly from the room.

AFTER A MOMENT OF STUNNED SILENCE, Tony trails after Lu Yao, gripping the railing, unsteadily descending the stone stairs to the ground floor. He staggers into the sunlight of Piazza San Marco. In the square Tony is enveloped in a deluge of people crowding in front of St. Mark's Basilica. Tourists pose beneath clouds of steel-blue pigeons hovering and swooping, while the souvenir stand operators peddle their cheap wares, amidst vendors of glowing yo-yos and hawkers of tours to Murano glass factories.

In front of the Basilica's hodgepodge of Byzantine domes and mosaics, Lu Yao turns to face him. Her slanted jade-green eyes narrow. The breeze from the canal blows a few strands of hair across her face, which she angrily brushes back with her hand. A hard edge comes into her voice. "You are a liar, and I foolishly trusted you."

"Lu Yao, I swear to you that I never knew about my grandfather."

"Ha," she says with a derisive snort. Her eyes narrow.

"Please. Sit for a moment, have some coffee. Let me explain—"

She cuts him off. "What is there to explain?"

The two of them wait in awkward silence for their coffees to arrive. Tony shifts uneasily in his chair as violin melodies pour from tented orchestra stands in the piazza. Lu Yao's sudden personality change has stunned him. When the surly waiter delivers their coffee, Lu Yao lifts her cup to sip while keeping her gaze fixed on Tony.

Tony feels himself flush. "Here's the deal. Because of my leg injury, I was headed for a medical discharge from the Army. The thought of retirement, at my age, is scary. Then, a general from the Pentagon invites me to a fancy Washington restaurant. He says that the Army still has a role for me, even in the physical condition I'm in. I was sent on assignment to Venice." He grins. "I'm really not cut out for this kind of work. I'm a soldier; as a spy, I suck."

In spite of her anger, Lu Yao laughs out loud; her face softens into a real smile.

Tony resumes, "As for my being descended from the illustrious Marco Polo family, this is all news to me. My father's name was not Polo, it was Perini; he was born in America. How do you say in Italian, *illegitimate*? He never knew who his real father was."

He pauses and inhales deeply. "In the past week, I've lost the father I hardly knew and a grandfather I never met. I know it sounds far-fetched, but I believe both men were murdered."

Lu Yao's light touch of her fingertips on his wrists makes Tony's pulse rate jump as he tries to react to her change of mood.

"I'm truly sorry for your losses," she says, giving Tony a bitter-sweet smile, adding in a voice so pleasing it is almost seductive, "For what important assignment did your Pentagon send you to Venice?"

Tony doesn't reply. He has an uncomfortable feeling that they are being watched. In Afghanistan, this sixth sense saved his life on more than one occasion. He pays the waiter and leads Lu Yao into the San Marco arcade.

She points at a mannequin in a store window. "With your blue eyes you should only wear navy turtlenecks and blue jeans. It's very fashionable."

Tony studies the darkened reflections in the plate glass of the shop window. "I don't want to upset you, but I have a feeling we're being followed."

"Yes," Lu Yao nods gravely. "The two heavy-shouldered Mongolians in woolen trousers, gray sweaters and jackets. They picked us up when we left the Correr Museum."

"WALK OR *VAPORETTO*?" Lu Yao asks, adjusting her sunglasses. "The bus boat ride takes five minutes to San Silvestro, or we can stroll back, keeping an eye out for our watchers."

"I may have trouble managing the bridges and steps," Tony answers. "Let's ride."

They plunge into the tide of tourists waiting for the number 2 line boat beginning the broad curve to bring it to the dock. The engine slows to an even purr, and then comes the heavy thump as the *vaporetto* slides into the Piazza San Marco quay. Tony and Lu Yao are caught in the boarding crush of passengers. They don't spot the two burly men who climb aboard as the boat pulls out.

The crowded *vaporetto* putters its way along, passing glittering palazzos. Tony senses that he has visited this identical locale in another time. The eerie familiarity of the flowing water conjures up darkened images of men heaping luggage into gondolas, bidding farewells, slipping through this echoing canal between shadowy high-walled palaces and tenements, past markets and dark shops; finally passing under the arched wooden Rialto Bridge on their way to boarding ships headed for grand adventures.

His reverie is interrupted by the angry horn of the *vaporetto* as it overshoots the San Silvestro landing area. The captain slips the boat suddenly into reverse. People on the deck totter as they attempt to maintain their balance. Slowly, the boat reverses itself in the water and heads the short distance back toward the *embarcadero*.

Tony's adrenaline spikes as he watches two men with Slavic tilts to their eyes forcing their way through the crowd towards him. Over the noise of the engines, he doesn't hear Lu Yao's screaming warning. The men pull out knives, their eyes fixed on Tony.

Lu Yao launches herself at the closest attacker, chopping him across the face with the stiffened blade of her right hand, a lethal strike driving bone and cartilage into his brain. She hits him a second time, a solid elbow against the side of his head, which is unnecessary, because the man is already dead when he hits the wooden deck.

Tony whips his marble-headed cane a complete 180-degree turn and slams the other Mongolian as hard as he can along the side of the head. There's a loud crunch and a spray of blood. He slashes the cane again with all his strength against the man's upper arm, shattering the bone. The wounded man growls and continues to crowd in against him, his knife chest high.

The rocking of the boat causes Tony to lose his balance. He falls backwards over the guard chain, grabbing a handful of sweater, pulling the Mongolian with him into the oily green water of the Grand Canal only seconds before the *vaporetto* is to hit the pier.

The water engulfs Tony. A current of raw fear grips his brain; he realizes that his assailant is wildly clutching his injured leg and the boat is about to crush them both against the dock. Tony kicks hard in the direction of the man's face. He feels the grip loosen; he dives deeper into the dark water, hearing the thud as a wave pushes the *vaporetto* against the embankment.

Tony swims under the *vaporetto*, towards the bow to avoid the deadly propellers. He glances up, searching frantically for daylight. It is difficult to swim using only his good leg. He finds no daylight. The *vaporetto* is wider than he had imagined. The pain in his leg is blinding; his lungs are bursting. An overwhelming weariness overcomes him. He can't hold his breath any longer. Tony is dimly aware that his body is shutting down; he knows he cannot prevent it. He gasps, aspirating water into his lungs. Every ounce of animal instinct and muscle memory propels one last kick.

Tony is unconscious when his head breaches the surface. He doesn't hear the wail of sirens filling the air as police boats race up the canal, their blue lights flashing rhythmically. Nor does he see the woman dive into the polluted canal and swim to his side with strong, smooth strokes, nor feel her cross-chest carry him to shore and administer mouth-to-mouth resuscitation until the ambulance boat him speeds to the Ospedale Civile at San Giovanni e Paolo.

...23

TONY'S HEAD IS IN A SWIRLING FOG filled with bright lights. His mind floats. He shouts soundlessly to drive the fiery shapes away; a bright stream of red tracer bullets light up the sky over the mud brick compound in Afghanistan's Nuristan Province. Enemy AK-47 and machine gun fire crackles in all directions. Even in his hallucinatory state, Anthony Perini hunches his shoulders as he re-lives hearing the whistling sounds of the Taliban's 120 mm mortars, and the ground rumble and quake following each dull-sounding mortar explosion.

"Major," Sergeant West yells over the noise. "The Taliban are firing rocket-propelled grenades from the orchard. They're surrounding us."

"Have Webster radio for air support," Tony orders, his mouth chalky-dry.

"Webster's dead, sir," the sergeant cuts in. "Satellite reception's piss-poor. We need direct line-of-sight. It's suicide using a phone out in the open."

Without thinking, Tony grabs his EMSS Iridium handset and dashes outside the bunker. He ignores the bloodthirsty yells and the dark, menacing figures waving AK-47's. Machine gun fire plows the earth around him. He feels a huge fist striking him as a bullet slams into his shoulder. Tony is spun around sharply and lands on his back in the dirt, stunned; the bright oozing of blood colors his field jacket. He rolls into a sitting position and grabs his phone. "Base, this is King Outpost. Under heavy attack. Need air cover and reinforcements. Do you read me?"

"We copy you, King Outpost. Hang in there. Posse's on the way."

Tony clutches his bleeding shoulder, crouches over and runs, trailing blood. Bullets lap the dust as he zigzags around the compound, checking his men. "Fire only at targets of opportunity," he commands. "Keep helmets and flack jackets on. Help is on the way. Be cool!"

To his machine gunners he cautions, "Lay down a curtain of lead when they start moving. Careful with your ammo. Don't run out."

They hear the sound of the back blast from a rocket-propelled grenade, and Tony watches as the helicopter lurches clumsily in mid-air, tilts over sideways, and crashes in a booming, orange-red fireball. A column of thick black smoke rises into the clear mountain sky. A cheer goes up from the Taliban guerilla fighters.

"The Taliban are massing," Sergeant West warns.

More helicopters can be heard buzzing in the distance.

A grenade sails past Tony and bounces into a knot of men. "Grenade!" he screams and leaps up. It is not a conscious decision. Tony tears off his helmet and hurls himself forward in an unsuccessful attempt to use it to smother the exploding grenade.

"ARE YOU AWAKE, Major?" Tony hears the field surgeon ask. He nods groggily.

"Your leg took the brunt of the fragmentation grenade."

"My men?" Tony whispers.

"As well as could be expected. Your company suffered casualties, but minimal, considering the circumstances." The doctor resumes his diagnosis. "The bullet from your shoulder is out and the wound is clean. It should heal nicely. Your leg wound is another matter—a ticket home. We saved the leg, but I'm afraid you have years of physical therapy ahead. And your body is speckled with grenade fragments just under the surface of the skin. By the way, sir, may I congratulate you for being awarded the—"

Tony's eyes close as he drifts off into an oxycodone reverie.

...24

"ARE YOU AWAKE? My name is Doctore Isabella Vilasanta. You are in the Ospedale Civile," she says. "Feeling better, yes?"

Tony looks up at the Italian doctor's finely chiseled nose and her carelessly brushed silver-blond hair gathered in a high bun, exposing her long, graceful neck.

"For a young man, you have too many scars on your body."

"How soon can I leave?" he asks, ignoring her comment.

"You are free to go, but there is something important to be discussed." Her warm smile evaporates. "I noticed a few angry-looking red patches on your leg, near the surgery; they felt warm. You also are running a low-grade fever. In that dirty canal water, your leg wound was reopened and exposed to bacteria. I have cleaned, disinfected and bandaged your leg and will give you more dressings and oral antibiotics to take with you. Sterile dressings will act as a filter to keep out bacteria, but you must also allow air to reach the wound. If you overexert, and the sweat cannot evaporate, your wound will stay moist; then infection can easily set in."

Tony starts to get out of bed. He experiences a stab of pain in his knee; a shiver and a chill pass through him. He bites his lip in silence, then says, "I've gotten through worse. Do you have oxycodone?"

He sees Dr. Vilasanta's eyes tighten. "Don't play the hero with me, young man. I am quite serious. With this condition, you run the risk of contacting cellulitis, which if not treated, can progress rapidly into a life-threatening streptococci disease called necrotizing fasciitis. There's a police official waiting to see you," Dr. Vilasanta adds, "but first, I want you to pay strict attention to what I am telling you. If you develop flu-like symptoms, fever or lightheadedness, and your leg wound becomes more painful to the touch, you must report to a hospital immediately. Understand?"

"Thanks, Doc. I'll be fine."

She adds skeptically, "If you do not pay attention, you will not be fine. I do not wish to alarm you, but necrotizing fasciitis streptococci is also called the flesh-eating bacteria." She touches Tony's shoulder gently. "And go easy with the oxycodone. It is highly addictive."

A DAPPER, MIDDLE-AGED MAN with his hair slicked straight back from the forehead enters Tony's hospital room. "My name is *Commissario* Alesandro Zambelli," he announces flatly, without extending his hand.

Tony tries to clear his head. He looks at the inspector with a puzzled expression. The man's eyes are brown and deeply set. They lend his face an air of authority.

"How is my lady friend?" Tony asks. "Is she all right?"

"If you are referring to the Chinese woman who towed you to the pavement at Galizzi San Silvestro and administered first aid..." Zambelli pauses for effect. "She has been questioned."

"What the hell are you talking about?"

"*Signor* Perini, please do not attempt to treat the Venetian constabulary as fools." Zambelli removes a tape recorder from his pocket. "Do you object to this interview being recorded?"

Tony props himself up in bed and shakes his head. *Be cool,* he warns himself.

The *commissario* pushes the start button. "What brings you to Venice, *Signor* Perini?"

"I'm a U.S. Army officer on leave. I always wanted to visit Venice."

"Can you substantiate this information?"

"Of course. Contact General Preston Morgan in Washington, D.C." Tony glances at his watch. "It's six hours' time difference. You can call him at his office." Tony offers Morgan's private number, and Zambelli notes it down.

"How do you know the Chinese woman?" Zambelli asks.

"We are staying at the same hotel; we met in a Chinese restaurant in the Rialto area."

"Did you know the lady prior to your visit?"

"Absolutely not."

Zambelli stares hard at Tony. "Are you not related to the Cullotta Mafia crime family?"

"Joey Cullotta is my father's cousin. I have no other relationship with him."

"You know of the Chinese Triads?" Zambelli presses.

"No."

"These Chinese gangsters are enlarging their sphere of influence in Italy. We do not intend to allow the Triads to infiltrate into the Veneto area. Isn't it passing strange that you, an American family member of the *Mala del Brenta*, and a Chinese woman, who according to witnesses killed a big man with one lethal blow, both arrive in Venice on the same day and are staying at the same hotel?" He pauses. "Doesn't that strike you as an odd coincidence?"

Before Tony can reply, Zambelli continues. "And while the two of you are traveling together on the number 82 *vaporetto*, two unidentified men attempt, not to rob, but to kill you." He smiles conspiratorially. "Wouldn't that suggest a competitive crime organization attempting to prevent your two families from joining forces to control Venice?"

"Did you question the men who tried to kill us?" Tony asks hotly.

"Unfortunately, both are dead. One drowned in the canal and the other was dispatched by the Chinese woman. Who knows who sent them or where they came from? Many strangers come to Venice these days with UN refugee status, or their documents are forged."

"And as for your Chinese accomplice," Zambelli scoffs, "I had her references checked. We telephoned her newspaper company in Hangzhou. They gave no answers. They advised that we should telephone the Ministry of Information in Beijing. My secretary called and was advised that the inquiry has been received. I'm afraid it has dropped down a bottomless well."

Zambelli pushes the stop button on the recorder. "Now let us check your references." Clamping his cell phone to his ear, he refers to his notebook, then punches in numbers.

"Morgan here," the voice barks.

"Ah yes," the policeman says, pushing the speaker button so Tony can listen to the conversation. "General Morgan, I am *Comma-*

sario Zambelli of the Venice constabulary. A moment of your time, sir. We have a man by the name of Anthony Perini under investigation in connection with a murder inquiry. The gentleman claims that he is a major in the U.S. Army, he is vacationing in Venice, and that you, sir, would vouch for his identification."

"*Commasario*," Morgan replies. "Do you have any idea how many majors there are in the United States Army? Literally thousands. How in the world would I know, off the top of my head, where the hell they all are?"

Tony hears Morgan hang up.

"You are free to leave the hospital," Zambelli smirks. "However, we will require your passport until the matter is resolved."

...25

"WHAT DID YOU EXPECT ME TO SAY?" General Morgan growls.

"I didn't expect you to leave me hanging out on a fucking limb."

"How could I tell the Venetian police that I've got an undercover agent operating in their country? It would be all over CNN, and by the way, it's against their laws. Have you made any progress in Venice, other than getting arrested?"

"My 'progress,' as you call it, is that I was nearly shot, almost knifed, and practically drowned. I spent last night in the hospital—"

Morgan interrupts, "Whatever doesn't kill you makes you stronger."

"Now you're quoting Nietzsche to me, great."

"Who's Nietzsche? I read it in a fortune cookie."

"I'm serious, General. The police took my passport, I'm under suspicion of being part of the Italian Mafia, and oh yes, I forgot to add that I'm the grandson of your agent, the Venetian."

The line is silent. "Nicolo's grandson?" Morgan mumbles, sounding stunned. "How is that possible?"

"If you don't mind, sir, let's save my family tree for another time. Your boss, Cody, stared daggers at me at Polo's funeral. What's his problem?"

Morgan pauses again. "Cody was head of some lobbying group. He is rumored to have a cushy job waiting with an oil company when he leaves office. I wasn't privy to it, but Desmond is leading a top level trade mission to Mongolia to secure oil rights for American companies. He's in Venice working out the arrangements.

"But back to your situation. The passport's no problem. We can fly you out of Aviano Air Base if necessary."

"I'll stay in touch," Tony says. "I'm going to check out an isolated little island near Venice. Strategically, the place is an ideal location for receiving, processing and shipping heroin. It's called *San Francesco del Deserto*—the Island of the Dead."

"Catchy name," grumbles Morgan. "For the hundredth time, Major, remember—your mission is reconnaissance only. Understand me?"

Morgan gets no response; the phone has been hung up. He reflects that there is not much boyishness left in this young officer. Instead, there is an audaciousness, a willingness to stand up for his convictions—a quality Morgan wishes he still had more of himself.

"LU YAO, ARE YOU THERE?" Tony calls out, rapping gently.

The door flies open. Lu Yao's face lights up with delight and concern. She clutches him into her arms. "You look gray and drawn," she says, studying him closely. "Are you all right?"

Tony dismisses her question, inhaling her musky fragrance. His heart feels squeezed. In that moment, Tony knows this is more than only a physical attraction. He admits to himself that he is smitten, like a seventeen-year-old boy. It is an urgent need to be near her; to be friends as well as lovers. But not lovers yet—it is too soon. He senses that she realizes it too, for her cheeks redden and she stares at him with her lips slightly parted.

"Can I repay your saving my life with Chinese food?" he asks, smiling. "And this time, I promise not to pass out."

"TAMIL ROSES FOR YOUR WIFE OR SWEETHEART?" hawks the wizened old man with the dark, wrinkled hands and face. He trails closely behind Tony and Lu Yao as they amble down Ruga Vecchia S. Giovani.

"Tamil roses for your sweetheart?" the flower peddler continues cajoling. To be rid of the annoyance, Tony purchases three long-stem roses.

"Thank you, kind sir," says the aged vendor with a wink.

"It's such a beautiful night. Let's rest and have a drink before dinner," Tony suggests. He presents the flowers. "A gift for saving my life, but more important, for retrieving my cane."

"I think you look pale," Lu Yao says with genuine concern. "Tell me how you feel."

"My leg is achy from wrestling with that maniac on the *vaporetto* and swimming in the dirty canal. I'm heavily bruised, slightly dented, and the hospital doctor thinks my injury might have become infected. Otherwise, I'm in good shape.

"Being with you, Lu Yao, makes me laugh and be happy for the first time in a long while. At Walter Reed, they told us that laughter is good medicine. It releases endorphins, natural chemicals that counteract stress hormones. So, for my health's sake, you must make me laugh."

Lu Yao giggles. "I've been reading through the lost diary of Marco Polo. There are sections that are funny, serious and saucy at the same time."

"Tell me the sexy parts," Tony pleads.

"Maybe later," she teases. "Have you ever heard of the Kingdom of Maffeo?"

"Never."

"I'll tell it as best as I can remember. When Marco Polo was in Baghdad on his travels, his uncle Maffeo took a trip south to trade in the southern port city of Al-Basrah, or as it is known today, Basra. Maffeo returned with stories of geysers that jetted out a black liquid, a type of oil he called *naft*, which seeped from the soil and burned more brightly than other oils, and for a longer time and with no suffocating odor.

"His uncle Maffeo was so impressed with the black oil that he traded ten precious bricks of orange saffron spice, which the Polos had carried all the way from Venice, in exchange for obtaining the deed to an area of sand the size of all your Veneto. But Marco Polo's father, Nicolo, laughed at Maffeo's trade in Al-Basrah, saying it was a waste of their valuable trading commodity for an empty desert. Nicolo called his brother's deeded land 'The Kingdom of Maffeo.' Maffeo defended his trade, saying that someday the acquired property would accrue great value to the Polo family. Marco's father laughed and said, 'And someday camels will fly.' "

"That's the same Basra that's in Iraq?"

"Of course."

"Wow!" Tony whistles. "Basra sits on some of the world's largest untapped oil reserves. In fact, the bulk of Iraq's estimated 200 billion barrels in potential deposits is there."

"Wait," Lu Yao continues, "you haven't heard the rest of the story. Marco Polo says that when they crossed the Gobi Desert in 1273 south of the city that is now called Bayankhonger—"

"Where is that?" Tony cuts in.

"Southern Mongolia, just north of our Chinese border. Marco also speaks of a quaint custom of the desert folk." Lu Yao blushes. "If a husband travels away from home and does not return within twenty days, his wife takes another 'husband' until his return, and the man who is away is likewise permitted to take unto himself a temporary 'wife.' "

"Let me think about that one and get back to you," Tony teases.

"But seriously, here is the important part. While their caravan rested, and Marco was being entertained by a temporary 'widow,' his uncle Maffeo explored the surrounding desert area of Mongolia, and when he returned he said he had found a new Kingdom of Maffeo. He reported eyeing fountains in the earth more numerous than in Basra, from which black liquid flowed in such abundance that a hundred shiploads of it could be taken at one time."

"Huge untapped oil deposits in Mongolia?" Tony says thoughtfully. "Our Secretary of Defense is leading an American delegation to Ulaanbaatar for an important meeting next week."

Lu Yao looks startled.

"Hungry?" he asks, taking Lu Yao by the arm.

As they enter the restaurant, the proprietor nods to Lu Yao, tilting his head in the direction of the restrooms.

"Let me freshen up a moment," she tells Tony. As she enters the ladies' room, the jar of potpourri is filled with geraniums, not lavender. It is the danger signal. Lu Yao unscrews the bottom of the jar and reads the message:

VENICE POLICE CONTACTED BEIJING
YOUR FALSE IDENTITY EXPOSED. YOU
ARE TO ABORT MISSION AND RETURN.
LI HU JENGH

Lu Yao scribbles a handwritten reply and replaces the bottom.

American oil executives going to Ulaanbaatar
for important meeting, led by Defense Secretary.
Does this alter mission? Shall I remain?
Will check back in one hour.
Cheng Lu Yao

"WHO WAS THIS GENERAL TSO, and why are we eating his chicken?" Tony asks.

"There *was* once a General Tso," Lu Yao replies. "Tsung-t'ang Tso was a 19th-century Chinese military leader from Hunan province. After each military victory, his wife would make this dish for his officers."

"A Chinese Colonel Sanders."

Lu Yao doesn't smile.

"What's the matter? Have I upset you?"

"I was thinking about the oil in Mongolia. What would happen if America gets involved in Mongolia seeking oil, like in Iraq? Bayankhonger is on China's doorstep. It makes me fearful."

"I have a friend, a Mongolian officer that I met in Afghanistan. He headed up the 150th Elite Peacekeeping Battalion working with the Afghan National Army. Vachir Borbaatar has a lot of contacts, and Mongolia is a small country. I can call and ask him if he knows anything.

"The check is paid and I haven't passed out, so are you ready to head back?"

Lu Yao folds her hands defensively against her stomach and says, "It's embarrassing. I'm having a little stomach discomfort. Please wait for me at the table outside in the piazza. Okay?"

SITTING IN THE PIAZZA, Tony is aware of a vague sense of unease. The sun has set; the campo is gray and bare. The rose vendor continues to pester strolling couples. On the corner of the piazza Tony notices another old man standing by a cart of knockoff designer

handbags, busying himself spreading a sheet on the ground and an-
choring each corner with one of his handbags. As soon as the sheet is
in place, he begins to pull samples of Prada, Gucci, and Louis Vuit-
ton from his cart and displaying them on the sheet. The bag seller
hawks his wares in Italian-accented English, "I have them all: Mis-
soni, Armani, direct from the factory. Good prices!"

Nothing appears unusual. Tony orders a coffee.

"Is this seat taken?" says a man who slips in silently by his side.

Tony recognizes the streak of chalk white running though the
man's black hair and feels the hard barrel of a handgun pressed hard
against his leg.

"Name's Fischer," the man chortles. "My friends under the table
are Heckler and Koch."

"Roses for your wives or sweethearts?" the flower man begs,
hovering near the table.

"Get lost, old man!" Fischer barks. "What do you think, we're
queer?"

Tony remains silent.

"For starters, Perini, keep your hands on the table where I can
see them. Next, where's my boss, Brad Schmidt?" Fischer shoves
the gun roughly against Tony's injury. The nerves in his knee quiver
and twitch uncontrollably.

"This pistol was my Navy SEALS special. It fires a 9 mm para-
bellum cartridge," Fisher adds, "and with the silencer, it sounds no
louder than a cork popping."

Tony is dimly aware of the ten o'clock bells ringing out from the
Church of San Giacomo di Rialto. The piazza is now completely deserted, save for the weary-looking old rose vendor sitting dejectedly
at an empty table, and the handbag peddler standing by his cart.
Tony's instinct is to take aggressive action, but he knows this ex-
SEAL to be an experienced killer. "Never heard of Schmidt," Tony
says.

Fischer taunts him, "Stubborn, like your old man."

Blood rushes to his brain. "My father—what does that mean?"

"It means what it means. We do what we're paid to do. Me and
the police broad. I hear the old guy we dumped in the inlet was your

grandfather. Nailing you, I hit the Trifecta," Fischer snickers, then coughs harshly as a thin coil of wire encircles his neck.

"Drop gun, fucker," the rose vendor whispers. "Or this wire cut your throat like butter."

Small red droplets appear at Fischer's neck. The handbag peddler joins them, picking up Fischer's gun and stuffing it in his belt. The rose vendor searches Fischer's jacket pockets, extracting two hypodermic needles. "Very nice," he says, studying the hypodermic before plunging the needle into Fischer's neck. The ex-SEAL slumps in his chair.

Tony sits bewildered. He watches the handbag peddler wheel over his cart and, together with the rose vendor, they load on Fischer's heavy body, then cover it with a blanket.

The Tamil rose seller turns to Tony, hands him the unused needle, winks, and says, "A souvenir. Cousin Joey sends his regards."

LU YAO REMAINS IN THE BOOTH sipping tea until the proprietor stops by her table.

"Would you care to view our special dessert menu?" he inquires.

She opens the menu and palms the piece of paper inside. In the ladies' room, Lu Yao locks the door and reads the message.

MONGOLIA PETROLEUM CONTRACT DUE RATIFICATION NEXT WEEK WITH CHINESE DAQING OIL COMPANY FOR EXPLORATION IN TAMTSAG BASIN AND BAYANKHONGER. AMERICAN OIL COMPANY'S PRESENCE IN BAYANKHONGER UNACCEPTABLE. WILL BE CONSIDERED A HOSTILE ACTION. REMAIN AT POST. KEEP US INFORMED. BE MOST CAREFUL.
LI HU JENGH

"WERE YOU LONELY?" Lu Yao inquires, looking around the empty piazza. "At least that flower-selling pest is gone."

"Very uneventful," he sighs audibly.

"Now, as promised," she whispers, squeezing his arm, "I will read you a bedtime story."

Leaning heavily on his cane, Tony leaves the empty campo with Lu Yao supporting him. Upon entering the Marconi, they climb the stairs and enter Lu Yao's room. She moves swiftly to the desk, shuffling through lightweight cardboard folders.

"I divided the manuscript into sections," she explains. "It is easier to study that way." Rifling through the folders, she hands one to Tony. "This one contains Marco Polo's description of the sexual customs of the ladies in Baghdad and of Turkish carpets. Read it while I shower," she grins, stepping into the bathroom. "I think it will hold your interest."

"Great. I'm fascinated with carpeting." He glances at the folder heading: Section II. *Concerning Carpets of Turkomania and Sexual Customs in the City of Baghdad.*

...26

FROM THE HOLY LAND, we traveled through the province named Turkomania, where the inhabitants worship Mohammed and fashion the sovereign carpets of the world, decorated with geometric designs and animal figures in the most beautiful colors. Some of the Turkomanian rugs were woven with wool that had been dyed in soft pastel shades and golden saffron tones reminding me of the colors of the Venice Grand Canal at sunset.

From the land of the carpets we proceeded to the Tigris River in the land of Mesopotamia and a busy city called Mosul. From there we continue to follow the Tigris south to Baghdad.

The inhabitants of Baghdad do not shield and sequester their womenfolk as most Muslims do. Each woman's eyes were visible above a mere half-veil of chador, which did not conceal her nose, mouth and chin. On their upper bodies they wore a blouse and waist-coat, and on their lower limbs the voluminous pai-jamah. However, these garments were not many-layered, but gossamer light and trans-lucent, so the shapes of their bodies could be easily discerned and appreciated. It was good that I wore the Arab clothes and was no longer wearing a tight Venetian tunic, because at the sight of these delightful creatures I would have bulged most disgracefully.

I observed that the majority of Muslims, men and women alike, do not speak of sexual relations. However, in Baghdad my sexual education was advanced when a friend of Uncle Maffeo introduced me to a free-spirited young woman of his acquaintance named A'idah, who served me much wine, which made me lightheaded.

A'idah told me that Persian girls call the act of sex 'making zina.' She inquired by what term do the ladies of Italy prefer. I said of the act, as yet, I had no personal acquaintance, but from my friends I was told that when men put their candles into the woman's scabbard and together they jumped about, it was called the 'Dance of St. Vitae.'

Feeling emboldened by all of the drinking and A'idah's candor, I asked, 'Is it true what my uncle Maffeo told me, that Muslim women are somehow deprived of their... enthusiasm for sexual pleasure because they are, well, somehow circumcised?'

'That is so,' A'idah answered. 'This is done for most women when they are infants, so they will never enjoy making zina, and will become faithful wives. But it is not done to girls of upper classes— like myself.'

Then to my embarrassment A'idah pointed to the female part below her waist and said, 'A handsome young traveler like yourself is surely acquainted with the anatomy of a female person. Then you know that down here,' she said, 'a woman has a tender protrusion called the zambur. What is it called where you come from?'

I stammered and blushed most crimson, and said, 'I do not know.'

A'idah continued, 'In every woman, that is her most sensitive place, the very nub of her sexual excitability. My own zambur is commendably large, and in arousal it extends to the length of my little finger's first joint.'

Just the thought of it made me excited, and my excitement was much in evidence.

The girl laughed and took my hand, leading me to a private area. Since we were both in the springtime of our youth, we were able to excite each other to completion many times until my member became raw and chafed. When I staggered to our quarters, Uncle Maffeo observed my giddiness and mussed clothing, and said, 'So young Marco's lance has finally found its target.' I did not reply, but went immediately to sleep for many, many hours.

...27

LU YAO ENTERS with a towel wrapped like a turban around her damp hair, wearing a white terrycloth robe. Her almond-shaped eyes are bright, her face flushed. She places her hand on his forearm.

"Tony, I have been so alone for so long. Since they dragged my parents to that terrible place." She closes her eyes and stops speaking, but the pressure on his arm increases. Her body moves against him; the warmth and softness, and at the same time the hardness of toned muscle.

"I have known men," she continues awkwardly. "I never found love until—" She looks directly into his eyes. "I never want to be lonely again, ever."

He feels her face pressed to his chest. Tony gently lifts her chin and her lips part slowly. He tastes her mouth. The uncertain flutter of her tongue becomes bolder. The sound of her breathing increases. He unfastens her robe. She shakes loose the turban; strands of hair fall across his face. Lu Yao turns away and with her back to him she slips the robe from her shoulders, takes a deep breath, and lets it slide down the length of her body. Her nipples are hard and her breasts firm and full. He runs his fingers over them, carefully, tenderly. He hears her gasp at his touch; a slow voluptuous shudder shakes her.

"Tony, I'm not very good at this." Her throaty whisper is barely audible. He feels her hand bunching into a fist, dragging out his shirt; her nails against his chest, then reaching down and unbuckling his belt, and he experiences the unfamiliar sensation of pure love and joy. And afterwards, the stillness of complete peace as she sleeps on the pillow beside him with her head against his heart.

THE SOUND OF CLATTERING WHEELBARROWS and the clamor of construction workers below their window awakens Tony. He listens to Lu Yao's soft snoring. His eyes wander to the

137

neatly stacked folders of Polo's diary on the desk. He skims the section titles Lu Yao has updated with current-day geographical references, noticing that Section VI is missing.

Prologue

Section I (Iraq) *Al Bashra, the Kingdom of Maffeo and the Black Liquid.*

Section II (Iraq-continued) *Carpets of Turkomania and Sexual Customs in Baghdad.*

Section III (Mongolia) *Concerning Genghis Khan's Grandson, Peter the Tatar.*

Section IV (Afghanistan) *Balkh and Badashan and the Opium Sap.*

Section V (Iran) *Concerning Traveling through Persia and the Assassins.*

Section VII (Ceylon) *Concerning the Largest Ruby in the World.*

Epilogue

Tony's attention is drawn to Section IV, *Balkh and Badashan and the Opium Sap.* Dressing quietly, Tony tucks the folder under his arm and wanders downstairs to the hotel dining room to read Marco Polo's Afghanistan narrative while drinking his coffee.

28

OF THE PROVINCES OF BALKH and Badashan and the Opium Sap. After twelve days' journeying we came to the mountain chain wherein lay the province of Badashan, inhabited by people who worship Mohammed. The men of Badashan were enamored of women with amply developed buttocks. This preference of the men caused the ladies of the region to wear trousers. Their breeches were voluminous because they swathed themselves in many layers of linen, cotton or silk, thickly pleated and scented with musk. The ladies did this to show they have large hips. In this region she who appeared more stout below the waist was deemed to be more beautiful and more glorious. Uncle Maffeo advised me not to attempt to unravel the multiple layers of cloth surrounding any of their lower bodies, as we could not afford to alienate the king if we wished to trade for gems and safely depart.

The fields of Balashan were teeming with enormous quantities of colorful poppies as far as my eyes could see. These flowers were very like our common Italian red field poppy, but of a silvery-blue color. Brightly-colored flowers bloomed at the tips of greenish stems. As the petals fell off, I could see exposed oval-shaped seed capsules which contained pods of a milky sap. Uncle Maffeo told me the sap from the poppy was called opium and was popular in ancient times for its pain-relieving benefits.

This opium sap was removed by slitting the capsules up and down with a special tool. When the sap oozed out, it turned darker and thicker as it became exposed to the sun, forming a brownish-black gum. I observed the men of Badashan collecting the gum with strange-looking scraping implements and forming it into balls and bricks. This gum was then filtered and boiled and dried, and in such condition could be made suitable to smoke in pipes.

My curiosity as to the local practice of smoking the dried poppy gum all but ended my travels. Without the company of women, the nights in Balashan were boresome. One night as I was returning to our Karavansari, I passed camel drivers passing an opium pipe and I paused to observe. Amongst the men smoking was one of our camel drivers, named Siamak.

'Ah, Master Marco,' he said, spying me, 'Among the remedies which it has pleased Almighty Allah to give to man to relieve his weariness and suffering, none is so pleasing as smoking the sap of the poppy. The taste is like flowers, Master,' he said smiling, with his eyes half-closed as if speaking in a pleasant far-off trance.

'May I take a turn at the pipe?' I asked our camel driver.

Siamak pinched off a piece of the opium brick, maybe as big as an almond nut, and heated the lump over a burning lamp. When the opium was hot and soft, he smeared it around a hole in the pipe, which was a long bamboo tube. Then Siamak handed me the pipe.

I took in a lungful of smoke. To my surprise, it was not harsh and did not make me cough nor choke. I felt a strange sensation, totally unlike anything I had ever experienced before. A gradual, creeping, drowsy gleefulness, similar in nature but not the same type of sleepiness brought on by too much wine. In fact, rather than sleep, I wished to talk, and talk I did, even though my words were fanciful and disconnected. As I continued to breathe in the smoke from the little piece of brown gum, I imagined that the dirty camel drivers were now bedecked in expensive robes and brilliantly-colored necklaces and rings abounding with gold, precious Persian turquoises and pink balas sapphires.

After a period of time that I could not rightly calculate, Siamak led me home, where my father and uncle were busily poring over travel maps. I hugged and kissed them on both cheeks. They thought me deranged.

'Gesu, Marco,' my father said. 'You smell most peculiar. What manner of mischief have you been engaged in?'

'From the smell, he has been smoking the opium pipe,' Maffeo said. 'Marco, the poppy juice is good to have where next we are headed into the Pamir Mountains to the Roof of the World, because in case of snow blindness a few drops in the eyes will relieve the pain. And a little smoking is less harmful than eating. When you smoked the pipe you inhaled but a relatively small amount, but be-

ware, eating of the whole medicament can paralyze your digestive organs, and you would rapidly fall into a state of physical and medical decadence.'

My father interrupted most sternly, 'A little smoking of the poison leads to a greater dependence, and the next step is opium eating. We are leaving tomorrow. We did not bring you on this trip for you to destroy yourself. Is that understood?'

And thus we continued our journey south of the Gobi Desert to Kamul, where the people are all Idolaters and live by the fruits of the earth. And it is in truth that I tell you if a foreigner comes to the house of one of these people to lodge, the host is delighted, and desires his wife to put herself entirely at the guest's disposal, whilst he himself gets out of the way, and comes back no more until the stranger shall have taken his departure. The guest may stay and enjoy the wife's society as long as he wishes, whilst the husband has no shame in the matter, but indeed considers it an honor. And all the women themselves are fair and wanton.

29

"INTERESTING?" Lu Yao asks, pulling up a chair.

"I'm reading Polo's description of meeting wanton women." Tony lifts her hand to his lips. "It must run in the family."

Lu Yao's face flushes brightly. "Big Auntie warned me never attach myself to white-faced foreigner; it's not good *Yuan fen*."

"What's *Yuan fen*?"

"The term *Yuan fen* describes relationships that are meant to be. You need both *yuan*, which refers to fate, or destiny, and *fen*, which means a partnering." Lu Yao's face grows serious. "When *Yuan fen* not good, it refers to lovers whom fate will not permit to live their lives together." She pauses, takes a deep breath, straightens her shoulders and asks, "Have you telephoned your Mongolian friend?"

"Not yet. I'm concerned about my room phone being tapped."

"Use the phone in my room, if you like. I will stay and finish breakfast."

"VACHIR, IS THAT YOU? This is Tony Perini calling."

"Major Perini," replies Vachir Borbaatar warmly. "How is your leg coming along?"

"I'm managing, thanks, Vachir. And how are things with you?"

"I have been promoted into a new position as vice-chief of intelligence, unfortunately," he chuckles, "with no increase in pay grade."

"What was the Afghan situation when you left?"

"Bad and getting worse, I fear. Many Afghans view the Alliance members as foreign invaders. The British failed twice in the 19th century, and the Soviet Union failed disastrously in the 1980s. The last successful conqueror of Afghanistan was our Mongolian Genghis Khan.

"The Kabul government has no real support and is viewed by growing numbers of Afghans as the agent of foreigners. Also, the recent air strikes that killed civilians make people sympathetic to the insurgency. Up to now, the Taliban didn't have the materiel to mount major offensives, but that may be changing as they obtain modern weapons smuggled through Pakistan."

Tony cuts in, "And those weapons are purchased from the proceeds of poppies converted into heroin and smuggled into America."

"My dear comrade," Vachir says, "expanding the war to stop the poppy growing is a weak argument. Your nation's demand for heroin is not the fault of the Afghan peasants who will take the financial hit for your interdiction. You cannot win counterinsurgencies against the will of local populations, and surely denying a livelihood to the poor farmers of southern and eastern Afghanistan is no way to persuade Afghans to your side. The 'bottom line,' as you say, is what kind of commitment are your American voters willing to make if a successful Afghan operation requires expending more blood and more treasure than you did in Iraq?

"Enough of this kind of serious talk. Tell me, for what purpose is your call?"

"Do you know a man named Gianpietro Scarlatti?"

"Of course, everyone knows *Signor* Scarlatti. He was the Italian ambassador to Mongolia in 1992. Scarlatti helped President Ochirat to get elected in a landslide victory. Regrettably, the gentleman has changed his allegiance and is now supporting the opposition Democratic Party chairman, Elbegdorj, in the forthcoming elections."

"Why do you say, 'regrettably'?"

"Our government is currently negotiating long-term petroleum exploration leases with Chinese oil companies. Scarlatti is funneling huge sums to the opposition party in the expectation that a win by Elbegdorj will result in oil contracts awarded to Scarlatti's American patrons."

"What difference does it make who gets the leases, if Mongolia benefits?"

"Big differences, I'm afraid. In the Gobi and in Mongolia under the permafrost are oil and gas deposits that make even Saudi Arabia look deprived. But the problem is that we have no infrastructure; that takes time to construct. China and Russia have their hungry eyes set on Mongolia. Russia's nationalized oil company, Rosneft, supplies more than 90 percent of our present oil requirements. Over the past months, Rosneft has increased prices twice—by an average of 20 percent each time. This has helped pushed inflation in Mongolia to over 15 percent annually. Rosneft recently told Mongolian officials that it would 'lower' oil prices if given the rights to run all the oil production in the country. Moscow also wants to build 100 gas stations throughout the country, which would solidify its overwhelming presence there. You must understand that we suffered 70 years of Soviet-inspired suppression, so it is a serious problem.

"We are similarly nervous of the Chinese. They are also itching to pounce on us. Half of Genghis' heartland, the half that lies south of the Gobi, has been absorbed already, so it is not prudent to turn our backs on the Chinese. Voltaire said, 'Better the devil you know than the devil you don't.' In commercial terms, there is great pressure on us to cooperate with the Chinese, because our valuable oil resources in the Gobi will find a natural outlet in China—with Chinese finance, Chinese transport, and Chinese oil exploration companies. Until we are able to harvest our own oil, China should be our trading partner, not the Russians nor the Americans."

"Doesn't China have a lot of other things to focus on right now?" says Tony. "Their problems with Tibet, pollution, the earthquake aftermath and their economic problems?"

Tony hears his friend sigh. "Oil is always the top priority. That is why there is the potential here for conflicting views of who rightfully should exercise authority over Inner Asia's borderlands. China may shrug her ample shoulders and point out that Mongols have been members of the great family of China for centuries, and this is merely returning to the status quo that was established by Genghis, the founder of China's Yuan dynasty.

Vachir adds wryly, "Of course, we have a different view: that China is really Mongolian. But, as you know, demography rules, and 1,300 million Chinese may, in the end, trump our two million Mongolians. In both nations, Genghis' spirit is still honored. If the Chinese Communist Party claims that Mongols are to be considered as Chinese, then China has a claim on Mongolia, even though we are at present independent. So you see the seriousness of the Russian—

Chinese problem. The last thing we need is for Scarlatti and the Americans to muddy the water."

Vachir continues, "One should never underestimate Scarlatti. In my new position I am in possession of worrisome intelligence reports, which have been dutifully passed on to your CIA."

"Tell me, Vachir."

"Scarlatti is connected to South Ossetian criminal elements seeking to sell 5 kilograms of bomb-grade highly enriched uranium, pilfered from the Russian military. Try to imagine the magnitude of this, Tony. Genghis Khan held sway over one-fifth of the world's populated land masses. Genghis would not be using the Mongolian crossbow as his weapon of choice. He would seek to control the lands with the most black liquid in the ground. It takes a ruthless, brilliant genius, not a savage, to accomplish this. And if Genghis Khan had gotten his hands on nuclear weaponry..."

Vachir pauses and adds ominously, "Gianpietro Scarlatti is the direct descendant of Peter the Tatar, the eldest grandson of Genghis Khan. Be very, very careful of that man."

TONY RETURNS TO HIS ROOM, boots up his laptop and sends an e-mail message.

GENERAL MORGAN
MY MONGOLIAN CONTACT REPORTS HE ADVISED CIA OF GIAN-
PIETRO SCARLATTI'S CONNECTIONS TO STOLEN RUSSIAN BOMB-
GRADE ENRICHED URANIUM SMUGGLED THROUGH SOUTH OS-
SETIA. WHY DOESN'T PENTAGON KNOW?
TONY

LU YAO REENTERS HER EMPTY ROOM, advances swiftly to the phone, and removes a small recording device hidden underneath. Taking out a pair of earphones, she listens carefully to a playback of Tony's conversation with Colonel Vachir Borbaatar, making extensive notes.

In the basement of the Hotel Marconi, a man with slightly Mongolian slant of eyes, dressed in the dark blue overalls of Artel Telefonia, closes the telephone panel box, picks up his cell phone and punches in a number. *"Apart from our shadows we have no friends,"* he says.

"And apart from our horsetails we have no whips. What have you to report?"

A SHROUD OF FOG envelopes the Rialto. Rain splatters on the windowsill. Lu Yao grabs an umbrella and slips out of the hotel's side entrance, headed towards the Chinese restaurant. Mist rising from the canal swirls about her. With no car traffic in Venice, and little vegetation to absorb the sounds, her footsteps echo loudly on the wet stone streets. She glances up and down the street, hearing nothing but the steady sound of rain dripping from rooftops on to the pavement.

In her peripheral vision Lu Yao observes two men moving in her direction. In two strides the first man is upon her. A strong hand roughly clamps her shoulder. She hears the click of a steel blade and sees a stiletto gripped in a threatening hand. The man spreads his legs as he prepares to strike.

Appearing frightened, Lu Yao turns away, then suddenly spins back. Using her umbrella as a staff, she lunges forward, smashing the umbrella point into his crotch, then digs her nails deep into his scrotum. He screams as she twists.

She backhands the second man in the face with the heel of her right hand, shattering the small bones in his nose. The Mongol moans and falls to the pavement, gasping for breath. Blood sprays across the cement.

Lu Yao shakes the rain from her eyes as she slowly rises and closes her umbrella. She senses there is another person behind her and pivots on her left foot, raising her elbow high, but not in time to deflect a vicious blow along her arm, causing an electric jolt across her shoulders. Lu Yao's body twists backwards as her back muscles go into spasm. She feels the ground rise up to meet her as she blacks out.

The Mongol leader bends over Lu Yao with his knife poised. The soft sound of a shuriken whistles through the air. It strikes the man, burying itself to the hilt. The Mongol jerks backwards, wheezing as the air rushes from his lungs. Then he slides dead to the pavement.

Three black figures appear on the rooftop, silhouetted against the night sky. Deadly four-pointed metal stars fly from their hands, raining instant death on the other two targets.

"WAKE UP, LITTLE SISTER," says the black-hooded Triad leader.

Lu Yao opens her eyes. Her vision is blurry, her back muscles pounding as she sits up and looks around.

The man speaks calmly. "*Hao-pu-hao,* all is well under the heavens." Then he fades into the shadows almost as quickly as he had appeared. All Lu Yao sees is the shape of a black shadow moving backwards out of sight.

Book III

With Heaven's aid, I have conquered for you a huge empire.
But my life was too short to achieve the conquest of the world.
That task is left for you.

—Chinggis Khan (Genghis Khan), 1227
The Secret History of the Mongols
Professor Igor De Rachewiltz's translation, 1972

...30

"EXCUSE ME, PLEASE," Carlos calls from the desk. "A call on the *telefono*. I connect."

"Major Anthony Perini. This is Ambassador Gianpietro Scarlatti calling. How are you enjoying your visit to Venice—beautiful city, yes?"

"Hello," Tony stammers, collecting his thoughts as a cold sweat forms along his scalp.

"The purpose of my call is that I would be grateful for the pleasure of you and your Chinese lady joining me for luncheon tomorrow at the Danieli. Is one o'clock convenient?"

Tony bites his lip in silence, then shrugs. "One o'clock sounds good."

"Until tomorrow then, Major. *Ciao*."

He rings Lu Yao's room. "You will never believe this. We were invited to luncheon by none other than Gianpietro Scarlatti."

He hears a sharp intake of breath. "That is not a funny joke."

"No joke. We are his guests at the Hotel Danieli at one o'clock."

The line is silent. "Are you still there?" Tony asks.

"I have heard that Scarlatti is very dangerous man," Lu Yao replies. "His bloodline is filled with terror, destruction and death."

"I know. My Mongolian friend, Vachir, told me Scarlatti was descended from Peter the Tatar, the eldest grandson of Genghis Khan. Vachir also warned me to be careful of him."

"You may wish to do your homework before bearding the lion," Lu Yao suggests. "In his diary, Marco Polo references Peter the Tatar."

...31

CONCERNING GENGHIS KHAN'S GRANDSON, PETER THE TATAR. I should now relate the truth about the Mongol slave known as Peter of the Tatar race. I released this man from all bonds of servitude. Likewise, I, Marco Polo of San Giovanni Christostomo, bequeathed to Peter the Tatar, as fruits of his labors, one hundred lire of Venetian denari. This noble person and trusted friend served as my guide, interpreter and protector during my journeys in the East and returned with me on the long journey from Cathay.

Peter's father, Jochi, was the firstborn son of Genghis, the Mongol leader once called Tamujin. In 1206, at the age of 42, Tamujin took the title Universal Ruler, which translates to Genghis Khan. Genghis Khan's subjects saw themselves at the center of the universe, the greatest of people and favored by the gods. They justified Genghis Khan's success in warfare by claiming that he was the rightful master not only over the 'peoples of the felt tent' but the entire world. As the first born, Peter's father, Jochi, was first in the family line to take over the mantle of Great Khan at the death of Genghis, except for an event that I will now relate.

As a young Tatar chieftain, Tamujin was a fearless leader with fire in his eyes. One day while Tamujin was away tending his animals, a rival Mongol tribe, the forest dwelling Merkits, attacked his campsite and carried off Tamujin's wife, Borte. She was handed over as a spoil of war to the Merkits chief's younger brother, Chiulger Bokes.

Two months later, Temujin assembled his allied tribes and with a small army they made their way north over the Khenti mountains to the tributary of the Selenga river, where the Merkits were camped. Tamujin's men crossed the river by night, each man holding a float of reeds and swimming across with a horse. Seeing the advancing troops at dawn, the Merkits scattered in panic and Temujin was reunited with his bride, Borte, who was by that time pregnant.

As related to me by Peter, one of Genghis' wives, Yisui by name, spoke to Genghis about the subject of succession. She said, 'When your body, like an old and withered tree, comes crashing down, to whom will you bequeath your people?' The great emperor understood. His four sons, Ogedei, Jochi, Chagadai, and the youngest, Tolui, were all experienced commanders. As Genghis Khan's firstborn son, Jochi was favored to rule the empire after his father died. At the familial kurultai called in 1222, the issue of Jochi's legitimacy was brought up by his brother, Chagadai, who spoke thus to his father. 'Are you saying we are to be governed by this Merkit bastard?' Jochi seized his brother by the throat and they were kept apart by two of Genghis Khan's generals, Boorchu and Mukhali. At that meeting, Genghis acknowledged Jochi as his legitimate firstborn. However, he worried that the quarrelsome nature of the two would split the empire.

By early 1223 Genghis Khan had selected Ogedei, his third son, as his successor for the sake of preserving the Empire. After the death of Ogedei, his youngest son, Tolui, became the khagan, khan of khans. And Tolui's son, Kubla, became the next in line of succession.

A wedge had been driven between Jochi and his brothers. Although Jochi's descendant, Peter, and his brothers formed the oldest branch of Genghis Khan's family, they were never permitted to claim their father's heritage and ended in servitude.

Genghis Khan's name struck dread and fear in all Europe, from the Pope and the emperors on their thrones to the lowliest peasants in the fields. When our caravan entered the blackened ruins of the Afghan city of Balkh, we were told that although the city surrendered without resistance to Genghis Khan, its citizenry were ordered outside the city under pretense of counting them. However, its young people were sold into slavery, the older people done to death with unspeakable cruelty, and the city burned to the ground. This story was related by inhabitants who had escaped the Tatar scourge and had begun to creep back and resettle Balkh.

In this city of Balkh I bought a slave called Peter, a Tatar man. Although the price was a third more, it may be taken as a certainty that no Tatar ever betrayed a master. And thus, Jochi's eldest son,

Peter the Tatar, became, not my slave, but rather my trusted guide and companion.

Peter had family rights to be khagan. While he didn't seek the role, he was fearful that Kubla Khan would discover his true identity, perceive it as a threat and arrange for his murder. Peter made me swear a solemn oath never to reveal his identity so long as we dwelled in China. According to the promise made to Peter the Tatar these many years ago, I transacted for my companion to be established as a lawful citizen of our city. Thus, Peter the Tatar, the direct descendent of Genghis Khan with lordly Mongolian ancestry, has taken a new name. He and his family are now held and recognized as Venetian citizens.

...32

"ACCORDING TO THE GUIDE BOOK," Lu Yao says, "Marco Polo lived on a street named Corte Prima Del Million O Del Forno. The home is located only a few minutes over the Rialto Bridge, and it's on our way. I would love to visit and take photographs."

As they climb up the steep steps of the bridge, Tony uses the railing for support. Lu Yao remarks, "Marco Polo is very popular in my country. More so, I think, than he is in Venice. There is a statue of Marco Polo near the West Lake in Hangzhou, the city where I was born. And, near Beijing, we have the Marco Polo bridge made completely of marble. I go there on Sundays," she says, caressing the white jade pendant hanging on the gold chain around her neck. "It's a peaceful spot on the banks of the Yongding River. I enjoy looking at the four hundred stone lions that adorn the bridge. No two lions are alike."

After crossing the canal, Lu Yao points to a street sign: *Corte Prima Del Million O Del Forno*. "Down this way," she says, walking under a Byzantine arch into a narrow courtyard. On the left is a weathered brick building the color of chestnuts. The structural stone is discolored by air pollution, years of buffeting winds off the Adriatic, salt air and flooding. Tony gazes up at the gothic curved-dome windows.

"Will you take my picture?" Lu Yao asks, standing in front of a sculpted stone block embedded vertically near the entrance.

Through the lens Tony sees that carved into the stone, along with small flora decorations, are two encircled symbols of unrecognizable creatures.

"I wonder what these upper carvings are?" Tony asks, after he snaps the photo. "Looks like turkeys, or chickens or geese."

"They are peacocks. In Buddhism, peacocks symbolize purity, but for Christians, the peacock represents immortality—eternal life.

That is why Polo may have selected these two engraved images for his portal: purity and eternal life."

"And the lower ones?"

"The bottom tableau portrays a wild boar battling a vulture," Lu Yao explains. "These animals depict the cosmic struggle between the Christian faith and the Islamic religion."

"With a billion Muslims in the world today, that's comforting to hear."

Lu Yao continues, "Some Muslim extremists and their supporters unfortunately preach that they have a right to go forward with a jihad against the West in the 21st century because of the Christian crusades against Muslims in the 12th century, and the terrible acts of cruelty perpetrated by the crusaders. It is evident from these carvings that Marco Polo divined this impending struggle."

Tony lifts his hands palms up. "This conversation is depressing me. I'm starved. Let's go back to the square and have espresso and sugared brioches."

After a surly waiter jots down their order, Tony asks, "At Polo's house, you mentioned the peacock's symbolism in Buddhism. Are you a practicing Buddhist?"

"No. Our Chinese Communist Party is officially atheist. My parents and my Auntie were atheists, but my grandmother practiced Buddhism. Women in the countryside had no education, no radio, no newspapers, no television." She smiles. "And certainly no laptops or BlackBerry devices. They seldom left their homes, so for women like Grandmother, Buddhism preached the Chinese virtues of peace and caring for family, and through their religion, they learned about the world."

"How about the men?"

"Men's jobs were to work hard and make money."

After a thoughtful pause, Tony asks, "So you practice no religion?"

"Not in the traditional sense. I work hard all day, then go to the gymnasium, swim my laps, go home, eat, watch a little television, go to sleep, and try to be a good person—that's enough for me."

"There's something serious that I need to discuss," Tony ventures awkwardly.

Lu Yao looks up, her green-flecked eyes widened.

Leaning in, Tony lowers his voice. "I don't want our relationship to end. Would you consider... coming home with me? Washington has beautiful parks, gardens, monuments, museums, and in the spring our cherry trees bloom around the Tidal Basin—"

Lu Yao stiffens, her face clouding over as she pulls her hand away. "You want me as your... concubine?"

"No," he whispers softly. "As my wife."

She struggles to keep her emotions in check. "My dear Tony, my heart wishes to follow you, but—"

"That's a start." He flashes a grin. "But I prefer the rest of your body as well."

"Life is not so simple," she says. "Remember *Yuan fen*?"

"Your Chinese version of kismet; the universal force governing things."

Lu Yao sighs and nods. "Maybe you come to Hangzhou; sit with me by the beautiful West Lake, under the blossoming peach trees. You will *also* find happiness there."

"Also?"

"In his diary, your ancestor, Marco Polo, wrote, 'In Heaven there is paradise. On earth there is Hangzhou and the beautiful West Lake.'"

"Sounds like a plan."

...33

GIANPIETRO SCARLATTI RISES TO HIS FEET, displaying old fashioned courtesy, but with a wintry smile and cold eyes. His blocky body is draped in a suit of dove-gray flannel, a white shirt and a blue silk tie. Scarlatti has a full head of dark gray hair, some soft wrinkles about the eyes and slight flabbiness in the neck.

To Lu Yao he says, "Your smile lights up the room, my dear.

"And you are the enigmatic Major Anthony Perini," he continues, shaking hands. Eyeing Tony's ring, Scarlatti raises his eyebrows, pausing thoughtfully. "That is a remarkable signet ring, young man. And is there a carved coat-of-arms inscribed?"

Tony nods.

Scarlatti stares searchingly at Tony; his face lights up with a smile. "*Un miracolo*," he sighs. "Of course, the glacier blue eyes, the same hawk nose and noble cheekbones," he says with his palms upwards in a gesture of understanding. "Come, give me a hug. Your grandfather was my lifelong friend." He laughs a low, deep laugh. "*Ecco,* another intrepid Polo returns to Venice. Now I understand why the fishes in the Venice lagoon have grown fatter since your arrival. Did you have the pleasure of knowing Nicolo Polo?"

"No," Tony replies cautiously. "We never met."

"Pity. Your grandfather was my comrade-in-arms during the war, and like myself, the last of a line." His black eyes fix on Tony. "Except for you, of course." Scarlatti continues, "I chose the diplomatic corps, while Nicolo, like a true Polo, craved adventure. Our two families trace back into the dim centuries, where history and myth blur. But where are my manners?" He signals the waiter. "May I propose an apéritif? Are you familiar with Kir?"

Lu Yao and Tony shake their heads.

"Kir was named after a friend of your grandfather's, a priest named Kanunnik Kir, a hero of the French resistance. After the war, Nicolo and I attended a reunion in France. Kir invited Italian parti-

158

sans, French resistance fighters and even some Germans who fought against the Nazis. When we got to Dijon, all they had to offer was a local wine mixed with cassis, which came from the wild blackberries in their area. Everyone loved the drink, so they named the drink after the priest, Kir; and there you have it."

"Should we call you Ambassador?" Tony inquires.

Scarlatti blinks like a reptile basking in the sun. "My friends call me Pietro. It is on behalf of my American friends that I arranged this luncheon. Please correct me if I am misinformed. I understand that you are in Venice to locate the source of drug trafficking into your country. Since I am that source, I propose to save you time and effort."

Tony's skin tingles with uneasiness.

"Allow me to explain. In your country one in five people dies from smoking; that is over 400,000 deaths a year. Yet your president and Congress do nothing to stop the manufacture of this poison—why? Because America is a capitalistic country, and tobacco companies are big corporations with highly paid lobbyists.

"But when it comes to drugs, there are no deep pocket corporate sponsors pressing their agendas on Capitol Hill, ergo the U.S. spends millions fighting drugs, and nothing has worked. They could reduce the heroin problem tomorrow by legalizing drugs. Give the drug business to Coca Cola and Pepsi." His eyes narrow as he smiles. "The corporations would market the heroin as 'diet nose candy' or 'caffeine free blow' and you would see prices and murder rates drop.
Poor black kids who stand on street corners making food money for their families would go back to school, and the millions of tax dollars spent on combating drugs could be better spent on education. However, your lawmakers find it politically expedient to make drugs illegal; they put a higher value on campaign contributions than they do on their responsibilities.

"I am a businessman," Scarlatti continues. His expression is neutral, his eyes hooded. "And, for the moment, drugs are one of my businesses. Like your grandfather, I also have a famous lineage. I inherited from Genghis Khan the ability to recognize opportunity and to seize it. In the morass that is Afghanistan, ninety-three percent of the world's heroin is produced." Scarlatti raises four fingers. "Three to four billion dollars a year—and growing. Most, of course, still goes to users in Europe and Russia, but obviously America is a prime target."

Tony feels discomfited under his stare. Scarlatti has made the same convincing arguments also voiced by some American police officials. He asks, "Doesn't it bother you that the drug money is used to supply arms to the Taliban?"

The smile is gone from Scarlatti's lips. For a moment the shadows darken under his eyes. "As a descendant of Genghis, I spit on the Taliban," he says angrily. "Most of the Taliban are ethnic Pashtuns. Genghis' family was of the Hazara tribe. It is no secret that we Hazaras are mocked and persecuted for being descendants of the Mongols."

He frowns and adds, "I take their opium poppies and convert them into dollars, which I funnel into Mongolia. Drugs are big business, but not the biggest business."

"Oil?" says Lu Yao.

"Correct, my dear. Mongolia is one of the few places in the world with significant unexplored reserves of oil. America must push forward and negotiate oil contracts, so Mongolia isn't forced to deal with China or Russia. And let me educate you that a twist or two of the oil spigots could spike the price at American gas pumps to over five, six, seven dollars a gallon. So, let me ask you, Anthony, would you prefer Chinese or Russian or American-friendly Mongolian hands on the oil spigots?"

Without waiting for a reply, Scarlatti scowls, his eyes projecting arrogance. "If Genghis were alive, he would not have treated oil as simply an unending pool of liquid money flowing from terminals in the Mongolian desert, nor permitted interference from foreigners. He would have used it as a weapon; a weapon that could be used to cripple the world's economies and make himself master of the planet."

Scarlatti shrugs. "Alas, I am no warrior, merely an enterprising businessman. After 9/11 your government shifted its focus from Afghanistan to Iraq. Was it to save the poor Iraqis from the terrible Sadaam Hussein, or to get your hands on the black gold—the oil? And when that failed, Washington turned to Mongolia. As I am the 'fixer' for the American-Mongolian negotiations, the oil people consider you an irritant."

Another mirthless smile. "My life has been as a diplomat. I resolve problems by satisfying opposite interests with compromise solutions. Here's my offer, Anthony. You will receive one million dollars if you say farewell to Venice, return home and take a well-earned disability retirement." Scarlatti's smile dissolves and is replaced by a stiff-faced look of attentiveness. "How much does a retired major make? I suppose you have your twenty years in. At fifty percent of your base pay plus disability, the total is less than $100,000. And then what will you do?"

"Are you trying to bribe me?"

Scarlatti turns towards Lu Yao, a glint in his eye. "This is a good faith offer. Wouldn't you agree, Captain Cheng?"

"Captain Cheng?" Tony repeats.

Scarlatti continues with a condescending smirk on his face. "Oh. I was under the impression that you knew that your lovely lady was an agent of MSS, the Chinese Ministry of State Security. Now, shall we order luncheon?"

Lu Yao recoils; the color drains from her face. "I'm sorry, Tony. I didn't mean to…" Lu Yao's voice trails off.

Tony glares at Lu Yao like a wounded animal, speechless with hurt and anger. An uncaring, irresponsible rage descends on him. He shoots her a look of poisonous fury, saying, "You'll pay for this," then pushes his chair back, grabs his cane, and storms through the revolving doors of the Danieli lobby, stumbling out into the open air.

Lu Yao rushes after him. Tears obscure her vision as Tony limps away under the arcades of the Doge's Palace towards St. Marco Square, swallowed up in the crowds.

Scarlatti laughs, tilts his head back and empties his glass of Kir.

...34

THE PAVEMENT THRONGS with noisy crowds. Tony feels the sickening acid of despair churning his stomach. He rushes headlong into a tour group gathered in front of a church in the Campo S. Zaccaria. He doesn't give a damn.

"This is Chiesa di San Zaccaria," announces the tour guide, an attractive woman with long red hair holding aloft a white pennant. "The church is dedicated to the father of John the Baptist, whose body it supposedly contains. As you can see, the church is a mixture of Gothic and Renaissance styles, and the walls are covered with paintings by Tintoretto, Angelo Trevisani, Giuseppe Salviati, Giovanni Bellini, and—"

Tony pushes himself free, turning blindly into Campo Lorenzo. He's breathless; the leg pain is searing. Small waves of faintness and nausea flow over him. He stops and rests on a bench in front of a narrow, gray stone church. Tony lowers his head and inhales deeply, trying to will down his racing pulse. The blind rage seeps slowly away, replaced by a sense of hopelessness, of regret for something that for a few precious moments held promise, but now is lost.

The tour group from Campo San Zaccaria straggles up to where Tony is seated. The guide says in Italian-accented-English, "Ladies and gentlemen, I know some of you are weary. This is the last stop on our walking tour. We cannot inspect the church interior, because it is under repair. However, it is important for you to view the facade of San Lorenzo, our oldest church in Venice, built in the sixth century."

The guide continues, "The celebrated Venetian adventurer of the 13th century, Marco Polo, so known and famous for the discoveries of new countries before Christopher Columbus, was buried in this church in 1324. Unfortunately, they lost his body during the 16th century rebuilding—it's assumed that he's still in here somewhere, but no one knows for sure."

Tony lifts his head sharply.

"Although Marco Polo received little recognition from the geographers of his time, some of the information in his book of travels was incorporated into important maps of the later Middle Ages, such as the Catalan World Map of 1375, and in the next century it was read with great interest by Henry the Navigator and also by Columbus.

"So, somewhere under San Lorenzo," she concludes, pointing to the church, "lies a coffin with the bones of the great traveler. When San Lorenzo was being remodeled, the coffins and *sarcofici* became part of the filler and the materials used to raise the floor of the church to its present level.

"Any questions? The restrooms are on the right side of the church. Please stay together until we get to the *vaporetto*."

After the tourists depart, Tony walks to the church entrance. Noticing a warning sign, he turns off his cell phone. As his eyes adjust to the darkened interior, he can see scaffolding in the center area. It is Sunday and there are no workmen around. Several people are praying, and lighted candles line the back wall. Tony makes his way down the nave, crossing himself, and takes a seat across from the chapel. For a while he stares at the statue of Jesus over the altar.

Marco Polo buried here? he muses. *It's more than coincidence —it's downright eerie.* Tony smiles at his imaginings and rubs his painful knee. *I'm not like you, Marco old boy. What I should do is take my medical discharge and get a job coaching lacrosse.*

He is considering leaving, when from the innermost recess of the church the bell tolls for repentance. There is a shuffling of feet as the few communicants leave their seats to go to the altar. The church is small. Its stained-glass windows shield the interior from the summer heat. Tony sees an old woman shuffling up the aisle. In the dim vaulted church, she reminds him of his grandmother, Nana Perini. Once, as a child, when his dog had died, Tony asked his grandmother why God lets bad things happen to good people. His grandmother told him that in her view, God stands ready to help us cope with our tragedies, if we can only get beyond our feelings of guilt and anger that separate us from him.

Tony feels a physical pang of longing as he thinks about Lu Yao and her view of religion. "I work hard all day," she had said. "I go to the gym, swim my laps, go home, eat, watch a little television, go to bed, and try to be a good person—that's enough for me."

He takes a deep sigh and gazes at the statue of Jesus, then makes the sign of the cross again, winks, and says, "Thanks. Maybe Nana's right. I'll try and take it from here."

Outside the church, Tony checks his phone; he has one call waiting.

"Tony, Tony," Lu Yao's message says. "Please do not be upset with me. I will explain everything. Please come to restaurant Sun-WuKong. I wait." He hears her voice break as she whispers, "I love you."

TONY'S HEART LIGHTENS as he bolts back towards the Piazza San Marco. He opts for the *vaporetto* rather than braving the slow tourist traffic through crowded narrow streets and bridges to reach the Rialto area.

Waiting impatiently in the queue at the San Marco-Vallaresso stop, he hears a rumbling boom in the distance. Black plumes of smoke rise from the San Polo district to the north.

"*Terrorismo?*" people shout in frightened voices.

As an explosives expert, Tony recognizes the all-too-familiar sound of a bomb blast. He estimates the distance to the blast site to be approximately 1500 yards. He fights down a sense of panic and foreboding; Lu Yao is waiting for him at the Chinese restaurant in the San Polo district. The wail of sirens can be heard filling the air as police boats race up the Grand Canal.

He rushes from the *vaporetto* line, signaling a water taxi driver. The boatman nods, throws his cigarette into the canal, and helps his passenger off the quay.

"Rialto landing," Tony yells. "And fast!"

The boat noses up and gains speed. Mixing with the briny sea air, he smells the acrid odor of smoke drifting downwind.

"No can make stop Rialto," the boatman says, pointing to a big fire launch pulling up to the Rialto landing. "I drop you San Silvestro. OK?"

Sirens are shrilling. Tony pushes a handful of euros in the boat-man's hand and jumps up on the dock as the taxi boat smacks the quay. Tony hobbles as quickly as possible up the Fondamenta to a narrow street that leads to the fire.

A block away, he hears windows exploding and the shouts of the firefighters; he smells wood burning. The orange glow of flames illuminates church spires and terra-cotta rooftops on Ruga Vecchia S. Giovani. As Tony reaches the square, firemen are connecting hoses and pumping water from the canal, aiming their nozzles at the restaurant's second floor windows. People cluster in groups, talking in sub-dued tones, gazing wide-eyed at the blazing Chinese restaurant. Media and TV crews are arriving; a big fire makes for good visuals and good ratings.

Tony searches for Lu Yao in the crowd. The whole building seems to shake. He detects a whiff of burned cordite and remembers that the restaurant is made of wooden beams and wooden walls embellished with Chinese decorations painted with layers of lacquer and gilt. *A fucking tinderbox,* he thinks.

Tony claws his way through the crowd, eying the disheveled restaurant owner wrapped in a blanket, talking to police.

"Where's Lu Yao?" He shakes the owner's shoulder and yells.

Tears pour down the old man's face. He shakes his head slowly and nods in the direction of the burning building.

Tony grabs a blanket, covers his head, takes a deep breath and disappears into the dense black wall of smoke, eluding the firemen trying to stop him from entering the inferno.

The smoke is too thick to see anything. He feels the intense heat licking at him, the tongues of flame on his legs. He calls out Lu Yao's name. A part of the ceiling collapses to his right. A shower of glowing embers fall on his blanket. Tony smells scorching: the blanket is getting hot. In a moment it will ignite.

He turns to the left, heading toward their favorite booth. There is another crash from above and a hail of sparks, smoke and more burning embers drifts down, stinging his eyes. Then he spots her; just an arm and shoulder visible through the smoke. Lu Yao is pinned under ceiling debris. Using the blanket, he pushes aside the smoking scraps of wood and plaster. Lu Yao's face is drained of all color; it's a gray-ish white.

He drags Lu Yao from under the charred booth, putting the pain out of his mind and concentrating on his grim task. "Hang in there, honey," he whispers through blackened lips. He's dizzy and his clothes are smoldering. Using his hands locked under her arms, he continues dragging Lu Yao towards the entrance. His strength is waning; then his leg buckles and he drops backwards into strong arms.

Ignoring the rubberneckers, Tony falls to his knees next to Lu Yao and cradles her head in his arms. His ear goes to her lips; she is breathing—just. He feels for a pulse, and it's feeble. "Oxygen," he yells. Nobody comes.

She is limp and still, but her eyes are open. Lu Yao smiles weak-ly. She is very pale now. Her hair is matted and flecked with gray ashes. Her eyes move in her head and then settle on his face. Her open lips are stark white. He bends close to listen.

"Big Auntie say," she whispers, "fall in love with white-faced foreigner, bad *Yuan fen*."

"I love you," he says softly, crying into her hair.

Lu Yao smiles peacefully.

He looks down at Lu Yao's face, and as he watches, she dies in his arms. Her eyes lose their focus; he can tell that she is gone. Tony holds her for long moments more. He hears the ambulance boat si-rens. Then he lays Lu Yao's head gently on the concrete. The para-medics cover her with a sheet and leave her there for the medical examiners and the crime scene investigators.

Tony's vision is blurring with tiredness; all of his body is one searing ache. Steam drifts from the ruined restaurant, mixing with the smoke, as Tony stumbles off. He sits at the edge of the grimy canal. The only sound is the creak of moored gondolas. Tony stares transfixed into the mist rising from the water and swirling about the Rialto Bridge. He lowers his face in his hands and begins to weep.

AT THE FIRST LIGHT OF DAWN, Tony reenters the Mar-coni lobby. The night clerk snores peacefully behind the front desk.

Tony reclaims his room key from the slotted wooden key box. After a thoughtful pause, he also withdraws the key to Lu Yao's room. He inhales deeply, aware of his shortness of breath as he labors up the stairs. With the tragic death of Lu Yao, waves of black despair engulf him. His anger is choking him; he needs to feel her presence.

In Lu Yao's room, Tony rests on the bed with his eyes closed, trying to breathe in her essence. All he can smell is the dank smoke odor from his clothes. He is bone-weary. On the dresser he spies Lu Yao's jade necklace. *Fucking Yuan fen,* he thinks bitterly. Gritting his teeth, he begins to sort through Lu Yao's personal possessions before the police arrive. In the top dresser drawer he finds the missing section of the Polo diary. Tony pockets the jade necklace and diary portion and returns to his room. Too keyed-up to sleep, he opens the missing section.

35

CONCERNING MEI LI AND MY PRECIOUS JADE, LU YAO.
After spending the best of twenty years in China, I was a wealthy
man, rich in jewels of great value and in gold. As Governor of Kin-
sai Province and the city of Hangzhou, I became acquainted with the
delicate and angelic ladies of the city, famed through the centuries
as the most beautiful in all of China.

The Chinese say, 'Shang t'ien t'ang hsia, su hang,' which means,
'Above are the halls of heaven; below Hangzhou.' The ladies and
wives are most knowing in how to flatter and caress with ready
words. So much were travelers partaken of their favors and by their
sweetness and charm that they never forgot Hangzhou.

It was my destiny to encounter a fine lady named Mei Li. In the
first moment of our meeting I knew that I was looking at the most
beautiful woman I had ever seen in my life, and that my heart was
hers. She had face and hands of ivory tint, and upswept mass of
blue-black hair, barely perceptible eyebrows, no apparent eyelash-
es, with rosebud lips, red and dewy-looking.

I would have been ready at any time for us to have 'broken the
plate,' as the Mongols called it, because their wedding ceremony
ended with the customary smashing of a piece of fine porcelain. But
Mei Li attached no importance to tradition or ritual. We made our
vows in private at West Lake and that sufficed us both.

On our first night together, Mei Li recited to me an ancient Chi-
nese bridal poem, which these many years later, remains perma-
nently inscribed upon my memory.

> *Let us now lock the double door with its golden lock,*
> *And light the lamp to fill our room with its brilliance,*
> *I shed my robes and remove my paint and powder,*
> *And roll out the picture scroll by the side of the pillow,*
> *The plain girl I shall take as my instructress,*

So that we can practice all the variegated postures,
Those that an ordinary husband has but rarely seen,
Such as taught by T'ien-lao to the Yellow Emperor,
No joy shall equal the delights of this first night,
These shall never be forgotten, however old we may grow.

While our Venetian women are no strangers to sexual pleasure, the women of Kinsai were more accomplished in the arts of blandishment and dalliance. Mei Li demonstrated to me sexual activities that had been written down one thousand years before, in the biography of the great Emperor Wu of the Han Dynasty. These sexual matters were expressed in the words of a beautiful young servant girl named Su Nii or 'Plain Girl,' who was the Yellow Emperor's chief advisor on male potency, women's desires, and provocative positions for the sex act.

One such position is known as the Turning Dragon, where the woman is turned upon her back. She raises up what Plain Girl described as her Jade Gate and the man inserts his Jade Stalk into her mysterious cavern; another is the Tiger's Tread, where the woman leans forward on her hands and knees with her buttocks raised, and the third is the Monkey's Attack, when the man raises the woman's legs until her knees touch her breasts and her buttocks hang in the air. There were many such positions described by the Plain Girl and revealed to me by Mei Li.

While we were lovers only, and not married, nevertheless I will invoke the privacy of our sexual relationship and not relate further particulars. My fondest wish was to journey home to Venice with Mei Li, my dearest companion at my side, and our infant, Lu Yao. I would not have been the first to come home with a foreign bride-to-be. Mei Li may have provided a curiosity in Venice at first, but I would have been lost without her.

The Great Khan showed displeasure on his countenance at our repeated requests for permission to leave. Seeing that the Great Khan was very old, we feared that if he were to die before our departure, we might never be able to return home should we have fallen under the ill will of his successor. So we bided our time.

Alas, no one can foretell the future. Mei Li was a woman of notable beauty and gentle spirit. She would go each day to Kinsai's ma-

jestic West Lake and feed the waterfowls: the storks, geese and gulls. I fear it was at West Lake where she contracted the bird sickness, the fly-borne kala-azar. During the first stage of her illness, Mei Li became flaccid, lacking vigor and energy. Then her glorious long black hair began to fall out. She became feverish and gaunt. None of the Great Khan's doctors were able to repair Mei Li's high fever.

To my infinite sadness, my dearest Mei Li died, and I lost the only woman who I would ever truly love. After Mei Li's tragic death, I let not a day pass that I didn't visit with our child, Lu Yao, who was then two years old and resembled her mother in her beauty and gentle nature.

Shortly thereafter, the Great Khan summoned my father, uncle and myself to his presence and described a mission he required us to perform: safeguarding a young princess on a long sea voyage to her betrothed. After which we would be permitted to return home to Venice.

Before our departure, Kubla Khan presented us with two tablets of gold sealed with the royal seal and written thereon granting safe transport, free and exempt from every burden through all his lands, and wherever we might go, we would not pay expenses for ourselves, and for all our train, and an escort was to be provided in order that we may be able to pass in safety. That same night, I secreted one of the Great Khan's golden tablets and stole unseen to Mei Li's fresh grave and wept freely for some long time. Thereafter, I dug deeply into the red earth atop my beloved's bier and buried the golden tablet in order to provide Mei Li eternal protection, and safe passport to heaven.

Because of the length of the impending sea voyage and the infinite perils threatening us, it was with sadness that I heeded the advice of my father and placed my infant, Lu Yao, in the care of the Chengs, a family of good reputation in Kinsai. My father also cautioned that my returning to Venice with a bastard Chinese child would impede my chance of securing a lucrative marriage arrangement. Every day of my life, I have cursed the advice given by my father, as well as my own submissiveness and self-interest.

As I kissed my baby's head for the last time, I placed upon her neck a locket of the purest precious white jade, a symbol of her name,

Lu Yao. The child was the seed of my loins, and I miss her most fiercely. Would that I had the strength to return to Cathay. I cannot speak further of this as it weighs mightily upon my heart.

...36

THE BUZZ OF THE BEDSIDE PHONE awakens Tony. He grasps at it, fumbling with the receiver. "Signor Perini," Carlos says, "There is a police inspector to see you."

He hesitates before answering. "Send him up."

After reading the diary section, Tony dropped off to sleep exhausted. His clothes still reek of smoke and damp ash.

Commissario Zambelli raps, enters, and gives a low bow. "Good morning, Signor Perini. It is urgent that we speak— in regard to the fire at the restaurant."

Tony doesn't reply. Moisture gathers at his eyes. Lu Yao's loss is a palpable pain, a hollow aching in his chest that restricts his normal breathing.

"With your permission, there are questions to be answered." The policeman looks up and meets Tony's eyes. "Can you tell me your whereabouts yesterday afternoon?"

Tony's expression darkens. "Am I a suspect?"

Zambelli gives a tight smile. "I am merely following standard police procedure."

Making no attempt to disguise his mounting irritation, Tony says, "I left the Danieli about 2:30, I don't remember the time exactly. I walked through a square called San Zaccaria, passed your Questura police station and ended up at the church where Marco Polo is buried."

"San Lorenzo?" Zambelli notes, writing in his notebook. "Were you alone? Can anyone support your testimony?"

"There was a tour group visiting the church, but they wouldn't remember me. And there was an old lady in the church who nodded to me."

"Do you have her name?" Zambelli asks neutrally.

Tony shakes his head. "Then I waited in line for a *vaporetto* in San Marco Square. When I heard the explosion, I hailed a water taxi,

172

got off as close to the Rialto as possible, and ran to the fire. The water taxi guy can verify my story."

"Of course," Zambelli nods, then adds curtly, "your Carlotta family controls the water men, so anyone will testify to anything. You must understand that this restaurant fire has a very high profile. It is the first major arson case since the 1996 disaster at La Fenice opera." The *commissario* pauses. "Yesterday's fire was caused by an explosive device. You are familiar with demolition, yes?" Zambelli eyes Tony, giving him the opportunity to respond.

Tony brushes the question aside. He is seething. He lets the silence expand.

Zambelli continues, "Italy is a NATO member; we routinely exchange information. I requested your military records. You instructed soldiers at the Infantry School in Fort Benning, Georgia— mines and booby traps. Is that correct?"

"Of course, but—"

Zambelli interrupts, "You admit that you are a demolitions expert?"

Tony starts to protest, but Zambelli holds up a restraining hand and refers to his notes. "At the Danieli hotel, you threatened the victim, Miss Cheng. We have a witness."

"Scarlatti?"

He nods. "You are quoted as saying to the Chinese woman, 'You will pay for this.' " Zambelli continues, "As to your character, you requested that I contact a General Morgan in Washington as a reference; the general did not recognize your name."

Tony decides to interrupt. This back and forth could go on for more time then he has patience or self control. "Are you here to arrest me?"

Zambelli ignores the question. "You may think me unsympathetic to a wounded war veteran, but my priority is my city. I fear for Venice, Major Perini. The Venetian Mafia and Chinese Triads grow more powerful each year; they are struggling for control of the lucrative contraband traffic in cigarettes, liquor and drugs from Montenegro. Our politicians are indifferent, the *carabinieri* are impotent, and our people are simmering with anger. We must be rid of these criminal elements." He stares hard at Tony. "And their accomplices.

"Suddenly you appear in Venice," Zambelli resumes, his voice rising, "a man who cannot explain his whereabouts prior to the fire; a man who is an expert in demolitions; a man who cannot be identified by his Army superiors. You are a member of the notorious Cullotta family who control the *Mala del Brenta* and who are at odds with the Chinese Triads.

"Then, *ché sorpresa*, the Chinese opponents, are sent a stern warning when one of their leaders is killed in an explosion. And there we have it," Zambelli states, opening his palms in a gesture that implies he has just revealed the major pieces of evidence.

Tony is exhausted from the physical and emotional trauma of the fire and Lu Yao's death. He feels the sickening jolt of despair in his stomach; he wants to grab Zambelli by the collar and shove him out of the room. He sees the policeman withdrawing papers from a folder. "What are those?"

"Your expulsion orders," announces Zambelli. "You are fortunate to have a friend in Ambassador Scarlatti. He has very powerful connections. Ambassador Scarlatti acquainted my superiors with the fact that you are the last descendant of the famous Polo family. They wish to avoid a scandal. While I am personally opposed, I am ordered to explain your options."

"Options?"

Zambelli hands Tony back his passport and flight documents and says with authority, "You leave Venice tonight on Alitalia's flight 7332 departing at 8:40 P.M. to Washington."

Tony hesitates before answering. "And if I refuse?"

"You have no diplomatic immunity, and Italy has no death penalty," Zambelli tells him sternly. "In our prisons, you will not find a Rustichello to write your memoirs, like Marco Polo did. Instead, you will find inmates packed into cramped, filthy cells, often with only holes in the ground for toilets. Medical services are taxed to their limit, and prison guards are barely able to maintain order. They are not called 'tombs of the living' for no reason. Signor Perini, I strongly advise you to be on the 8:40 flight to Washington."

Tony nods, but says nothing.

Zambelli leaves, closing the door quietly behind him. The sad moan of a fog horn sounds in the distance. Tony's body aches from strained muscles, burns and bruises. The pain in his leg is flaring up; he gulps two oxycodone tablets, undresses, and showers, training the hot water on his stiff neck and shoulders.

Stepping out of the bathroom, he spots an envelope that has been slipped under the door. Tony tears the envelope open and digests the contents. It reads, "Do you wish to avenge Lu Yao's death?" Underneath the message is a phone number.

"THANK YOU FOR TELEPHONING," says the hoarse voice.

"Who is this?"

"Someone who requires that unwanted ears do not intercept our conversation. Captain Cheng Lu Yao's unfortunate death occurred because adequate precautions were not observed. Please tell me, Major Perini, are you on a secure line?"

Tony listens in sullen silence. The mention of Lu Yao's name stirs up raw emotions. "Yeah, this line is secure. I'm sitting in front of the Hotel Marconi near the——"

"I know where it is," the voice interrupts. "A red water taxi will dock in front of your hotel. If you have true interest in avenging Cheng Lu Yao's death, board it." The call ends.

Tony takes a deep breath of the fresh, moist air and thinks about his loss. Rage-generated adrenaline seeps into his bloodstream, temporarily lifting his melancholy mood. As Tony rubs his leg, aching from the unaccustomed exertions of the night before, he spots a red motorboat docking at the landing.

"Signor Perini?" the water man asks, helping him on board and casting off the bow lines. The pilot heads north on the Grand Canal, passing the palazzo Ca'd'Oro, then the boat slows to a crawl, makes a sharp right, and enters the mouth of a narrow canal thick with algae. The boat glides past overhanging balconies and weather-worn stone figures set into crumbling brick and stucco, then bobbles and drifts broadside to weed-encrusted stone steps and the pungent smell of stagnant water.

A young Chinese man steps out of the shadows and reaches for Tony's hand. Without a word, he is guided down a dark, narrow street to the front of a small nondescript hotel, then led through an empty lobby to a room in the rear. The man knocks twice, bows, and disappears.

"I KNEW YOUR GRANDFATHER," asserts the short, heavy-set man wearing a black suit with a white shirt and dark-colored tie. "I see the resemblance."

Tony notices that the room is sparsely furnished: a bed, an empty desktop, two chairs, no television, no clothing, no suitcases.

"My name is General Li Hu Jehng. I was Cheng Lu Yao's superior officer. Lu Yao was like a daughter to me; her father, Middle General Cheng, was a courageous patriot who was executed during the Cultural Revolution."

Listening to Jehng talk about Lu Yao makes Tony feel uncomfortable. He remains silent.

"The reason for my unexpected visit to Venice," the general continues, "was to convince Captain Cheng Lu Yao to revisit her impulsive decision."

Tony frowns. "I don't understand."

"You were not aware that Cheng Lu Yao had tendered her resignation?"

"Lu Yao resigned?"

"Captain Cheng notified me that she could no longer perform her duties; she had fallen in love with an American military officer. I came to Venice to explain the seriousness of the situation and to order Captain Cheng to complete her mission." Jehng's voice wavers. "Instead, I now have the sad duty of flying Cheng Lu Yao's body home."

Tony feels his breath tighten in his throat. "What mission?"

Jehng's sharp eyes fix on Tony. "I trusted your grandfather. Can I trust you?"

"Lu Yao's death will not go unavenged. I've made a sacred promise—to myself. If that's not enough for you, too bad." Tony rises to leave.

"My apologies. You are much like your grandfather. When it was in our mutual interests, we shared information. Your grandfather said he trusted me more than his paranoid, politicized CIA bureaucracy. I understood. We have similar problems at our Ministry of State Security—"

Tony interrupts Jehng's reminiscing. "What was Lu Yao's mission?"

General Jehng looks mildly annoyed at the interruption. "As you know, China has 1.3 billion people. Two of our major concerns are energy and security. Even though we have completed the Three Gorges Dam, which is the largest hydroelectric power station in the world, the dam will not reach full capacity of 22,500 megawatts until 2011. Even then it will only supply part of our needs. China requires increased oil supplies to fuel our expanding economy, and at costs that do not trigger discontent at the gas pumps.

"We have reached tentative agreements with the Mongolian government for Chinese companies to service the Mongolian oil fields. But there is a problem: The man, Scarlatti, has emerged as a catalyst for your American oil companies to secure drilling rights in Mongolia. His Hasara party is doing well in the polls. A win will guarantee the oil goes to America rather than Russia or China. He is bribing officials to favor his clients. In fact, your Secretary of Defense Cody is flying into the American air base at Vicenza tomorrow night with Neff, the president of Canton Oil. The next day they will fly with Scarlatti to Ulaanbaatar, Mongolia."

"How do you know this?"

"Do you take us for a backward nation? After we staged the greatest Olympics ever, then invested over a trillion dollars to support your economy. You should never underestimate China. Your NSA is not the only security service who can intercept transmissions. Cody and the oil man are being picked up by Scarlatti's launch at 7:30 tomorrow evening at Piazza Roma to join the ambassador at the Danieli for dinner..." Jehng pauses. "Tibet is giving us enough of a headache. We certainly cannot permit a Genghis Khan-worshipping Mongolia on our northern border armed with nuclear weapons."

"Nuclear weapons? Jesus Christ! And you talk about the CIA being paranoid?"

Jehng answers quickly, "We may be paranoid, but with good reason. Again, Scarlatti is at the core of our problem. Our Ministry of State Security has verifiable intelligence that five kilograms of bomb-grade enriched uranium was pilfered from the Russian uranium enrichment facility at Krasnoyarsk and smuggled over the border to Mongolia."

"Five kilograms of enriched uranium isn't enough to build a nuclear bomb," Tony says.

"You are correct. Fifteen kilograms is required." Jehng adds, "Scarlatti's ancestry is the Hazara tribe of Genghis Khan. Does the name Abdul Qadeer Khan mean anything to you?"

"No."

"Abdul Kahn is the father of Pakistan's nuclear industry. He developed atomic centrifuges that produced fuel for Pakistan's nuclear arsenal, now estimated at 50 to 100 warheads. Dr. Kahn is of Hasara heritage, and he is now actively assisting his fellow tribesman, Scarlatti, to develop a nuclear bomb."

"My specialty is demolitions," Tony explains. "But I'm not totally naive about nuclear bombs. They are very complicated to assemble."

"Naivety is a luxury I can ill afford. Dr. Kahn has accepted large payments and in turn, has provided Scarlatti with 6 kilograms of enriched uranium, technicians and equipment. The bomb you Americans dropped on Hiroshima used 64.1 kilograms of enriched uranium. Our experts say that a nasty bomb can be built using less than 15 to 25 kilograms of the material.

"Dr. Khan also developed for Pakistan the electronic trigger that provides the split-second timing essential for unleashing a chain reaction. If this chain reaction is controlled within the bounds of a nuclear reactor, as you know, it generates power. The same reaction, when left unhindered, produces the catastrophic effects of a nuclear explosion."

"Do they have 15 kilograms of highly enriched uranium?"

Jehng does not answer immediately. "To complete this hellish scenario, North Korea has agreed to ship sufficient enriched uranium to Mongolia to complete the bomb. Try to imagine the magnitude of a descendant of Genghis Khan's controlling a nuclear bomb. If Genghis were alive today, he would use the threat of a nuclear holocaust to dominate the lands with the most oil in the ground. It takes a ruthless genius, not a savage, to accomplish this. Scarlatti plans to employ oil as a weapon that could be used to cripple the Chinese and American economies—"

Tony interrupts, "You never told me Lu Yao's mission."

"Her mission was to terminate Gianpietro Scarlatti. Unfortunately, Scarlatti struck first."

Tony hesitates before responding. "Lu Yao's mission will be fulfilled—on one condition."

"I'm listening," Jehng answers guardedly.

Tony takes an envelope from his pocket. "Have your people in Washington prepare this for me in a secure metal briefcase. I will pick it up at your embassy."

After Tony leaves, the general sits with his head down and his hands steepled together in contemplation. Jehng's somber thoughts are of Lu Yao—the daughter he never had, the child of his friend and commander, Middle General Cheng, who unlike Jehng, had refused to compromise his integrity to get along with the cultural revolutionaries. Everyone important in his life is gone. The intelligence chief heaves a deep, lonely sigh and tries to shake off his fit of melancholy.

...37

"*SIGNOR* PERINI HAS CHECKED OUT," Carlos reports to Gianpietro Scarlatti. "I personally instructed the water taxi pilot to take the *signor* directly to the airport."

On the trip to Marco Polo Airport, Tony observes the still waters of the Grand Canal shimmering with the reflections of the great *palacios* lining its banks. Soon they are out in the wide lagoon passing Murano. In what seems only minutes, the water taxi enters the canal leading to the long arrival walkway. Tony can spot the Alitalia flight for Paris. The fuselage section is green and red and silver.

He heads straight to the ticket counter and checks in. Next comes security and customs and the Alitalia departure lounge. Tony purchases coffee and a newspaper, then takes a seat with his carry-on bag at his feet.

"Attention please," says the airline attendant. "This is a pre-boarding announcement for Alitalia flight 7332 to Washington, DC, with a stopover at Charles de Gaulle Airport in Paris. Passengers with infants or small children, or passengers needing wheelchair assistance, may begin the boarding process at Gate 41. Have your boarding passes and passports ready. Thank you."

Tony picks up his suitcase and ambles to the men's room. Inside, two men are waiting. "Put up the 'Out-of-order' sign and lock the door," Joey Cullotta orders the man dressed in blue jeans and a navy blue turtleneck sweater, wearing dark glasses.

Joey hands Tony a pair of white overalls with *Servair Air Chef* in blue lettering printed on the back. "Hurry," Joey warns, glancing at his watch. "Give me your ticket, boarding pass, suitcase and passport." He transfers the documents to the handsome young man.

"Meet my... partner, Georgio," Joey says. "He speaks a little English, enough to get by. Georgio will take your place on the flight. In Paris, he will leave the plane, use his own passport, and return.

"*Rapidamente!*" he tells Georgio, pushing him towards the door and giving him a hug.

Joey is also wearing the catering company's uniform. He waits a few minutes, then removes the sign from the men's room door. "Let's go."

Both men quickly cross the Alitalia waiting room area, entering the "Employees Only" door that leads down to the ground level. Outside, Joey Cullotta takes the wheel of a white Servair Air Chef van, and the two men drive off the tarmac and out through the airport gate.

"Thank you, cuz," Tony grins. He takes a piece of paper from his pocket. "Now, here's a list of what I'll need."

AT 2 A.M., PIAZZA SAN MARCO IS DESERTED. Tony slips quietly into the entrance of the Correr Museum. The soft yellow glare of the sodium street light reflects through the window on the stairwell, illuminating the steps up to the museum. Tony withdraws gloves from his backpack and puts them on. He uses the narrow black metal railing for support as he climbs to the second floor.

The museum area is protected by a sophisticated alarm system, but Dante Foscari's office alarm has not been reconnected since the recent fire shorted it out. The lock pick Joey provided makes fast work of the office door. Once inside, Tony closes Foscari's drapes and clicks on a pen light. Reaching again into the backpack, he removes three short strips of plastique, a digital detonator, two coils of wire, and a small lithium battery-operated power supply. Tony carefully positions the plastique over the safe's hinges in such a way that the explosive will slice through the hinges without damaging the safe's contents. He finds a throw rug and places it against the safe to dull the sound of the explosion.

Inserting the detonator, Tony connects it to the power source and flips the switch. A ten second count begins. Wisps of smoke rise from the hinges. Kneeling, Tony grasps the safe's handle and gently pulls it up and open. He takes out the foot-long box, unclasps and opens it. He sighs as he shines his pen light on the 12 inch ivory-and-gold tablet inscribed in Chinese letters beneath the image of a gyrfalcon.

Tony places the box in his backpack and slips silently out of the building. Mario is waiting, as arranged, on his boat near the Valaresso *vaporetto* stop.

"I DO NOT UNDERSTAND," remarks *Commissario* Alesandro Zambelli. "Please tell me, *Doctore* Foscari, why a thief would break into your office, open the safe and steal only one object, leaving behind valuable coins and manuscripts?"

Foscari shrugs his shoulders. "It is puzzling, I must admit."

Zambelli takes out his notebook. "Please describe for me the missing object?"

"Yes, of course, *Commissario*. What was removed from my safe was a golden tablet, called a *paiza* or passport, given to the Polo family in reward for their service to Kubla Khan. This tablet of authority notified all subjects of the Khan that the Polos, as his ambassadors, must be honored and served throughout all of his empires as though they were the Khan's own—"

"*Doctore*," Zambelli interrupts, "what is the value of the stolen tablet?"

"It is impossible to put an exact price on it. What price the priceless?"

Zambelli continues, "But, *Doctore*, if it went on auction, what might it fetch?"

"The price depends on how much a buyer wants the tablet and how much money he has."

Zambelli frowns. "That is not much help to us. And why, *Doctore*, is your alarm system not functioning?"

Foscari looks annoyed. "If you recall, *Commissario*, the as yet unsolved arson fire in my office was nine days ago. This is Venice. Where can you get electricians when you need them?"

After the inspector has gone, Foscari walks slowly to his office window overlooking the Piazza San Marco, gazing at the canal. A flotilla of gondolas glides past.

Foscari nods thoughtfully. "*Buon viaggio, Anthony, buon viaggio.*"

...38

"GENERAL MORGAN, Perini here."

"It's about time. I didn't send you to Venice for a vacation—"

"Listen up, sir. I don't have much time. We can take down this drug operation today, but I need your help." Tony reads off a number and explains what he needs Morgan to do.

"Keep calling this guy until you get him, General, and make damn sure he keeps a buttoned lip. And, one more thing," Tony adds. "I need to be extracted from Italy no later than tomorrow morning. I will be at the Aviano Air Base before dawn. Please notify the base commander and arrange my transportation home. Gotta run." He hangs up.

"PATCH ME THROUGH TO COLONEL BORBAATAR. This is Major Anthony Perini with an urgent message."

Vachir Borbaatar answers quickly. "What is the problem, Tony?"

"You remember the 5 kilograms of uranium that was pilfered from the Russian military and found its way into Scarlatti's hands?"

"Yes," Vachir replies quietly.

"Scarlatti has set up a facility near Ulaanbaator to assemble a nuclear device—"

"What nonsense is this!"

"I have it directly from Li Hu Jehng, head of the Chinese Ministry of State Security——"

"I know who General Jehng is," Borbaatar interrupts.

"The Chinese discovered that 5 kilograms of bomb-grade enriched uranium is being flown in to Mongolia today from North Korea. Scarlatti has some kind of tribal connections with the Pakistani scientist Abdul Qadeer Khan. Technicians from Pakistan with bomb-making experience have started work at Scarlatti's Ulaanbaator facility. The Pakistanis are supplying additional uranium in sufficient quantity to construct a nuclear device."

"WHERE?" roars Borbaatar. "We will mount an assault."

"Write down these GPS coordinates," Tony explains as he outlines his plan. "We have six hours' difference in time. Arrange for your operation to commence at 1:30 A.M. your time. As a signatory to the Treaty on Nonproliferation of Nuclear Weapons, you will need to contact the International Atomic Energy Agency for assistance in disposing of the uranium."

"Let's synchronize our watches," Vachir says, smiling thinly.

AT 7:15 TONY PICKS UP HIS CELL. "Joey, start moving. It's time."

Standing on the fore deck of Scarlatti's launch, one of Joey Cullotta's men holds a pistol to the boat pilot's head. "Tell the police you had engine trouble; that's why you were late."

Piazzale Roma is nearly deserted. A few passengers wait at the number 1 *vaporetto* stop.

Cullotta steps out of his car, puts on gloves and pulls down the brim of his hat. He watches Cody, the American Secretary of Defense, and Neff, the head of Canton Oil, exit their chauffeur-driven military sedan, chatting amiably as they stroll towards the Grand Canal embarkment.

Joey blocks their path. Cody says curtly, "Who the hell are you?"

"*Dobry vyecher*," answers Joey Cullotta in Russian, loud enough to be overheard by the passengers on the quay.

"What do you want?" growls Cody.

Joey draws a Yarygin Pya Russian pistol from his pocket; there are two soft pops as he fires directly into Desmond Cody's chest, hurling him backwards, a spidery vein of red spreading across his shirt. Robert Neff freezes; he seems to be paralyzed. Neff starts backing away from the pier. He raises one of his arms feebly as if to protect himself.

Joey whispers, "Tony Perini sends his regards." Then he extends his arm so it is only a few inches from Neff's head and pulls the trigger. He tosses the gun into the canal and walks across the plaza to where his black Alfa Romeo is waiting with the door open. He jumps in, and the driver speeds off.

AT 1 A.M. ULAT TIME in Ulaanbaatar, fifty elite Mongolian commandos assemble in the cold early hours at the rebuilt Soviet military base near Ulaanbaatar. Dark military transport trucks idle nearby, white puffs spewing from their exhausts.

Dressed in a black leather coat with a gray fur collar, Colonel Vachir Borbaatar addresses his troops. "You have each been selected for this mission because of your special skills. What we do today can affect the future of our nation. Underneath our eyes, in the area north of the capital, in the area of five hills, enemies of Mongolia are developing nuclear weapons."

There are angry mutterings from the men.

"In thirty minutes," announces Borbaatar, glancing at his watch, "we will assault this weapons-making facility. I caution each of you to be mindful that this operation poses a serious danger for the population of Ulaanbaatar. There is the possibility that bullets striking the uranium containers can set off a nuclear explosion. That is why each of you has been carefully picked. You know your assignments," the colonel concludes, shouting, "Mongol Brothers mount up!"

A FLOTILLA OF POLICE BOATS flashing blue lights surrounds Scarlatti's island, *San Francesco del Deserto*. Three A129 Mangusta assault helicopters circle noisily overhead. Inspector Zambelli rechecks his watch. He reluctantly picks up a bullhorn from the police boat cabin roof, put it to his lips and shouts, "This is the police. The island is completely surrounded. Please come out with your hands up and no one will be—"

A sustained burst of automatic weapons fire answers Zambelli's pronouncement. The side window of the patrol boat explodes in a cloudburst of glass; the police boat pilot falls groaning to the deck, clutching his bloody shoulder.

Zambelli bellows on his phone, "Fire the flares; I need an ambulance boat, officer down."

Almost immediately two blue flares light up the sky over the island. Zambelli raises his head fearfully. He observes multiple muzzle flashes coming from the direction of the island defenders. Then Zambelli hears the high piercing noise of exploding flash grenades being hurled from the helicopters. For 60 milliseconds, he feels like he is looking directly into the sun. Then the air fills with white smoke and the smell of aluminum dust. The sounds of sirens in the distance are carried on the streaming wind.

Zambelli watches as the assault airships land, each discharging twenty fully-armed *Polizia di Stato* from the Central Directorate for Anti-drug Services. The men are clad in black combat fatigues and carry short-barreled weapons. In a coordinated sweep, the anti-drug police round up the retreating guards and occupy the heroin processing facility, finding no resistance from the frightened illegal immigrant workers inside.

TWELVE HOURS EARLIER Zambelli received an important call from Preston Morgan, the American Undersecretary of Defense.

"*Commissario* Zambelli," Morgan said, "you called me with reference to a Major Perini. I'm Preston Morgan in Washington."

"Yes, sir," Zambelli replied.

"Can I trust you on a matter of vital importance?"

"I don't understand?"

"Drugs are being smuggled into the United States from the Venice area—"

"How can that be?"

"Never mind how," Morgan growled. "Listen to me, man. I have it on good authority that heroin is being processed on a place called *San Francesco del Deserto,* an island near Venice owned by an important Italian—"

"There must be some mistake."

"If this conversation is over your pay grade, Zambelli, I'll contact Interpol and the head of the Italian Central Directorate for Anti-drug Services. But I'm short of time, and I was told you were anxious to clean up drug trafficking in the Venice area."

"Yes, sir."

"So listen up. Here's what you have to do."

Zambelli listened, his mouth agape.

Morgan ended by saying, "NATO soldiers are dying in Afghanistan because of weapons bought with drug money coming from your island of whatever-it's-called. I know Venice is a close knit society and all that shit, but if one word of this leaks out and the operation is compromised, you will not only have your government to deal with, but me personally, and I am a former Green Beret in Vietnam. Do I make myself perfectly clear?"

Zambelli understood a death threat when he heard one. He had to choose between offending an important Venetian citizen like Gianpietro Scarlatti, or the possibility of leaving his nagging wife a not-so-grieving-widow. He also thought that if things went well, he would achieve recognition, promotion, and more income. *It is my duty to protect my dear wife,* he rationalized.

WEARING NIGHT VISION GOGGLES, Colonel Borbaatar studies Scarlatti's one-story brick building in the distance. Floodlights illuminate the exterior. Razor-sharp wire fencing surrounds the facility.

"Sir," reports a scout. "I make out four sentries. Three on walking patrol, and one smoking a cigarette at the front gate."

"Bowmen," Borbaatar commands, "move to within striking distance and prepare to release on my count of three."

Eight wiry Mongolian soldiers flex on their thighs their 3-foot recurved bows of the kind that rank with the Roman sword and the machine gun as one of the three weapons that changed the world.

"Borbaatar continues, One... two... three!"

Eight arrows whiz through the air, leaving the bows at 300 kph —about a quarter of the speed of a bullet—silent and deadly. One arrow strikes each guard in the throat, and one arrow in the chest. Not a sound is heard. The colonel waves his men forward.

Outside the gate, Borbaatar's Mongol warriors are positioned in a column, armed with bows and sharp knives. A battering ram is on the ready. Two soldiers with metal cutters attack the wire fencing, opening the way for the men with the battering ram to press forward.

In an instant, the door bursts open on its hinges; canisters of smoke grenades are tossed inside. By the time the smoke clears, five men in gray security uniforms lie bloody on the ground—their throats cut. The Pakistani technicians huddle together with their hands in the air.

A large black van with the Mongolian military logo on the side pulls up to the entrance. Men wearing security tags and dressed in full protective suits and hoods take charge. They confer earnestly with the colonel, who smiles and nods in agreement.

Borbaatar orders his men to stand guard around the building perimeter. Other government vehicles appear and dim their lights. The dead bodies are loaded into one of the trucks. "No Admittance" signs are posted at the entrances, and the Pakistanis are herded into unmarked vans.

The colonel assembles his men. "Today," he tells them, "we are setting in order the means to protect our entire nation under the protection of the Eternal Heaven. You are the instruments of this triumph. Your descendants will be proud." He raises his fist into the air and shouts, "*Apart from our shadows we have no friends. Long live Mongolia!*"

The warriors echo, "*Apart from our horsetails we have no whips.* Long live Mongolia!"

MARIO PILOTS THE BOAT to the Danieli landing. Two of Joey's men disembark and silently slip out into the darkness. To Mario, Tony says, "Wait for me here."

His cell phone rings. "Tony, this is Vachir calling from Ulaanbaator. I wish to report that the mission is successful. In behalf of the Mongolian government, we thank you."

"That's good news, Vachir." Tony breathes a sigh of relief. "Have you contacted the International Atomic Energy Agency to dispose of the uranium?"

After a long pause, the Mongolian colonel replies, "There has been a change of plans, my friend. All of the Pakistani technicians are requesting political asylum and seek employment within the Mongolian defense establishment."

"And they also wish to avoid prison?" Tony asks caustically.

"Please understand that we are a small nation with a 3 million population, bordered by the hungry Russian bear to our north and the creeping Chinese Dragon to our south—"

"What are you telling me, Vachir?" Tony cuts in.

"Mongolia must have its own nuclear deterrent. The bomb you Americans dropped on Hiroshima was code-named 'Little Boy.' Ours is code-named 'Little Genghis.' "

TONY ENTERS THE DANIELI. Two of Scarlatti's strong-arm men are seated in the lobby. Spotting Tony, one whips out a mobile phone. The henchman listens, nods, and ends the conversation with a short grunt. The men remained seated, looking edgy.

Scarlatti blinks for just a fraction of a second as he watches Tony approach his table. "I congratulate you, Anthony. You are resourceful, just like your grandfather."

"I never finished my Kir," Tony tells him.

Scarlatti flags the waiter. "Two Kir," he orders curtly.

A flicker of annoyance shows in the watchful dark eyes. "I would enjoy chatting with you, young man, but I'm expecting dinner guests."

As Tony sips his drink, he asks casually, "You and my grandfather were wartime buddies? Why did you have him murdered?"

Scarlatti whispers, "You're in way over your head, boy. You don't know what you're doing, but I'll give you an answer. Nicolo was a noble fool. He uncovered my drug business and threatened to notify his Washington superiors." Scarlatti gives a fatalistic shrug. "Sometimes in life we must do unpleasant duties."

"And the broken neck?"

Scarlatti glowers dissuasively. "An old Mongolian ritual. The killing of a noble person demands that no blood be shed. Death by the snapping of the neck is a sign of respect."

Tony can't bring himself to respond. His anger is choking him. He inhales a deep breath. "By the way, Ambassador, your American dinner guests are indisposed—permanently."

Scarlatti pauses, his face cold with contempt; anger contorts his face. "You have no idea what trouble you have loosed. Your impetuous actions will cost your country the oil leases in Mongolia. And when gas prices go through the roof, they will have you to thank for it.

"No matter, I planned to nationalize the oil fields eventually and throw out the Americans. That wouldn't be possible with the Russians or Chinese. So what now, do you intend to revenge your Chinese woman and try and kill me? I think not." Scarlatti looks around the room for his bodyguards.

Tony's phone rings. He listens for a minute, nodding his head. "That was Inspector Zambelli of the Venice police. The police raid on *San Francesco del Deserto* was productive; your immigrants have been arrested, your heroin confiscated, and your property impounded."

Scarlatti's face is bleached of color. Tony moves his chair closer and withdraws Fischer's hypodermic needle, hiding it under the table. "And, oh yes, Ambassador, I also received a call from Mongolia. Your facility in Ulaanbaator has been raided and taken over by the government. They are seeking your extradition—"

Tony never sees the knife that flashes in front of his face. He instantly recoils, feeling a sharp stinging in his jaw and the taste of blood. Instinctively, he plunges the hypodermic deep into Scarlatti's thigh. The ambassador sags, glassy-eyed.

"Too many Kir," Tony says to the waiter." Can you help me with my friend?"

The two men drag the limp Scarlatti out through the lobby. Hotel guests ignore Tony. They gape in openmouthed horror at the sight of Scarlatti's two garroted henchmen grotesquely sprawled on the Danieli's priceless Ushak rug, their pooling blood commingling with the saturated brick-red colored background of the Western Anatolian carpet.

At the boat, Mario jumps up to assist. The night is dark and moonless. "Under the Rialto Bridge," Tony orders.

Scarlatti is groggy. His eyes are slightly out of focus, his speech slurred. Tony leans close and whispers, "I know you will understand, Scarlatti, I do this as a sign of respect."

Tony reaches over his shoulder and cups his hand under Scarlatti's chin; he places his other forearm at the base of the man's neck and with a clean jerk, pulls sharply back. Scarlatti's neck breaks with an audible snap. The boat passes under the Rialto Bridge in the darkness and slows to an idle. Gianpietro Scarlatti's body is dumped into the black waters of the misty canal. The mournful blare of a police foghorn can be heard in the distance.

Book IV

One generation passes away, and another generation comes; But the earth abides forever. The sun also rises, and the sun goes down, And hastens to the place where it arose.

—Ecclesiastes 1

...39

IN THE ADRIATIC DARKNESS, the military jet takes off from the American air base in Aviano. It is a converted Gulfstream V used by the U.S. military under the designation C-37A.

"Estimated flying time to Andrews," announces the pilot, "will be approximately seven hours. Our arrival is scheduled for 11:00 A.M. Washington time."

Swiveled reading lights angle down from the ceiling. Tony thumbs through the Polo diary, pausing at the section, "Concerning Our Travels through Persia." He shakes his head, thinking, *It will only take me seven hours to travel four thousand miles from Venice to Washington; it took Marco Polo seven years to travel six thousand miles from Venice to Beijing. Incredible!*

CONCERNING OUR TRAVELS THROUGH PERSIA. Leaving Baghdad, we rode on camels. I will mention that riding a camel is no more difficult than riding a horse. A camel walks with a mincing gait and wears a supercilious sneer. It is easiest done with both legs on the same side, in the way a woman rides a horse, sidesaddle. Unlike the single-humped camels that we had seen in the Holy Land, the camels in the Persian region had two lopsided humps to store fat, in addition to long necks and pointed teeth.

When we departed the Persian region of Kerman, we followed the Silk Road, along which all land trade with China had traveled since ancient times. The route was so named because the silk of Cathay was the most costly merchandise carried along the trade route; silk was worth more than its weight in gold.

Here, in the western part of Persia, we first entered into the domain of the Mongols and the powerful monarch of the East, Kubla Khan, who governed the largest far-flung empire ever ruled by one man in all the years in which the world of men had existed.

Along the Silk Road, we passed our first Mongols on patrol; men with eyes like slits. The shaggy Mongols wore skins and leathers and were coated with dust, and they stank. Their faces were the color and texture of tanned leather and they had long wispy mustaches; none wore a beard. Each man carried a sharply curved and recurved bow slung on his shoulders, with its bowstring across his chest, and a quiver of short arrows. Their war cry was, 'Mongol Brothers mount your horses.'

I will now relate a strange tale of Ala-'u-'d-Din Muhammad, known as 'The Old Man of the Mountain,' and the Assassins. This murderous band got their name from the hashishiyun of Persia: Assassins—'those who eat hashish.' These men would kill at the instigation of religious fervor induced by the drug hashish.

The Assassins came from the Ishmaili Moslem sect who resided in the Persian region called Mulehet, south of the sea of Caspian, in the stronghold of Alamut. According to what the locals told me, the Old Man, who by name, Alaodin, had made, in a valley between two mountains, the biggest and most beautiful garden imaginable. Every kind of wonderful fruit grew there. There were glorious houses and palaces decorated with gold and paintings of the most magnificent things in the world. Fresh water, wine, milk and honey flowed in streams. The loveliest girls versed in the arts of caressing and flattering men played every musical instrument; they danced and sang better than any other women. The Old Man had persuaded his men that this was Paradise. The Prophet Mohammed had taught that those who went to Paradise would find as many beautiful women as they wanted, rivers of wine, milk, honey and fresh water.

Young men who were being trained for a mission of assassination were given a sleeping draught and taken into the garden while unconscious. When they awoke, their ravishing surroundings persuaded them that they were in Paradise itself. They remained in this happy state until a victim was designated, when they would once more be drugged and removed, still asleep, from the garden. The certainty, born of experience, that Paradise existed and would be their reward, not only strengthened their determination to succeed in their task, it also removed all fear of failure—knowing what awaited them in the next world, they did not fear death.

Twenty years before our arrival in Alamut, Hulagu Khan the Tatar, Kubla's brother, sent a large army to attack the Old Man's fortified castle. The siege lasted three years; the Old Man of the Mountain, Alaodin, was captured and put to death with all his men, and the castle and the garden of paradise were demolished. And thus ended for all time, God willing, the reign of the Assassins, the men who performed their deeds under strong intoxication from hashish, resulting in their own deaths, but with the promise of immediate entry to paradise.

"YOUR ATTENTION, PLEASE," announces the pilot. "We have received an important transmission. Venice police report that terrorists have assassinated American Defense Secretary Desmond Cody and Robert Neff, President of Canton Oil. All aircraft departing the Veneto area are advised to be on alert status. We will keep you informed. In the meantime, please extinguish all reading and over-head lights. Thank you."

In the darkness, Tony clutches Lu Yao's jade amulet worn on a strap around his neck. He closes his eyes and plunges into a dream-less sleep.

The jet descends, banking through the cloud bank over Andrews Air Force Base. The noonday sun beats down on the tarmac as Tony departs the plane and lurches, a little jet-lagged, through the terminal. The *Washington Post* headline grabs his attention.

AMERICAN OFFICIALS ASSASSINATED IN ITALY

WASHINGTON POST, May 17. International attention was focused on Venice today following the bizarre double murder of American Defense Secretary Desmond Cody and Robert Neff, President of Canton Oil.

Eyewitnesses interviewed by the media report a Russian-speaking gunman fired on the two Americans at close range in an apparent assassination. The killer pitched the alleged mur-der weapon into a canal before escaping the scene at Venice's Piazzale Roma. Police divers raised the weapon from the muddy water. The shell casings found confirm the death weapon was a 9 mm Russian-made Yarygin Pya revolver.

Defense Secretary Cody was traveling to Mongolia to help negotiate important leases for American oil companies. Unnamed government sources report that Russia and China were also seeking access rights to the oil-rich Mongolian Gobi Range and that Secretary Cody's murder may have been orchestrated by the Russian government to impede American entree to the Mongolian oil. The State Department has filed a formal protest. The president appointed Assistant Defense Secretary Preston Morgan to fill the job of Desmond Cody, subject to confirmation by the Senate.

...40

"MAJOR PERINI, SIR?" the armed MP sergeant asks. "Please come with me."

"Am I under arrest?" Tony smiles, mildly surprised by the official reception.

"No, sir," the sergeant responds stiffly. "I am instructed to drive you directly to the Metropolitan Club to meet with Acting Defense Secretary Morgan."

"Please take me by way of the Tidal Basin."

"I'm sorry, sir, I'm supposed to—"

"Sergeant," Tony cuts in angrily. "You'll do as I damn well order you, or shoot me while I grab a cab. Do you read me?"

"Yes, sir," the MP answers woodenly.

Looking out the window, Tony observes wistfully the cherry trees framing the Tidal Basin in the foreground of the Jefferson Memorial and the Washington Monument. The trees are now empty of their delicate pink and white blossoms. *Lu Yao, my dear,* he muses, *you would have loved Washington in the spring.*

He closes his eyes and takes a deep breath. "Okay Sergeant. I haven't showered, shaved or changed clothes in three days. I smell like a polecat and will probably fall asleep at the table from jet lag. Sorry for delaying you. I'll tell Morgan we were held up in traffic."

"YOUR PLANE LANDED AN HOUR AGO. Where the hell have you been?" Morgan demands, glancing at his watch, then glaring at Tony, not bothering to stand. "I waited thirty minutes, then I ordered. You hungry?"

Tony shakes his head. "It's good to see you too, General," Tony says, placing his carry-on bag on the seat beside him. "Congratulations on your promotion. I'm not trying to be disrespectful, sir; I'm just tired." Tony notices that Morgan is drinking O'Douls, a nonalcoholic beer. He signals the waiter. "Black coffee, please."

Morgan sits motionless in the chair, his face without expression, but not his eyes. They are observant and angry. "Consider this an official debriefing, Major. The President wants to know what the hell happened to Cody and Neff in Venice, and so do I."

"The *Washington Post* said it was the Russians."

"That's bullshit and you know it. I have reliable contacts inside the Kremlin. They were just as surprised as we were."

Tony shrugs. "What do the Italian authorities say?"

"That Venice *commissario* couldn't find his ass with both hands."

Tony sips his coffee and remains quiet.

Morgan studies the young man seated across from him. *He doesn't trust me. He's so like Nicco.* "Look, son. I have a confession. I admit that I bear responsibility for your grandfather's death. Alcohol dulled my skill craft. Our communications were intercepted by Neff's people. My carelessness got Nicco killed. I have to live with that, but what's done is done."

Morgan coughs and lowers his voice. "I've been in this job less than twenty-four hours. The President expects prompt response from the Pentagon—from me—or he turns the Cody-Neff mess over to the CIA, and I can kiss my Senate confirmation goodbye. The truth is, I don't know what to tell him. It's not just career-ending—it's personally embarrassing."

"General Morgan, what I'm going to tell you is off the record. If you quote me, I'll deny it. Are we on the same page?"

Morgan swallows the insubordination and nods.

Tony continues, "Cody and Neff, with Scarlatti's help, resorted to murder and bribery in an effort to steer Mongolian oil contracts away from the Russians and Chinese. Advise the President that his administration doesn't need to be coated with the brush of an international bribery scandal. Let the news of their death play itself out; in a week it will all be over."

"And what about Scarlatti?" Morgan asks.

"He was a lineal descendant of Genghis Khan. Not one of these DNA-related characters you read about in the newspapers. Scarlatti was a tactical genius: selling drugs to Americans, then using drug money to try and corrupt the Mongolian election and put in his own slate until he was ready to take over. He had dual Italian-Mongolian citizenship. Once he took over, Scarlatti told me he planned to nationalize the oil fields and throw out the Americans. He couldn't do that to the Russians or Chinese."

"Go on, I'm listening."

"Scarlatti built a nuclear bomb-making facility near Ulaanbaator, Mongolia. The technicians were trained by Abdul Quadeer Khan, the Pakistani scientist who sold atomic technology to Iran, North Korea, and Libya. With nuclear bombs, Scarlatti could dissuade Russia and China from encroachment into Mongolia and also threaten the Middle East oil-rich nations with the specter of nuclear weaponry in the hands of another Genghis Khan."

Morgan stares open-mouthed.

"Fortunately, the Mongolian government was alerted and has taken over the facility."

"Are you telling me little Mongolia has a fucking nuclear bomb?"

"Yes."

"And Scarlatti?"

"Word on the street," Tony laughs, "or shall I say 'word on the canal' has it that the gentleman in question suffered an unfortunate accident. It seems Scarlatti suffered a broken neck in a fall from the Rialto bridge."

"You are a sly son-of-a-bitch," Morgan says. "And you remind me of you-know-who. Let me ask you something, Anthony. I have this new job at the Pentagon, and the truth is, I don't know who to trust and who's feathering their own nests for post-retirement employment.

"You are also a disrespectful subordinate, but I trust you. I want you on my staff with a promotion and all the perks."

Tony signals the waiter again and asks for paper and a pen. As the general looks on curiously, Tony scrawls a message, dates it, signs it, and hands it to Morgan.

"This is the resignation of my Army commission, effective today," Tony says.

"I don't understand."

"General, I have a few loose ends to clean up. The less you know, the better. *Capisce?*"

As Tony leaves the restaurant, Morgan notices his limp is more pronounced.

After hailing a cab, Tony says, "Walter Reed Hospital."

"I'M SORRY TO HAVE TO TELL YOU, MAJOR PERINI," the doctor states. "There has been a rapid and severe progression of your staphylococcus infection."

"What are you telling me?"

The doctor clears his throat and grimaces. "As a result of having your open wound exposed to a polluted environment, you have contracted an extremely dangerous bacterial staph infection that destroys skin and the soft tissues beneath it. It is called necrotizing fasciitis, and is most toxic when occurring in someone with an underlying illness, or your case, a severe battlefield wound."

He pauses, takes a breath, and continues, "Our tests show that the severity of tissue damage is widespread. I want you admitted at once and prepped for surgery. If we move quickly, we may be able to remove the infected tissue, reduce the number of bacteria in your body, and stop the spread of the infection. I regret to tell you, Major, amputation may be necessary, depending on how severe the infection is and how far it has spread."

"And if I put it off?"

"Unless you're suicidal, that's not an option. I'll send an admitting nurse to assist you."

Tony exits the doctor's office, limps to the hospital entrance and flags another cab.

"2133 WISCONSIN AVENUE," Tony tells the cab driver. "And please wait for me."

He presents his ID to the guard at the Chinese embassy and is promptly admitted.

"Here are your *special* travel documents, hotel accommodations, passport, West Lake directions and tourist visa," the slim young military attaché says. "General Li Hu Jehng sends his regards." The attaché hands Tony a metal briefcase. "Please handle this most carefully, Major."

"Okay, pal," Tony directs the cab driver. "BWI Airport."

...41

TONY SLEEPS FITFULLY during the four-hour flight to Florida. With a thud the wheels hit the tarmac. He awakes confused, hearing the rumble of thrust reversers being engaged as the pilot applies power to slow down the aircraft.

After sitting in one position for hours, he feels lightheaded when he stands up in the aisle. A stab of pain jolts his knee joint. Removing his flight bag from the overhead rack, Tony takes another oxycodone tablet, then puts on sunglasses and a Miami Marlins cap.

At the Budget Car Rental counter in the Melbourne Airport, he presents the false ID that General Jehng had authorized, and he picks up keys to a reserved silver Hyundai Accent. Tony drives to the short term parking area, puts his travel documents and forged passport into the glove compartment, locks up and limps back to the terminal. Detective Lou Brumberg is sitting in a police car studying his watch.

"Sorry I'm late," Tony says. "I appreciate your picking me up."

"No problem. Are you okay? You look worn out."

"A lot of traveling," Tony answers. "Do you still have Dad's car?"

"I've kept the battery charged; it's parked in the lot next to headquarters."

"Lou, you're the only one, besides his lawyer, who doesn't buy the suicide. Why?"

"Dominick would never have used a silencer to kill himself. No way. He said putting a silencer on an automatic was like tits on a bull—only good for movies and spy novels."

"I don't understand."

"A silencer captures and dampens gas exploding out of the barrel from a muzzle blast. On a gun like your dad's, the silencer would have forced the gas back down the barrel to the cylinder; there wouldn't have been much noise reduction. Dominick wouldn't have

204

wasted time screwing around with a silencer. That's why I know somebody else pulled the trigger."

"Lou, I know you've spent your own time working this case, and I appreciate it. Any credible leads?"

"*Nada*. No body—it was cremated; no eyewitnesses; no support from the department; and no uncompromised evidence in the house. According to Dom's will, the place is now a domestic violence shelter. I know it's hard to swallow, but after a while, you gotta try to move on with your life. I'm sorry."

Tony asks to be driven to the police parking lot adjoining the Fort Pierce Station on US 1. Brumberg flips him the car keys and said, "Let me know if I can be of help, Tony. But watch your back. The bastards who murdered your dad are still out there."

"Which car belongs to the chief?"

"The black Lexus in the reserved space with CHIEF on the license plate."

ON THE PHONE, Tony says, "Captain Thompkins? Tony Perini here. Dominick's son."

"Sorry about your dad. Terrible thing."

"That's why I'm calling, Captain. I just got back from—"

"Yeah. I heard you were out of the country," Thompkins cuts in. "How can I help you?"

"In Venice, I ran into a man named Karl Fischer." Tony pauses, waiting for a reaction.

"Never heard of him."

"Before he died, Fischer confessed to the murder of my father and grandfather."

"Who's your grandfather?"

"The man whose body was found in the inlet."

"Go on, I'm listening."

"Fischer told me why my father was killed and who authorized it." Tony lets the tension build. "I know that Dad would have wanted me to discuss it with you first before reporting it to my superiors at the Pentagon. He trusted you and Detective Unger."

"Who else knows—you know—knows the whole story?"

"Nobody yet. I just got into town, and I'm scheduled to see Dad's lawyer, Harold Richmond, tomorrow to sign a bunch of papers. I'll leave him a copy of Fischer's confession—"

"Not a good idea," Thompkins interrupts. "You know them Jew lawyers. Got a car?"

"Yes, sir."

"I'm tied up for the next few hours, but I would rightly appreciate it if we could meet and talk this over, away from the station house. Too many ears here—you know? How about at eleven o'clock tonight on the road behind headquarters— at the Indian Springs golf driving range."

"Where the high fences are?"

"Good boy. See you then."

TONY STEALS INTO THE DARK POLICE PARKING LOT. Detective Brumberg had told him that it wasn't fenced or guarded. Tony locates the chief's car, puts on gloves and withdraws several objects from his metal briefcase. He carefully arranges and connects the objects under the carriage beneath the driver's seat.

AT ELEVEN O'CLOCK, Tony is sitting in the driving range parking lot under a street light when a police car stops. A beefy patrol cop with a long scowling face approaches his car.

"Would you open your trunk latch and step outside your car, sir," the officer orders.

With his Mag-lite, the officer searches the trunk, removes a tire iron, and stows it in the police cruiser. "Nothing in the trunk, Chief," the man reports on his police radio. "Now, if you will please put your hands on the roof, sir." The officer expertly searches Tony and methodically checks out the car interior.

"No wire on him and no weapons, Chief," he says on the radio. "This guy can hardly stand up straight; he looks real sick. The car's empty, nothing under the seats; it's clean. Okay, I'll check the glove compartment too…. Nothing but a master lug nut, some old service records, registration papers and a ball point pen. Car is totally clean. Right, I'll confiscate his cell phone."

To Tony he says, "Sorry about this, sir. Now, if you will please get in your car and follow me, I'll take you to meet the chief."

Tony trails the police cruiser over the Indian River Bridge down Seaway Drive, then south on A1A, stopping at a turnoff road to John Brooks Park. Tony spots the chief's black Lexus parked off to the side of the sandy beach road. The officer motions him to continue down the road toward the beach. Then he salutes and drives off.

In the bright moonlight, Tony eyes a woman in the driver's seat. Billy Ray Thompkins is seated in the back, rolling down the window.

"Come on in, Tony," he says, flipping on the overhead light. Thompkins makes no effort to shake hands. Tony sees telltale bulges under both of their jackets.

"You know our Chief of Detectives, Connie Unger?" Thompkins asks.

"Yes. I've heard a lot about you," Tony says, watching her eyes tighten.

"Okay," Thompkins says. "What can you tell us about your father's murder?"

"It was all political," Tony replies. "The brains behind the drug operation was an Italian named Scarlatti, a former ambassador with connections all over east Asia."

"Was?" the chief asks. A flicker of surprise shows in his watchful gray eyes.

"Yes, Scarlatti's body was recently discovered floating in Venice's Grand Canal."

Billy Ray Thompkins studies Tony's face, but says nothing.

"Powerful American oil companies wanted to outmaneuver China and Russia for control of valuable Mongolian oil rights. Scarlatti was the 'fixer.' He held dual Mongolian and Italian citizenship and had important connections in the Mongolian government—also in Washington. Some American officials believed Scarlatti was so vital to our national interests that he had to be protected at all costs. When my grandfather, and then my father, got close to exposing Scarlatti, they were both murdered."

Tony can feel the tension building.

Thompkins says, "Go on."

"Secretary of Defense Desmond Cody was in bed with Canton Oil Company. He had a big payoff and a cushy job waiting after he left office, so he outsourced the murders to one of the Pentagon's mercenary sub-contractors. Karl Fischer was an ex-SEAL. He did the job."

No one says a word. It is like all the air has been sucked out of the car.

Finally, Billy Ray asks, "Yeah. What else?"

"You two were close associates of my dad's; I knew you would want to know."

Even in the semi-darkness, Tony sees Unger and Thompkins exchanging looks.

"What are your plans now, Tony?" Chief Thompkins asks.

"I'm going on a long vacation, but first I wanted to personally thank you for all you did for my dad." He opens the car door, smiles at the two police officials and hobbles back to his car. The pain in his leg is a white-hot shooting agony, but he tries to show no outward reaction.

Tony drives back on to A1A and pulls over to the shoulder of the road. Reaching into the glove compartment, he removes the ballpoint pen, takes a deep breath of sea air, then clicks the pen twice. A radio signal zips down to the package he had placed under the police chief's car. The radio signal closes the circuit and sends an electrical charge from the nine-volt battery into a blasting cap embedded in one pound of Composite 4 explosive.

An audible explosion shakes the ground, echoing up from the beach. Thick black smoke fills the night air, obscuring the moon. Then the gas tank of the police chief's Lexus explodes in a woofing clap of sound and more dense smoke.

Tony continues north on US 1, carefully observing the speed limit. In the distance sirens pierce the evening air. At the Melbourne airport, he parks his father's car in long term parking, picks up his rental car and drives two hours to the Orlando Airport, where he waits for his flight to San Francisco and then on to Shanghai.

...42

IN VENICE, DOCTOR DANTE FOSCARI opens the FedEx International Priority package addressed to him. Inside the layers of protective cushioning, Foscari extracts a chrome-finished cremation urn decorated with etched blue seagulls, a small jewelry box, and a letter.

>*Dear Doctore Foscari:*
>
>*Enclosed you will find a cremation urn containing the ashes of Dominick Perini. It is my wish that my father's ashes be buried in the San Michele Cemetery next to the grave of Nicolo Polo in order that father and son will, at long last, be reunited.*
>*The box contains the Pigeon's Blood ruby ring engraved with the Polo family crest. Please accept this signet ring of Marco Polo's as my gift to your Correr Museum in replacement for your recent loss of the golden tablet of Kubla Khan.*
>
>*Anthony*

FROM THE SHANGHAI PUDONG INTERNATIONAL AIRPORT, Tony takes a taxi for the sixty-minute ride to the Radisson Plaza Hotel in the nearby city of Hangzhou. As soon as Tony presents himself and his passport, the young lady at the Radisson check-in hands him the FedEx International Priority package he had shipped from Washington.

Dominick Perini had explained to his son how drug smugglers in Fort Pierce had out-shipped money to the Caribbean, hidden in large books with their insides razored out. Tony had secreted the golden tablet of Kubla Khan into a large volume describing the Yangtze

209

Three Gorge Dam Project. Then he had sealed the surrounding pages shut with a tacky glue.

In his hotel room Tony forces open the book covers and with a penknife slits apart the book pages. Encased in bubble wrap, the gold and ivory tablet has arrived undamaged. The throbbing pain in his leg is becoming barely manageable. He swallows two more pills, takes the bubble-wrapped tablet and asks the doorman to help him into a taxi.

"Tell him West Lake, the Pagoda of the Six Harmonies," Tony says to the doorman.

FOLLOWING GENERAL JEHNG'S DIRECTIONS, Tony stumbles down the path from the Pagoda of the Six Harmonies to the small cemetery near the lake. The short walk leaves him light-headed and wobbly. Searching amid the markers, Tony locates the fresh grave marker of Cheng Lu Yao beneath a weeping willow tree. The scent of peach blossoms wafts through the air. With his penknife, he digs out a twelve-inch-square tuft of grass, inserts the golden passport of Kubla Khan, then carefully recovers the grassy mound. He sits under the swaying willow branches, looking out across the lake. Pain and delirium cloud his mind.

The emerald green hills in the distance are covered with lush forests, reflected in the still waters of the lake. Tony squints to see the gilt-painted pleasure boats on the water and the shoreline studded with gardens and fanciful buildings. He pops another oxycodone and fingers Lu Yao's jade pendant. As a light haze embraces the cemetery, he visualizes Lu Yao standing in front of him with a peach blossom in her hair.

"I've missed you so, my dear Lu Yao," he says. "Are you well? Yes, I'm fine. Well... maybe not fine," he smiles, "but I feel better just being here with you. Your peach blossoms are beautiful; our apple blossoms in Washington are also beautiful." Tears are creeping into his eyes.

"Come, sit by me," Tony whispers. "I know you are not a believer, my dearest Lu Yao, but I wanted you to have Kubla Khan's tablet near you for safe passage to heaven, just in case—you know?"

He pauses; tears now stream down his face. "I had to come and thank you for offering me the gift of your love."

Tony presses his side. "My leg doesn't hurt anymore," he chuckles. "But I feel a little dizzy. Maybe if I rest here with you for a while—"

"MOMMY, IS THAT MAN SLEEPING?" the little boy asks.

Their Chinese guide answers, "The gentleman under the weeping willow tree may be resting and enjoying the magnificent view of the celebrated West Lake. The explorer, Marco Polo, praised Hangzhou as the most beautiful city in all of China. We have an ancient saying, *'Shang t'ien t'ang hsia, su hang,'* which means, 'Above are the halls of heaven; below Hangzhou.'"

The guide glances up at the darkening sky. Black thunder clouds swirl ominously across West Lake, howling and rustling through the branches of the weeping willow and flowering peach trees. Thunder crashes and raindrops fall. There is a lightning flash; the shower becomes a storm.

Opening an umbrella, the guide says, "We must return quickly to the bus. According to Chinese mythology, *Longwang*, the Dragon God, is furious and is weeping bitter tears."

The man in the blue jeans and navy turtleneck sweater sits very still, with his back propped against the quaking weeping willow, his head tilted up towards the sky. His glacier blue eyes are closed. He no longer sees the pagodas along the shoreline, or feels the rain water dripping from the weeping willow tree, nor hears the waves lapping up against the shore. In his hand is a white jade amulet. And on the dead young man's pale face is a faint smile.

Epilogue

ONE THOUSAND MILES TO THE NORTH, along the Yongding River, a massive series of lightning bolts strikes Beijing's oldest bridge. The marble balustrades supporting 485 curved stone lions on the handrails crumples under the blast, cauterized into molten slabs.

"Here is the damage assessment, sir," General Li Hu Jehng's aide reports. "Successive lightning strikes hit 16 kilometers to our southwest, over the Yongling River. The Marco Polo bridge is irreparably destroyed. No other damage in the area is reported."

"Only the Marco Polo Bridge?" Jehng asks, shaking his head.

"Yes, General."

"An omen, I suppose." Jehng coughs and turns away so his aide doesn't see the tear gathering in his eye.

SIX HUNDRED MILES TO THE SOUTHWEST, along the old Silk Road in the Taklamakan Desert of Central Asia, Dr. Miriam Jolson is traveling in a jeep with her guide on a rest and recuperation leave from Afghanistan. She has elected to follow Marco Polo's path through what is now the Xinjiang Uyghur Autonomous Region of the People's Republic of China—one of the largest sandy deserts in the world.

"When the traveler man, Marco Polo, crossed the Taklamakan desert," her guide intones, "it was much hazardous journey. *Takla Makan* means go in and you'll never come out. But they did not possess jeeps, eh?" He smiles a toothless grin.

"What is that awful sound?" Jolson asks, feeling the desert wind suddenly rising up.

"The Gobi has a reputation as an abode of spirits. We best go now," her guide says nervously, putting the jeep in gear. "Desert spirits angry."

As they drive away, the whirling sands give out an eerie, keening sound like people being tortured and crying.

* * *

FIVE THOUSAND MILES TO THE WEST along the Grand Canal, Mario, the water boat pilot, snuffs out his cigarette and stares at the darkening eastern horizon. *"Gesu, aqua alta,"* he exclaims, docking his boat against the piling and lashing it down securely with extra lines.

The sky becomes pitch black as the sudden storm roars in off the Adriatic, bringing heavy rains and large half-dollar-size hail. The squall line rises over the Lido, creating large, choppy gray waves. The wind picks up, rocking *vaporettos* and blowing small boats against the walls of the *palazzos*. San Marco Square fills waist-deep with flood water. Lightning crashes repeatedly into the San Marco District in the area around Campo San Lorenzo and the Church of San Lorenzo—the burial site of Marco Polo.

In the hurricane-force, wind-driven rain, the roof of the Church of San Lorenzo tears loose. Tons of water gush into the nave and three arcades. The weight of accumulated water and the fierce, buffeting wind cause the ancient religious building to buckle and vibrate. Moments later, a solid column snaps at the midsection and crashes down, followed by a loud rumbling thud, as the entire church structure topples into the waters of the Rio della Pieta Canal. The canal waters, roiled by the rushing tide, propel the burial crypts of San Lorenzo into the Grand Canal; they float past the great bronze horses of St. Mark gleaming in the sunlight, drifting towards the Lido and the eastern coast of the Adriatic, heading towards Cathay.

For an instant, the wind changes direction. Everything becomes eerily silent. The storm abates and the sun shines brilliantly from behind the clouds.

As the storm dies away on the Western horizon, *Doctore* Dante Foscari looks out the window of his office at the Correr Museum in time to see a magnificent rainbow arching over the white-columned facade of San Giorgio Maggiore. Then he returns to reading the final page of the lost diary.

I NOW STAND WEARY at the end of the road, heaped not with praise. And yet I would gladly do again what I have done, u daunted by what others say. I believe it was God's will that I should have traveled thousands of miles, through uncharted deserts, over steep mountains, exposed to extreme weathers, to wild animals and uncivilized tribesmen. And to come back, so that men might know the things that are in the world, since no other man, Christian or Saracen, Mongol or pagan, has explored so much of the world. And now you have heard all that I have to tell you.

The sun is setting, the mist rises from the canal and I sit in the dying sunlight with my memories of bygone times. I know full well that my next trip will not be in this lifetime. My bodily remains are consigned to rest in some underground crypt, but my soul is destined to journey east once more to the West Lake, where above are the halls of heaven, and below in the earth, 'neath the flowering peach trees, lies the grave of Mei Li, the companion of my heart.

I subscribe myself,

Messer Marco, son of Messer Nicolo Polo, great and noble citizen of the city of Venice.

In the year of our Lord, 1318.